D0912390

*For my beloved husband and kid.  TLC.*

Time comes into it.
Say it. Say it.
The universe is made of stories,
Not of atoms.

   – Muriel Rukeyser

Don't you know *yet?* Fling the emptiness out of your arms
into the spaces we breathe; perhaps the birds
will feel the expanded air with more passionate flying.

                              – Rainer Maria Rilke

# CONTENTS

# THE ALTIPLANO

The road before them dissolved into two sets of tire tracks pressed in the sand, one going to the left and one to the right. The American family looked through the front windshield at the greatest expanse of nothingness they had ever seen. Sands every shade from silver to lead stretched in all directions and would have gone on eternally had not snow-capped volcanoes pricked the horizon, their conical perfection burning the sky, too harsh for reality, too exact for dreams. The tracks represented not so much a choice, as the utter impossibility of choice, rational or otherwise. The family was, at long last, on their way back to the United States after a year and a half in Chile, and they had 12,000 miles between them and their home in upstate New York. The road was too rough to return to Chile, so they chose the tracks leading left. Within twenty feet, the car's underbelly got hung up on the high median, and their tires spun uselessly in the sand.

Try though they might, they could not get the car to budge. The mother jumped out and rolled rocks behind the tires while her husband gunned the engine. The wheels merely spat the rocks back at her. They traded places, and she gunned the engine while the father and the oldest son pushed from behind. Nothing. The middle child, a girl, and the youngest boy were sent under the car to dig out the middle, and scramble back to safety. The car lurched a few feet forward and got hung up again.

There was no one to go to for help, no people, no buildings, no cars, not even animals, just silent volcanoes, and distant sun, now cold and murky as gruel. They made camp. By the next day, all five were dizzy and slightly nauseated by the altitude. While the father brewed cocoa leaf tea for the children, a cure recommended by their Chilean friends, the mother unfolded a canvas stool at the edge of camp and sat with her back to them, staring at nothing.

Her acute attention to things beyond them was, in itself, not unusual. She was an inventor who had invented nothing. The father's job as an urban developer enabled them to travel all over the world, always returning to their house in upstate New York. But something essential about her had changed in Chile. It made the children uneasy. They pulled tightly together, as was their custom when they encountered adversity, but when they wandered over to her, she waved them away.

Like a three-person posse, the children wandered off, the younger boy and girl following the older boy's lead, their wiry bodies hovering together in a close triangle, more part of each other than not. They drew lines in the silvery sand and examined bristly shrubs and rubbery green mounds that grew at disparate spots, looking like flora from another planet. Out of the corner of their collective eye, they watched her. The texture of her body was different. It was as if the electrons and photons that held her together were circulating at greater distances from each other, becoming loose and disorganized. The children squeezed closer together to compensate, a trickle of dread infiltrating them.

Sometimes over the course of the afternoon the mother talked to herself, her face active, her fingers tapping a silent tune on her thumb like a violinist. Most of the time, however, she stayed still, staring at the distance as if it was a destination. Whenever they looked over their shoulders at her, she was smaller, having moved farther off. The invisible tether between the children and their mother was stretched to its limit, so they squeezed even closer to each other.

Later in the afternoon, a cloud of sand spun up from the ground at a distance. It was a truck driving toward them. The wind brought the distant rumble to them in spurts before changing directions. They all shouted and waved, jumping up and down — everyone but the mother — that is. She watched the truck and its plume of dust in alert silence. But the truck was far off, following another track, and it kept going, the drivers not seeing them, or not stopping if they had. Distance erased it, and no other trucks came their way that day.

The children wandered more listlessly. As the father prepared their dinner, his spoon scraped against the aluminum pan, and the camp stove flame guttered in the wind. When he offered the mother a bowl of soup, she waved it away. This wasn't unusual. She often didn't eat, but still the children watched her. Just before sunset, she stood, and moving slower than a plant grows, raised her arms above her head. She stood that way for so long, the children stopped watching and helped their father pour a few cups of precious water into the pan to wash the dishes. That is how they missed the exact moment their mother took flight.

She left a small spray of dust next to the overturned camp stool, and by the time they all looked up, she was in the distance already, running on long legs, fast and fluid, approaching the velocity of the spirit with elbows chopping the air, shoulders raised, head thrown back. She seemed to gather intensity as she ran, to crackle with light like a cloud before a storm. Then, with an explosion no louder than a cat's purr, she burst into flame and disappeared. But for a black plume of smoke, she was gone. Simply gone.

"No!" Ovid, the oldest boy, cried. He coughed and stumbled forward. "Wait for me!"

For a second, the rest of them stood immobilized.

It is here where the children's vision departed from one another, here where they did not see as one, but as three, six, nine—a kaleidoscope—broken shards of glass, where their separate visions defined them, where they were no longer a single thing, no longer a part of their mother, and never a part of their father, liberated and lost by a single stroke of fire.

"What happened? What happened?" Terry, the youngest, cried.

No one answered. They ran to the spot where she had been.

They found only a few dental fillings, five hooks and eyes, and several hundred safety pins still hot to the touch, all covered with a film of greasy residue. They stared wordlessly at each other, at the sky, at the horizon. Here is where they would always feel the incompleteness of unique experience, where they would always, in their memory, scan the peripheral vision of their downcast eyes and feel the nonnegotiable canyon of the unseen, the insatiable ache of the just-missed.

The three children turned and discovered their father for the first time, no longer the male counterpart to their mother, but an irresolute, middle-aged man named Walter, blank-faced and limp. Rather than shocked, he appeared bewildered and resigned, as if he had always expected some such end to his marriage.

Ovid condensed into a ball of fury and ran in circles over the ground of her disappearance. At first the younger siblings just stared at him in horrified silence, but as his muttering escalated into hysteria, Walter stepped forward, back, and forward again. "S-settle down," he said, trying to place his hand on Ovid' shoulder. Ovid kept running in circles, his momentum casting Walter's hand aside. When Ovid came back around, Walter took a deep breath and grabbed Ovid's arm, but Ovid shoved him, and what started as a rescue attempt became hand-to-hand combat. As they wrestled in the sand, Fallon, the middle child, clasped Terry's hand and edged closer. For a time, Ovid overpowered Walter, and the second natural order of the day was contradicted; but Walter held on grimly, and eventually Ovid collapsed under the full weight of Walter's six six-foot-four height.

Some indeterminate time later, the light began to fail, and the desert chilled. Occasionally, to make sure she was really gone, Fallon or Terry would return to the spot where the woman who gave birth to them had gone up in smoke. They could not absorb her absence.

An event so enormous and irrevocable has a way of exposing the inadequacy of human response.

A blue rag scuttled across the sand to Ovid's feet where he now sat leaning against the front tire. He picked it up and wept into it. Fallon scanned the surroundings to see where it had come from. In the cold descending breeze, in the white peaks of the volcanoes, in the colorless drift of the sky, she traced the hieroglyphics of her mother's being, a cipher, a code she would spend the rest of her life deciphering.

In this limbo, at the age of twelve, the first light of Fallon's consciousness dawned. It wasn't until she was twenty-five that the second light dawned.

# 1

# BLUE WOMAN

August in Manhattan was unbearable. By eight a.m., people were already sweating, and by noon, heat smote the pavement like a hammer on an anvil. Fallon had gotten up to run in the cool of the morning, tepid though it was. After she graduated from college, she followed her college friends to Manhattan and picked up a waitressing job with the idea that she would make do while studying for the MCATs and apply to medical schools. Three years later, she had yet to take the test, and not one application had been made.

After her mother spontaneously combusted on the *Altiplano*, Fallon had turned her head, and seen herself reflected, beautiful and male, in the face of her older brother, and known that through him, she could survive. Ovid, a child truly cast in the image of Eustacia's mind, was the supreme architect of Fallon's childhood, even more so than her mother. Only Ovid could open a space in the air and lead her into a land of his own invention. With fantastic words of his own derivation, he took her from a ship made of blankets and living room chairs to other planets. She could follow the quick flashes of his mind and magic anywhere for at least an hour before her brain tired from trying to keep up. His knowledge was not merely invented, for he had read their 20-volume encyclopedia from cover to cover when he was in Chile. His mind held onto facts in a way hers never had. Even when she was a baby, her head always turned to him, as though he was a sun that shone especially for her.

But thirteen years later, her human mirror was always on the verge of collapse, leaving her own survival in question. Whenever she reached down into his emotional pit to raise him up, he'd pull her down into it, both emotionally and physically. Even before their mother dispersed, he had pummeled her with angry words and fists. But afterwards, his anger cooled to disgust and disdain, mitigated occasionally by fits of tenderness, which were almost worse. The period between when her family arrived home and now had been rocky, to say the least, and Fallon had escaped with her sanity barely intact.

They had never traveled as a family again. They barely talked for the rest of the drive home. In the first year of being home, whenever they tried to talk about Eustacia's death or *whatever it was*, they would be collectively seized by a torpor so profound that they would all start yawning and have to sleep. In later years when they awoke from their collective shock, they argued, each one having a different story. The arguments grew so violent they never fully concluded, so the event, unmined, unmitigated, unnamed, became a rock around which they tried to flow onward, mostly unsuccessfully.

When he turned eighteen, Ovid attempted and failed a variety of colleges and eventually returned home, ostensibly to take care of Walter. It was a fiction which Fallon and her father maintained by unspoken mutual consent. Terence turned heavily to marijuana smoking, dropped out of high school, and left home for California. When news of him arrived (rarely), there was always some hint of flimflammery.

Fallon, the only one to successfully complete college, was sinking into s quicksand where medical school seemed less and less possible. For the last three years, feeling she wasn't smart enough to become a doctor, she tried to think of something she could do instead. But absolutely nothing came to mind that truly mattered or even remotely interested her. Even though it took millions of people to run this city, she couldn't imagine what they all did. It all seemed so meaningless. When she asked someone at the occasional party what they did, they gave her long, abstract titles that made her blood turn dry as chalk, answers like "I'm Assistant to the Director of Administrative Service Marketing," or "I'm Manager of First Option Subsidiary Rights Auctions." Their answers gave her tunnel vision and filled her ears with static. Yes, but what do you do? She wanted to ask. Actually. At your desk. In the morning? What difference does it make in the world?

She hated waiting tables. She felt degraded and useless. She told herself it was a good interim job until she entered medical school because it let her move, it was steady cash, and she was taking care of people in an elemental way. But it bored her, and boredom was a stasis more painful than sitting for too long. Nevertheless, she couldn't make herself apply for the MCATs. Whenever she tried, thoughts of her mother's and Ovid's brilliance mutely unmotivated her.

Yesterday, frustration with her job peaked, and today, her first day off in weeks, she determined the sun would not set before she filled out the registration forms for the October MCAT. Running was her salvation, so she propelled herself out of bed before the heat of the day took hold. As usual, the first fifteen minutes of her run were groggy and out of sync as if she was running ten yards behind herself; her right foot scraped her inner ankle twice, and her hands doggy paddled tensely near her armpits.

By the time she reached the park, her shoulders relaxed, her fingers uncurled, and her hands carved vertical orbits to either side of her hips. Her body had always been smarter than she: her stomach ached before she recognized her stress, and it called for the right foods just when she needed them, like dark leafy greens and chocolate before her period. Now, she rose onto her toes so as to leave the ground more easily and barely came down before she left the ground again. Her lungs delivered air and her heart pumped blood in perfect symbiosis, and she could do anything, anything,

anything, anything. Her body had won awards for her college track team after all, and she had graduated cum laude from a prestigious college. Everyone said she had a healing touch. Today she'd register for the test and begin studying.

She not only registered for the exam and ran the application to the post office before 10:30 but she pulled the study guide out from under the bed, wiped away all the dust, and plunged in. The first half hour, her brain resisted the abstract concepts, but an hour in, it clicked into gear. By noon she was absorbing material, maintaining focus, and feeling hopeful. That's when the shrill notes of the phone shredded her concentration.

When she answered it, she recognized the quality of the silence. A gasp for air between sobs.

"The sky is so high," Ovid said, "and the clouds are so far away." He broke into the kind of dry, painful sobs only men make. Each beat of her heart tapped her eardrums and stabbed her temples. The air of the apartment lost its last bit of oxygen. Outside, the heat of the day pounded the city full blast, and inside, her tiny air conditioner gave up with a mechanical sigh.

She worked her way around the bulky furniture to pull the blinds against the summer blaze, and she collapsed onto the velveteen couch, searching for the right words to release him from his grief. "What's going on?"

"I don't know," he said and sobbed more.

Connected to him like twins by an umbilical telephone line, she could picture him at home, his clean-shaven jaw, his olive skin, his hazel eyes turned green with tears, his disproportionately large hands making sweaty fists. He sounded high again.

She had experienced enough depression to know something of how he felt, but unlike him, she had always been able to function in the world. Sure, she procrastinated and felt plagued by the fact that she hadn't graduated magna cum laude; sure, she was stalled at this dead-end job; but she at least provided for herself, whereas Ovid did not.

"I just don't know what to *do* with myself," he said.

She knew the feeling too well.

"I keep seeing this blue woman dancing at the edge of the woods," he continued.

Fallon pushed herself out of the couch. She darted to the kitchen sink, wet a towel, and twisted it around her neck to cool off.

"On our land?" They owned a stone house on fifty acres in Oneonta, New York, inherited from their mother's side of the family. "Are you serious?"

"She's like a piece of the sky come down to visit," he said. "And I just want her to wait for me. But every time I run up the field to get to her, she vanishes."

He must be seriously high, Fallon thought as he rambled on. He had always leaned too heavily on marijuana, but he had never outright hallucinated.

It was some crazy neighbor performing one of those new age rituals that are becoming so popular. Lately, the whole country seemed to thirst for the lost magic religion used to offer. As he talked on, Fallon momentarily entertained the idea that the blue woman might be a piece of the magic from Chile reaching forward into the banal American reality that now characterized their lives. She shivered. Those things were only childhood perceptions, not possible in this heavily furnished apartment, this massive concrete city.

He collapsed into sobs again.

Her love for him surged around her like a river to buoy him. She might not be as smart as he was, might never go to medical school, but she could serve the world by saving him, and in the process save herself. She said the first thing that came to her mind. "Can you feel your feet?"

"What?" The word cracked across the line.

She gripped the brown couch cushion and drew her feet up to sit yoga style. The cuticle of her pinky toe had all but swallowed the nail. She picked at it, drawing blood.

"Your feet. Can you feel them? Touching the ground," she said more quietly.

"Of course, I can feel my fucking feet. What kind of an idiot question is that?"

"I just thought if you could ground yourself, it might help," she said.

"Don't give me that new-age pablum!"

There it was again. His words hit her as his fists had that distant summer afternoon the last time their fight got physical. She had tried to walk away from it. He had walked behind her, punching her in the back. Finally, she had curled herself into a ball and his fists hailed down on her like ice. She made a mad dash for the house and called the police. When Walter got home and found the police in his driveway, he was furious with her.

"I was just trying to help," she said to Ovid, now. Shame washed through her. Why had she allowed herself to be lulled into a sense of false security by the flattery of him turning to her for help? She thought for a second that he might listen to her, might even admire her form of intelligence, so different from his and her mother's.

"I don't know why I even bothered to call you," Ovid went on. "You want to help? Come home and help me take care of the house."

A blowtorch of rage roared to life under her skin. Every time he felt the scales of power tipping in her direction, he slammed them back hard to his side, changing moods with a speed that gave her emotional whiplash.

"No one asked you to go home," she said. "Dad can take care of the house himself."

"He's not strong enough, Fallon. You've got to face it. He's getting old."

"So? Sell the house."

"Sell the house? Mom's house? My God, you're cold."

"It's just a thing. An excuse to avoid getting a job." The words were out before she could think better of them.

"Oh, like you? Big time, successful *waitress*? Yeah. Wish I was more like you."

"She's not coming back, you know," she shouted.

"How the fuck do you know? You never understood her. You don't know what happened."

"Nobody knows, but I'm not wasting my life trying to find an answer or waiting for her to return."

They shouted at each other for more than an hour, going around in circles, repeating the same things, arguing about what they had or had not said, unable to hang up or resolve anything. He launched into his usual litany of criticisms and she fought back as best she could. When she finally hung up, she had a full-blown migraine. Each beat of her heart sent knives into her eyes and the crown of her head. The MCAT study guide on the floor tore when she tripped over it on her way back to bed.

# 2

# NO OBJECT IS SOLID

The next day, she spun and shapeshifted over the black-and-white tiled floors during the lunch hour rush at the North Star Pub. Commercial air conditioning blasted away the heat of summer, and her mind cut a path as sharp as glass. She remembered all her orders, even the incidentals. The shine off the thickly varnished bar expunged the taint of yesterday's argument with Ovid. The room bustled with customers, and her ten tables were full. When she folded herself up like an umbrella to squeeze between people and unfurled to deliver ketchup or salt, nothing could touch her, not Ovid's insults, not society's dictates, not even her own expectations. She was a thing in motion, a thing that couldn't be pinned down, a thing that could size people up in a split second and deliver whatever they so desired without the exchange of even one word. It was almost fun.

"For you, I'd recommend the Stilton cheese platter with Branston Pickle," she'd say, or, "Try the kidney pie. It's not really made with kidneys, and it comes with gravy that is out of this world." She enjoyed their cries of delight when she turned out to be right. She knew intuitively which rude customer needed to be mollified, and which ones actually wanted to be abused in return. She swept the tips into her apron pocket without looking at them so that the amount didn't spoil her mood. Spinning, she was momentarily free, momentarily happy.

During a lull, two younger dark-skinned men who accompanied an elderly white man ordered Sambuca, not your usual drink for an Irish pub. The younger men lit the Sambuca for their elder and he warmed his pale hands over the blue flame. When she delivered their check, the old man said, "We loved watching you. You're so graceful. We couldn't decide if you were a man or a woman. First, we thought, he's just a feminine man. But you'd spin around, and we'd think, no, she's a masculine woman. Beautiful."

Warmth infused her, and inexplicably, she wanted to cry. She thanked them and twirled away.

It was a good day until she waited on the stockbrokers. Most of them were regulars. They usually took a table and kept it for hours. They ordered so many drinks she was amazed they could walk back to work, and yet they did. It gave her a new understanding of the stock market. People's fortunes were made and lost on their gin-and-beer-soaked whims.

When one of the brokers grabbed her hands, she became acutely conscious that her hands smelled sour from the rag she mopped tabletops with.

"Smile," he said with his perfect white teeth and coiffed hair.

Her mood darkened like a thunderclap. She wanted to laugh, spray acid, and disappear all at the same time. She wasn't paid to smile. She was paid to serve, and serve she did. She looked away, hoping the poison had not yet risen to her eyes. Now shame suffused her. Why was she so angry at a man who was only trying to be nice? Why did she hate this Wall Street broker?

Because he was rich. Because he made loads of money shifting money around, creating nothing, and he was valued for it by society in a way she never would be, because she was his servant, and he therefore felt entitled to take her hands and command her expressions.

She smiled at him anyway, let her hands go limp so that he dropped them, and twirled away. Now a giraffe from the Central Park Zoo, she stretched her body long so that she could hold her tray above the crowd and squeeze through without spilling. Back at her service station, she wondered how much longer she could stand living in this crowded city and working this useless job. Ovid's words reverberated, "Oh, like you? Big time, successful *waitress?*"

She knew she could be so much more, that somewhere inside resided the kind strength that caused her to leap at the chance to attend the boarding school Ovid had refused eighteen months after they returned from Chile. Walter insisted that Ovid needed boarding school where she didn't , but he couldn't be forced to go, and the deposit had been paid. She left home without a backward glance. No matter how crazy and depressed she got, her body's decision propelled her all the way through college graduation.

There was a switch inside that made her adventurous, driven, and functional at times but she didn't know where it was or how to turn it on or off.

"Whew!" Will, the head bartender, said in the resounding silence after the lunch rush was over, pursing his lips and making an exaggerated gesture of wiping his brow. The prissy look was so comical in contrast to his bushy beard and broad frame that it teased a smile from her in spite of herself.

"There's the smile that makes it all okay," he said.

She made a face.

"What's wrong, beautiful?" Will asked.

"Nothing."

Will was the kind of man most people felt immediately comfortable with, a man who still wore a beard, a ponytail, and sandals, but who laughed at hippie jokes. He was ruggedly handsome, having spent a lifetime outdoors. Indoors, he was a wizard at organizing and strategizing. With his burly build and his knack for storytelling, he was often the center of a crowd of laughing men at the bar, but that didn't prevent him from noticing when a customer left his food to visit the bathroom, so he'd cover it with a plate to keep it warm. That's what drew Fallon to him.

"You hungry?" she asked.

"Starved."

"I saved you a meat pie someone forgot they ordered."

"My favorite," he said.

"I know."

When Will ducked behind the bar to eat, and she stacked empty plates left over from the rush, the angst from yesterday's fight with Ovid surrounded her like a mist. Ovid seemed to be going off the rails in a way he never had before. He'd always had bouts of depression that left him catatonic on the couch for weeks. He talked on occasion about ending it all, but he never hallucinated. What was going on? Had he gotten a batch of doctored pot? Was he on medication gone awry?

As always, when he'd expounded on all her intellectual and moral failings, her first reaction was to fight back, but when anger's tide receded, it uncovered her own mirroring disgust with herself. Guilt about her selfishness tugged her. Maybe Ovid and Walter really needed her. Ovid was convinced that if only she would return and obey his every command, he could make the long defunct family farm generate some kind of income. She thought his ideas ludicrous, but if she was serious about helping him, shouldn't she go home?

A stubborn, wordless part of herself refused.

Sometimes she wished she could tear a hole in the fabric of the universe, step through, and disappear like her mother had. She didn't want to die, exactly. She just wanted to stop for a while.

*No object is solid*, her mother told her one night during that fateful year in Chile. Eustacia Kazan was uncharacteristically tucking Fallon into her bed, which scraped against the red tile floor whenever she jiggled. Fallon lay under the blue wool coverlet absorbing the attention her mother usually reserved for Ovid, noticing how her mother's face shone, still beautiful at the age of fifty, with a small brown mole at the exact center of the lower lash line of her right eye. She couldn't remember her mother's physical voice. Instead, she remembered her mother's words as thoughts pressing through a veil straight into her mind.

*There are those*, Eustacia had said, *who, if they look hard enough, can see the seething atoms, the electrons spinning around the nucleus, and all the space in between, more space than substance. More space than substance!* She gave Fallon a little shake. *The only reason objects feel solid is because the negative and positive charges of the electrons push off the electrons of neighboring atoms.* She demonstrated with her hands squeezing emptiness between her palms, *and they repel each other the way a magnet repels another magnet. This tension, like the skin of water holding up a paperclip, is what prevents us from falling through.*

*So, if you can see the atoms spinning, all you have to do is figure out how to change the charge of the electrons to part them. You could pass through walls.* Her mother sighed and looked at the ceiling, momentarily deflated. *But perhaps this would require the genius of God.* Fallon waited. Eustacia lit up, pointing to herself. *Then again, I am a molecule of God, so it could be done. You have to be very smart, Fallon, very, very smart, like Ovid.* Or like Eustacia, Fallon thought. *And there is something about this country. I'm sure it will teach me finally how to command quarks and leptons.*

Fallon felt closer to her mother that year in Chile than she had ever felt in her life. Eustacia's eyes glittered brighter than usual that night, and the skin of her face was taut, as if the bones were trying to surface and dance for sheer joy at the idea of unravelling the molecular code of the universe and commanding the fabric of the physical. Eustacia wasn't actually looking at Fallon. Instead, she was looking at the pillow beside Fallon's head as if the pillow's atoms were, indeed, spinning, but it was close enough for Fallon to feel special. *It's a cipher, you see. Do you know what cipher means? It means both code and zero. Isn't that fascinating?* When she spoke, Fallon could almost feel the atoms spin inside her own head, feel both their complexity and their space. It terrified and exhilarated her. She wanted so much to be worthy of her mother's love and admiration as only Ovid was.

Wasn't her shapeshifting some version of what her mother had talked about? Hadn't the old man and his two dark-skinned lovers testified to her doing just that? If her mother parted the curtain and returned, would she recognize how much she was her mother's daughter and applaud? She felt like she needed her mother's blessing to go on, like she had been on auto pilot since her mother's death – or whatever it was. But the autopilot light had gone out. She was grinding to a halt -- or rather, the stakes of adulthood demanded more than mere survival. The canyon of the unseen had to be negotiated, and she didn't have a clue where to start. It hurt her head to think about it.

Her last table flagged her and signaled another round of drinks. She spun around and faced Will, who was rinsing glasses and scooping ice.

"What do you need?" he asked. He still had crumbs from the meat pie in his beard.

She tapped the corner of her mouth to alert him.

"I was saving those for later, but if you insist," he said, wiping them away. She smiled again.

"A gin martini, straight up, extra olives, and a Tom Collins."

"You got it," he said, not breaking his rhythm. He poured the liquor with a comically grandiose flourish, like a man conducting an orchestra.

The door jangled as the evening bartender, Collin, walked in. In contrast to Will's sturdy build and long hair, Collin was clean cut, with a narrow waist, short-cropped hair, and creased jeans. While Will's blue eyes were always warm, Collin's blue eyes were cold and expressionless. Rumor had it he was a Vietnam vet, which maybe explained his coldness. Fallon was glad she was off tonight. Will had a double shift.

"O Captain! My Captain!" Will called.

A tiny smile jerked the corner of Collin's mouth. "Came in early to eat," he replied.

"Absolutely. Take your time," Will said.

Fallon typed an order into the computer. When she turned back around, Will had already filled it. Fallon let out a big sigh.

"What's that about?" he said softly, his dark blue eyes dilating slightly.

"What?"

"That big sigh."

She hadn't been aware she had made one. "I'm fine. Had a fight with my brother last night."

"Just give me the word, and I'll drive right out to Oneonta and pop him for you."

"God no," she said, coloring. Her eyes shifted away from his. Usually, he just listened sympathetically without judgment.

"Well. Hang in there. We still on for later when I get off work?"

"Oh! I forgot! I don't know," she said. "I didn't sleep too well. My head hurts."

"Another time, then," he said, His glow dulled a fraction, but his tone remained light.

"Yes. Definitely. I'm sorry."

"Nothing to be sorry about," he said. The door jangled, and he turned to greet the new customers, "Welcome to the North Star Pub, pull up a seat."

For the first six months she had worked at the North Star, she hadn't realized he was sweet on her, because he always had a discerning eye and a kind word for anyone who emitted even the smallest nuance of discomfort, and she emitted a lot. They went out sometimes after work, but she hadn't seen him as boyfriend material. For one thing, he was ten years older than she, and for another, he didn't quicken her heart like Christo, an old high school crush she'd slept with only last week. The mere thought of her physical intimacy with Christo dizzied her. "I don't know why you bother," Fallon overheard Collin say as he squeezed behind Will and tucked a small comb into his tight back pocket. "She's obviously frigid."

Will smiled like a man with a well-kept secret and dried a glass.

When the other waitress came in for her evening shift, Fallon handed over her checks, divvied up her tips, and said goodbye to Will. He waved a blondly furred hand at her as she swung the door open. Collin nodded curtly. She stepped from the air-conditioned, frosted-glass interior onto the cobblestone mall of South Street Seaport. The summer heat blasted her like a kiln. Five p.m. was when the heat peaked. She was just sifting the hot air slowly into her lungs when a man hurtled toward her and snatched her purse.

Without thinking, she lit out after him, light on her toes, back arched, hands slicing the air. She gained on him easily, summoned all her aggression, and threw her voice like a karate chop, "Hey!" He faltered for a second, and she grabbed her bag with such force that she swung him around to face her.

The weak-chinned man with stringy hair assembled his face into a look of mild surprise, let go of the bag with a shrug, and sauntered into the crowd.

"You shouldn't do that!" she yelled after him as childlike outrage mushroomed inside her.

Will arrived panting. "You certainly told him. Bet he'll never do that again," he said ironically.

"Did you see that?" she turned to him.

"Sure did. He was on you the second you left the bar."

"I'm such an idiot," Fallon said.

"Are you kidding? You're like Arnold Schwarzenegger... only more graceful . . . and a whole lot prettier. Want me to call the cops?"

"Never mind. What's the point? He's long gone, anyway." She took a deep breath as sweat brimmed from her pores and trickled down her face and neck.

"Why don't you come back to the pub and collect yourself. I'll buy you a beer."

"No, that's okay, thanks. I'll just go home."

"You sure?"

"Yeah, thanks, Will."

"Well, I'd better get back. Take care, Fallon, you Amazon you."

She smiled, all muscle and sinew, but after he left, her heart slowed, her blood spun down, and the light inside her went out. An invisible hand had flipped the switch to off.

Sweat glued her T-shirt to her back. She turned away, feeling like a failure, knowing Will had feelings for her, not knowing why she didn't feel the same. Maybe he lacked the proper depth and complication she was used to in a person. She felt no attractive darkness, only quotidian sunlight and simplicity. How could he ever truly understand her or she him? She was a child of air and ciphers, loss and misery, and he was a folktale hero who comes to town a tinker and turns out to be a king. As she descended the subway stairs, her habitual gray curtains closed around her.

# 3

# CRUSHED

Her mental curtains didn't insulate her from the heat of the subway station. Steel and cement tunnels snaked underground, becoming a vast heat sink. The cement floor was grimy with spit, urine, and oval patches of gum stamped black by millions of feet. Serving Wall Street customers drink after drink all day long, coupled with the heat and press of people without a whiff of nature, brought the apocalypse near.

She kneaded the soft leather bag she rescued from the purse snatcher. Ovid had made it for her a few years ago, cured the leather himself, oiled it until it was supple, and hand-stitched it. He was always doing things like that. Once he hitchhiked to Oberlin, Ohio, during her junior year of college to help her build a platform bed in her first off-campus apartment. He came with a loaf of his homemade Swedish rye and home-churned butter tucked into his jean jacket. The loaf was mashed, but warm from his body, and she and her housemates relished it. Her housemates all fell in love with his thickly lashed eyes, his Michelangelo body, his unselfconscious, poet-physicist charm. He cut the Heathcliff bad-boy figure women were bred to adore. With him alive, part of her mother lived on.

She was proud to show him off, but a little worried that he would be embarrassed by her success at college in contrast to his own failure.

She and her housemates had taken in a stray kitten, but their landlord refused to let them keep it. Ovid buttoned the tiny black baby into his jean jacket, where it slept miraculously content, and he hitchhiked home with it. In fact, the kitten poking out of his collar right under his chin might have garnered more rides home than on the way out. Months later, when she came home for spring break, they got stoned together, and he confessed that he'd found the kitten frothing under the bed. He held his brow as he told the story and shook his head. He had treated it with flea powder before he read the label and learned that it was lethal to kittens. He was always injuring himself and others.

She closed her eyes to the subway tracks and forced her mind away from all that. She made herself liquid to merge with the water-laden air so she wouldn't be hot anymore. It was a trick she learned during those long camping trips her family took. Sometimes, the roads were so dusty they had to travel with the windows closed though it was broiling inside. Air conditioning was a luxury they never afforded themselves. One day, as they negotiated the hairpin turn down a steep mountainside, the sun beat through the rear window onto her head making it burn. As she wiped the sweat off the back of her neck, she discovered a pocket of cool air trapped under her hair. Some law of physics had been enacted, and when the grit between her teeth and her sticky skin got to be too much, she'd dip two of her fingers into that cool pocket at the back of her neck, and it gave her some measure of relief.

Now, swaying in the heat of the underground station like seaweed on the ocean floor, she kept her eyes closed as the presences of others pressed in on her. They talked, blew their noses, listened to headphones, and cocooned in mental buffers that allowed them to stand nose to ear on subway cars all over the city without killing each other. People outside the city simply didn't understand. New York wasn't violent. It was a miracle of patience.

*No object is solid,* she thought, opening her eyes to the brown and pink faces around her. Her electrons repelled the floor's electrons so that she hovered an incalculable millimeter above the ground.

*If you can see the atoms spinning,* her mother's words insinuated themselves into her mind again, *if you look hard enough, all you have to do is figure out how to change the charge of the electrons to part them.*

Standing on the subway platform, the thought hit Fallon like a minor explosion. Her mother had been talking about the atomic bomb. Worse, she had been talking about it like it was a wonderful magician's trick like you could blow everything apart and put all the pieces back together with the mere opening and closing of a curtain. A bitter smile creased her lips. Splitting the nucleus of an atom released an ungodly load of energy. She stared hard at the man in front of her, who stared dully at the cement floor. His nose, that black woman's finger tapping on the handle of her briefcase, that teenager's ear, capped by a headphone—each held a nuclear explosion's worth of energy inside, energy that maintained balance when properly harnessed. When disrupted, though, it became a mushroom cloud of destruction. She teetered on the edge of rejecting and accepting her mothers's assertions. She closed her eyes and let go. A cool expanse burgeoned within her. Creative and destructive energy were one and the same; the only difference was order.

At last, the train roared into the station, pushing hot air before it like a dragon, a tail of heat curling behind. Fallon stepped into the air-conditioned interior and secured a slippery plastic seat.

The bell chimed, warning of the doors' imminent closure, when a flash of movement caught her eye. Her mother came hurtling toward her, jumped the turnstile, and sprinted for the train. Head thrown back, elbows slicing the air, she ran just as she had run before she combusted on the *Altiplano,* more air than substance, molecules in a furious reel, faster than her knees could pump. As the doors closed, she slipped through the crack and grabbed a pole, spinning around it and grinning as people made way for her. All of Fallon's mental and physical circuits jammed as the possible and impossible collided. However, when Eustacia's face came full circle, it wasn't Eustacia at all. It wasn't even a woman, but a young man with shoulder-length red hair, a long-distance runner by the look of his emaciated build. *No object is solid.* The garlicky scent of his sweat wafted toward her.

Fallon blinked to reorient herself, but the floor of the train tilted off plumb. Was it the purse snatcher following her? He looked at her without recognition, and she decided she was imagining things. Well, she smirked to herself, she was definitely imagining things. But that was the problem: she couldn't tell what she imagined and what really happened half the time. Or rather, things she knew to be true, that she had seen and felt with her physical senses in Chile, were not possible in America.

Of course it wasn't her mother. How could it have been? She had been gone thirteen years. Once the atoms fly apart, no one knows how to put them back together. Not even her mother. She and her two brothers had both seen it and not seen it. But if she could fly apart, why couldn't she fly back together? Anything was possible. That thought filled her with dread instead of relief. If anything were possible, how could you take a step without fearing that the ground might open up and swallow you, or that a circus clown's head might emerge from your right toe?

She shook her head. Those things didn't happen anymore, if indeed they ever happened at all. She couldn't decide if she wanted them to or not. Eventually, one just had to go on. The mind writes off the impossible as something for which a rational explanation is temporarily unavailable, a mere misunderstanding. That's how the extraordinary becomes ordinary, forgettable, inconsequential. After thirteen years, there just wasn't any reason to wonder any more.

"Fallon!" A man's symmetrical face came into focus, golden haired like the sun, smelling of salt and seaweed. She blinked, waiting for the illusion to pass. Instead, it solidified into two peridot eyes that hid an ocean of loss and soft lips—so like Ovid's—that offered tenderness if only she could reach it.

"Christo?" She remembered their bucking attempts to make love last week with a twinge of arousal twined inextricably with shame. Like two ships chained to opposing docks, they could mirror but not meet. Here was a man she should be able to instantly merge with, because he came from the same desolate inner landscape. They had been born on the same day. His brother was schizophrenic, and his mother had recently been hospitalized with a psychotic breakdown. They had gone to high school together and had run into each other some weeks ago, rekindling an unmanifested high school crush.

"What are you doing here?" he asked, his lips tucking in at the corners with what could have been pleasure or disdain.

"I work near Wall Street, remember?"

She would never have considered dating a stockbroker if he hadn't been her high school friend first. She found people who worked out of the profit motive suspect. But maybe she was too judgmental.

"What about you? Just getting off work?"

"Nah. Meeting with my mother's lawyers," he grimaced. "I had to get power of attorney over her because of her," he hesitated, "incapacitation."

"Why haven't you called?"

"I was going to, but . . . " he trailed off.

She resonated with the damaged ones. But it never worked out because they couldn't see each other through the damage. She should let him go. Yet, even as she told herself this, her eyes traced the clean line of his jaw, the tendons of his neck that disappeared into his loosened collar and tie. Once she and Ovid had broken a thermometer, and a ball of mercury rolled across his desk, liquid yet solid, not really touching the surface it rolled over. They had rolled the ball around in the palms of their hands, marveling at metal in this liquid state, childishly ignorant of the poison they cradled. Now, the sight of Christo's lips turned her blood to mercury that slipped through her body as rapidly and lightly as silk in the wind and lifted her off the ground.

"Are you doing anything tonight?" she asked.

"I shouldn't," he replied. He had broken up with someone not too long ago, and they both knew it was too soon.

As he spoke, his pulse beat at the base of his neck, and warmth radiated off his skin and embraced her, reminding her of his long legs hidden beneath broker-suit slacks.

"Neither should I," she said.

At an East Village bar, she drank wine, and he drank beer with shots of tequila. He told her about his troubles managing his mother's apartment building. When he wasn't working as a stock trader, he managed the building, hired plumbers and carpenters, interviewed tenants. He needed to evict some bum tenants but couldn't until he obtained power of attorney. She admired his ability to navigate the adult world in ways she had never been able to.

In a drunken haze, discourse turned to argument. Fallon defended the tenants he wanted to evict and said something he thought was arrogant. She wasn't sure it was possible for her to be arrogant since her general opinion of herself was so low, but it was horribly possible that she was so unaware that she wasn't at all like she thought. Shame crystalized to anger. Years of defending herself from Ovid triggered her warrior gear. She couldn't help it. When backed into a corner, words flew from her mouth like small knives.

Though their date clearly was shipwrecked, they clung to it like storm-tossed survivors.

They decided to play pool. But she couldn't anticipate how one round surface would impact another. Christo leaned over the green felt to take a shot, lined up the pool stick and pulled it back slowly, thoughtfully. With a quick, soft jab, he struck the ball, and it hit the other ball in exactly the right place, with exactly the right force, neither too hard nor too soft. The movement was so sensual and held so much intuitive knowledge of the laws of physics that she had to touch him tonight. She drained a glass; alcohol-induced euphoria gave her courage.

They ended up at his apartment, empty but for a mattress on the floor in the living room, and they tried unsuccessfully to make love again. Their senses were so blunted by alcohol that neither of them could reach climax.

"I can't believe I'm doing this to Renée," he muttered as he lost consciousness, the smell of alcohol sugary on his breath.

She lay awake in the pink light shining in from the street, her face on his hairless, lightly muscled chest, trying to withstand the tide of nameless longing that came crashing in. Their two bodies made a solid island in an amorphous sea.

In that murky year after their mother's death, the siblings fought more violently. One time, Ovid straddled Terry and was punching him and, when she pulled him off, he turned on her. They raged all over the house, and she retreated all the way up into the bathroom, and backwards into the bathtub. He pinned her by the collar, and as he pulled back his massive fist to punch her, she realized that she wasn't going to be able to dodge it. In that long moment, some cool part of herself told her that if she relaxed her neck, it would hurt less. She did. When his fist smashed into her jaw, it jarred her brain, but it didn't leave so much as a bruise. However, when she touched it, pain shot up into her teeth.

Ovid was contrite afterwards. An hour later, he brought her a miniature couch upholstered in blue velvet that he'd made. His face was open and his eyes round as he offered it to her. She wondered how he could change so quickly, for her own anger still beat in her chest and hardened her to him. A shy smile loosened his face as he showed her how it unfolded into a tiny bed with a tiny, embroidered sheet and two matching pillows. She wished she could shrink herself down, crawl into that bed, and live in a world made with such infinite care.

Christo's heart beat resonantly in her ear. If only his body would open just like that couch and fold her inside. But there was no space left inside of Christo, so she fell asleep.

In the morning she awoke alone. She had dreamt vividly of a woman looking at her with one enormous, yellow-irised eye. The eye closed and opened into two, closed and opened into four, closed and opened into a multitude of yellow eyes. Outside the window of Christo's apartment, oval yellow leaves blinked in at her from the branch of a tree. It was too early for the leaves to be turning, but those yellow leaves called her back to herself. What was she doing here? He was like that third glass of wine you told yourself you shouldn't have, but the second you told yourself that, it sealed your determination to have it any way. Why did she say yes to Christo but no to Will?

The toilet flushed. Christo came out of the bathroom dressed for work and walked, blank-faced, to the door. She sat up in bed, sheet wrapped around her body, hair dark and sharp-tipped with last night's sweat. He paused with his hand on the doorknob and looked back. She tried to smile. Wordlessly he returned, squatted by the mattress, kissed her softly on the neck, and left. Butterflies taste with their feet, sea turtles breathe through their asses, and no one really understands gravity or love, least of all her.

# 4

# OVID'S BIRDS AND BEES

"Cloe-ray-ee-ah – noo-dee-lah-bia," Ovid whispered to himself that cloudy October day in the greenhouse he'd attached to the farmhouse in Oneonta. "Chloraea nudilabia," he repeated as he bent over the orange orchids that grew in a thick cluster at the end of a stalk. Their fleshy lobes filled his vision. He moved to the next flower, white with green veins: "Chloraea ma-ge-lan-ica," he whispered in its ear. It was a subtle flower whose beauty was easily overlooked, like Fallon. He straightened to look up at his Berberis linearifolia, which cascaded from a birch log he'd suspended from the greenhouse roof to replicate their natural habitat. The orange mane of flowers filled his chest with pride. Probably no one in the northern continent had produced such a magnificent bloom. He scratched his black goatee and brushed a forelock off his brow. He stretched to massage a sore muscle in his shoulder.

He'd first seen Berberis orchids in Chile when his mother brought the family to the Nahuelbuta National Park in the highest part of the Cordillera mountain range in Southern Chile. The giant monkey puzzle trees shot their singular trunks to the sky, their evergreen foliage branching like umbrellas. Spanish moss festooned southern beech trees, and long strands of orange orchids weighed down their branches.

*These are epiphytes, my dears. That means they grow on other plants, but they draw nutrients from the air.* Her words were like his own thoughts, now.

A wave of longing plunged through him. The truth Eustacia had told was huge, full of contradictions, containing multitudes—just like the world. There was nothing she didn't know. He was her only *true* child, more of her flesh and blood than Fallon or Terence. No one else had a mind like hers, no one else echoed his thoughts and drives so perfectly. Why had she left him? Why hadn't she come back? How could he follow?

It was October already. He hadn't spoken to Fallon since their fight almost two months ago. Winter would be here before he knew it. He had so much to do before it came. He needed help, goddamn it. Screw Fallon. She didn't care about anyone but herself. Well, he didn't really want her help, anyway. It was Terence he needed. They'd gone into business together for a short time fixing houses, building cabinets. But he never returned Ovid's phone calls.

He bent low over a stalk of white Gavilea venosa. Breeding and hybridizing orchids was a fine art. Just the right environment had to be achieved. He wanted to invent the first blue orchid, a difficult feat because they lacked the genes to make true blue or black, though lots of stores achieved the illusion with vegetable dye. His early attempts had failed, but when he finally achieved it, he would name it Chloraea eustacia. She too was fed by air.

He looked around the plasticized greenhouse. He'd love to build an entire conservatory right in the center of Oneonta. It would have four parts: an indoor natural water park, a learning lab, a café, and a hotel. It would make Oneonta a destination spot for the entire Northeast. His thoughts spun high. Instead of using eye-burning chlorine to sterilize the water, they'd use ultraviolet light, and the water slides would tumble through a rainforest of orchids and vegetation. Schools would bring their science classes for hands-on labs, and afterwards they'd play. If you just wanted to come for lunch or coffee, there'd be a section for that, a verdant retreat from bitter northeastern winters. People could write and read in a Garden of Eden. Guests could stay in a hotel that would actually be a giant greenhouse, sleeping with plants all around them. It would only cost a few hundred million. If he could only get the right investors, it was so viable, and it would be so massively profitable. He could feel the joy of creation expanding like the space between stars, a whole galaxy of ideas. He was an endless font. He *must* call the mayor to find out who the money people were in this town.

Cold calling. His thoughts crashed into the huge roadblock. The phone. Its blackness loomed before him. His energy fractured and dove. He should just pick up the phone. But he couldn't. It wasn't a choice. He didn't know how to talk to people. He always made them angry. He didn't know why. That's why he needed Fallon to come home. She could make the calls, set the thing up, get the engineers, and he'd tell them all how to do it. He just needed someone to clear the paths. He could lead the way. She wasn't doing anything important in New York. This venture was greater than both of them, a monument to their mother. But Fallon wouldn't listen to him, damn her. She didn't believe in him. Didn't trust him. Was too dull-minded to see the potential. She was not an entrepreneur like he was, willing to take chances. Again, a wave of longing for Eustacia tossed him, nearly knocking him to the ground.

He looked at the hole he had made in the wall between the greenhouse and the kitchen. When would he ever finish building the door between? When would he replace all this plastic with glass? When would he develop a heating and cooling system that was energy efficient? And the bees. He had to empty the supers. It was October already, and getting cold. The honey would granulate if he didn't empty the supers soon. Every cell of his body sagged with fatigue as the list multiplied.

His fatigue found no bottom as he pushed through the plastic into the kitchen. He'd never get the honey out of the combs if it crystalized. Not without heating it. And that would ruin the nutrients. All that work for nothing. He had been avoiding the bees because they had been getting more aggressive lately. He had to research that. Was it possible that the Africanized bees were making it farther north? They had been crossbreeding with bees in Texas, and there had been a few killer bee attacks that ended in death over the last ten years. Maybe he was doing something wrong. He was such a loser. There was so little time! The smell of burnt bread assailed him. Shit!

The oven door screamed as he yanked it wide. The hot air blasted his face and dried his eyes. He reached for the pan, burned his thumb, yelped, grabbed a towel, and pulled the pan out. He tipped the loaf pan upside down, emptying the bread onto his towel-covered hand, knocking on it to test for doneness. Instead of a dull thud, it rang hollow. Overdone. Obviously. Dark brown on top and black on the bottom. Ruined. He tossed the heavy brick into the garbage as his emotions spiraled further downward, the floor opening up, the panic rising, pain without end.

Something blue flashed outside the window, stopping the downward spiral.

The blue woman danced nude at the edge of the forest again. A gust of wind rippled through long brown grasses, and rushed up the field toward her, bringing more leaves down. The hemlocks roiled against the gray clouds of an oncoming storm. Who was she?

The first time he'd seen Blue, as he called her, he thought he was seeing things. But the grass bent down where she had danced. He asked his neighbors whether anyone new had moved in. It was at least a half mile to the next house, and the answer was no. He caught his breath. His energy eddied with her as she danced and turned her hands overhead like a Spanish dancer, her torso wiggling like a blue eel of pleasure. She was slight, with conical breasts too small to sag, but large enough to fill a mouth with floury softness. Her round belly gave succulent sway to her back and buttocks. She gyrated, a perfect black triangle covering her pudendum, a silver chain glittering just under her navel as she swiveled. Was her skin naturally blue? Or had she painted herself? She had been turning up more often lately, and her dancing always caught him, distracted him, saved him from the downward spiral. He calmed and opened the door. He jogged slowly toward her, hoping she wouldn't notice him this time, but as soon as she did, she darted into the woods. "Wait," he called, half to himself. "Don't go."

He picked up his pace and dove after her into the lemony scent of the hemlocks, as dark as the enchanted forests of Grimm's fairy tales. Where had she gone? He caught just a flicker of blue up ahead. He followed. No, she was over there. Was that laughter? Was that a flash of her black hair disappearing beyond that tree? He spun and turned, following, until she led him to a vast oak tree he'd never seen before. The trunk was as wide as both his arms outspread. It must have been hundreds of years old. What a fantastic tree. He spun around. She had evaporated. His chest ached, whether from running or from a sense of loss, he could not tell. But this tree. He knew every inch of their fifty acres. How had he never seen this tree before? It would be perfect for a sky dwelling. He would build it. He'd saved the wood from that old barn they bulldozed down the road. He would build it for her, and she would come to him there.

He went back to the house and gathered the tools, the beehive completely forgotten.

"Ovid? Ovid!" Walter bellowed, age clotted his voice with phlegm.

Dropping his tools in a bucket, Ovid opened the kitchen door, and the smell of wood with a hint of mold enveloped him. His black T-shirt was drenched with sweat. He had nearly finished the roughed-in frame of the tree house. Not bad for a day's work, but the days were too short. It would be dark by five.

"I'm right here. What?" He tripped over the vinyl "slate" tiles. God, he had to rip the vinyl up and mill that old chestnut log he'd been saving to make new floors that would match the old. He had to find a chestnut tree farm where he could get more logs directly. Nothing would do but his own handiwork.

"Where's my thing?" Walter cried.

"What thing?"

"The thing I left on the table. You know the—thing!" Walter

made incoherent hand gestures toward the wood-grain Formica table, which sagged under two-foot-high stacks of junk mail. Increasingly, over the last few years, Walter struggled to find the right words, and sometimes he plugged an extension cord into itself and wondered why the radio wouldn't work. He was only seventy but appeared to be developing dementia. Ovid knew it was the beginning of the end for Walter; the thought ricocheted off concatenating bumpers as if caught in a pinball machine.

"I don't know what you're talking about." Ovid tried to stay patient, but his temper flared.

"Yes, you do. It was right there. On the table. This morning."

"There was nothing on the table this morning."

"Don't contradict me! I put it there myself!" Walter thundered. "The drill! The drill! Where did you put it?" When they were children, Walter's temper tantrums had been infrequent, but the dementia triggered them more often, followed by adamant denial.

"I didn't put it anywhere!" Ovid shot back.

"Yes, you did. I left it right here!" He pointed to the table again.

"I'm telling you there was nothing there when I got up this morning."

"Are you telling me I'm a liar?"

"I'm telling you you're a fucking idiot," Ovid exploded.

Walter stepped back in surprise. "You've got an anger problem, young man."

Ovid shook his head, laughed, and stalked back outside.

It was nearly dark. He *had* to take care of the bees. Cloudy days were not the best for collecting; the bees got grumpy. But the forecast said it was going to rain for the rest of the week, and he could almost feel the honey crystalizing. He should stop and change his clothes. Strong scents disturbed bees. He should get the smoker started, but he was out of bark and could take a few stings. He just wanted to get it done while he was motivated.

Still angry, he yanked one super out and examined it. A bee stung him. The pain started small and expanded as the venom spread. Another stung him, a warning to slow down. He almost liked the sharp clean feel of it. Some swore it was good for arthritis, not that he had any. He set the super down behind him. As he cautiously pulled out the second super, he accidently trapped a bee against the frame, squashing it. Three more bees stung him, a triangle of pain. Stay cool. He wasn't allergic. No danger there. Don't swat them, just back off, slow down, flick the stinger out sideways so that it doesn't squeeze in more venom. He knew the drill. He backed up and tripped over the super on the ground, sending the second one flying and planting his knee and directly into the first. The bees buzzed angrily and dive bombed him from all sides.

"Dad!" he yelled. Two bees flew into his mouth and stung the back of his tongue. Danger became crystal clear. He must get away. Roaring filled his ears, and strength surged through his arms. He swatted them away, yelling. They flew up his nose, into his ears. They collected on the bare skin around his neck. He wiped off a blanket of them as his throat swelled.

"Dad!" he yelled, his voice barely audible. The bees dove faster, frenzied. He struggled to keep his throat open, siphoning a straw of air through it. He stumbled toward the house, hands outstretched. Dimly, through the swarm, he could see the front door open, heard Walter call. Oh no. An old man like that. They'd kill him. It would be his fault. He waved Walter away while pain lit up his body. A tidal wave of nausea engulfed him. His vision narrowed to a tunnel. Sound stopped. The tunnel constricted until there was only a tiny spot of light at the end. Then it went out.

In Fallon's apartment the phone rang. She knew instantly something was wrong, and she picked up fast.

"Fallon! I don't know what to do. The hive is attacking Ovid!" Walter said.

"What? My god, don't call me, call 911."

"911. But what should I do right now? He's on the ground! They're all over him."

# 5

# TIME TRAVEL

F allon was numb when she bought the bus tickets home. Small country roads spread like capillaries between New York City and Oneonta, so there was no direct route, forcing her to call all the stations between to figure out the connections. It would take her all night and she would spend hours waiting in small bus stations in one- stoplight towns.

Her worst fear had been realized: Ovid's life was in danger, and now she had to go back to save him. She had always known it would come to this, but at the same time it was unbelievable. As she sat on the bus, befuddled by fumes from the urinal at the back, the engine's growl conjured the hum of the ocean liner they had taken to Chile. A sing-song voice narrated the past, and without knowing it, she succumbed:

It was only upon their arrival aboard ship at the port of Santiago, Chile, that she had managed to capture her mother's attention long enough to inform her that Terence was missing. She was ten and Terence was seven. So involved were her parents in their last-minute disputes and plans that she could not make her voice heard above the folding and unfolding of maps, papers, and documents. Aghast, Eustacia and Walter Kazan immediately dropped all their papers and luggage and raced around the ship, frothing and gesticulating, too agitated to make themselves understood, until finally, the crew herded all four of them off the ship with the rest of the passengers.

The city was inhabited by yellow birds that day. Every windowsill, every iron railing, and every statue was covered with birds. The trees were clouds of rippling yellow, the traffic lights were bright garlands of feathers, and the Plaza de Armas looked like a field of overgrown dandelions. But whatever this city offered, it took back the same night, during the curfew imposed by the military dictatorship.

The family's panic over their missing child did not prevent Eustacia from taking a deep breath and declaring with a sense of rightness and finality, *"Children, we have come to the right place at last, I can feel it. The holy grail is just around the corner."*

"What are you looking for," young Ovid, only eleven, had asked.

*"I have no idea, my pretty boy, but I'm sure I'll know it when I find it."*

Eustacia aspired to be an inventor like her father. She stood for hours in her various laboratories across the world, wherever her husband's job or her intuition took them, thinking very hard. She intended to invent the single most brilliant thing ever to have been invented.

For now, however, they would have to wait for their car and wooden packing crates to clear customs and for their youngest child to be returned to them, as they were sure he would be. After a few hours, their car cleared customs, but they were told that the crates were being held indefinitely. Still no child. Finally, as the sun was setting, the captain of the ship delivered Terence, wearing the captain's hat. The elderly man shook the parents' hands with a disapproving look, spoke some words in Spanish that no one understood as he smiled at Terence, took back his hat, bowed, and left.

*Where have you been, you naughty boy?* Eustacia said, smiling. *Did I pack you by accident into our wooden crates?*

"No," Terry began, but was interrupted.

*You know, it's funny*, Eustacia said, slapping her thigh, *when I was packing the crates, the job seemed endless. At several points I had the distinct feeling that I was packing the same things over and over again. Little Brother was hovering about, I'm almost sure.*

He had, in truth, been hovering around his mother as she packed. The crates were the size of double-wide coffins. He'd been taking all his toys and valued possessions out of them each time his mother put them in. She hadn't noticed what was happening, though she had shooed him away several times as one would an annoying idea. The phone rang, and she left to answer it.

*I know what happened. He must have crawled into the crate when I was called away to the phone. He must have lain down with his toys so as not to be separated from them forevermore. When I came back you had already nailed the lid on, Walter. You must have shut him inside! How did you survive, you little urchin?* she asked, pinching his cheeks.

"Why, it must have been the ketchup you packed in the same case, Mother," Ovid said, jumping between them.

"No, I—" Terry tried to argue.

Fallon vaguely remembered playing with Terry over the two weeks aboard, but she was too tired to sort it out.

"See how red his cheeks are?" Ovid argued.

*Indeed, I do*, Eustacia laughed. *A brilliant deduction, my boy.* She clapped him on the back.

Fallon's memory of Terry gallivanting around the ship shimmered and faded until he disappeared before her eyes. Walter smiled faintly and shook his head. Eustacia spoke, and the story was made manifest. She was pleased with what she saw. And that was their first day.

If Eustacia was negligent, it was benignly so, and there was some sort of dubious comfort in the fact that they were named after her body parts. Eustacia was so amazed and fascinated by the fact that her skinny body could produce entire beings, she wanted to canonize the organs which made it possible. Thus, she was ready to write Ovum down on the birth certificate when Walter intervened and begged her to name him Ovid, after the poet. By her second child, a year later, she came to understand that the whole process did not start there, and she was delighted to discover the mystical timing of her descending eggs. She wanted to name her daughter Fallopia, but Walter suggested Fallon. It was an Irish name, and her mother was Irish. It meant "grandchild of the ruler" and Eustacia liked that. Her third child came three years later. She would have named him Utero but Walter suggested Terence, or Terry for short.

Walter was an amiable man, easily confused by the emotions of others. He was tall and good-looking like his wife, with a well-developed jaw and shapely nose; together they made a handsome couple. But unlike the pinball speed of his wife's mind, his mind was slower and more methodical, brilliant in a different way. Walter's profession as an urban planner made it possible for them to travel. He liked nothing better than to devise suburbs where people stayed neatly in their houses, and cars were directed, through skillful signage and street curvature, to flow smoothly and unimpeded. The family had lived in many countries, but always returned to their house in Upstate New York.

Reunited with their errant son, they drove their Dodge Dart to the outskirts of the city to find the earthquake-proof house Walter rented for them. The development sat under the protective, circling arms of Manquehue, a brown foothill at the base of the snow-crested peaks of the Andes, which had hosted an ancient and superior civilization that built terraced gardens and temples only on the highest and steepest mountaintops.

At first the house looked to be nothing but a drab, flat-roofed rectangle, squatting among other rectangles. But they were impressed by the river-stone patio and drive. Carved double front doors opened into a red-tiled hall that wrapped around a glassed-in garden. A full wall in each room consisted of a sliding glass door that opened onto a backyard on one side and a stone patio on the other. It was vastly different from their colonial farmhouse in upstate New York.

Walter's workplace had left a note about the international school the children were to attend, so after the family dropped off their luggage, he drove them immediately to the school, to register them. The school, Nido de Aguilas, or Nest of the Eagles, was perched atop another foothill of the Andes on the other side of town. Because they were halfway around the planet, the seasons were reversed. What was summer in New York was winter in Chile. The children, lulled into a stupor by too many new sights, too much distance, and seasonal reversal, barely saw the few landmarks Walter pointed out to them so that they could take the public bus to school the next day.

In a daze, they were interviewed by the principal of the school and registered for classes. Maria Ester, a new co-worker of Walter's, met them at their house that night to teach the children some Spanish so they could manage the bus by themselves in the morning.

Sitting with them in wood carved dining chairs, Maria Ester, a dark-skinned, high-boned woman, taught them how to say *"permiso"* when they boarded the bus and *"pare, por favor,"* when they wanted to get off. Schoolchildren rode for free. *Pare, por favor.* Stop, please. *Pare, pare.* The words reverberated in the children's collective mind.

The next morning, Eustacia laid out their navy-blue national school uniforms, Walter forced them to eat a huge breakfast, and the two parents loaded them up with gigantic sandwiches wrapped in wax paper, rolled them out to the local bus stop on Las Condes, and wished them the best of luck.

Standing at the bus stop surrounded by mist, they did what they had always done when their parents brought them to other countries. They stood close together, tangled their fingers in the hems of each other's garments, and moved like one organism, an amoeba, now one edge leading, now the other. They filled their heads with fog so they thought nothing, felt nothing, feared nothing. When the dark green bus roared out of the mist and ground to a halt before them, sighing fumes of gasoline and oil, they boarded without question.

Other school children in navy uniforms with clean faces and wet, combed hair crowded the bus, along with a few adults holding chickens in cloth sacks. Once aboard, the smell of gasoline and some other musky animal scent engulfed them. They squeezed into one seat together and hooked their sleepy stares straight ahead. The bus passed beneath cool eucalyptus groves with sickle-shaped leaves and overpowering scent, drove past pink and blue stucco shops, crossed bridges spanning the churning Mapocho River several times and wended its way through cardboard shantytowns and upscale suburban developments. With all the fog, they recognized little from the day before, and as more and more children got off at different schools and the bus climbed higher into the hills, they floated further and further out into mental space, like astronauts cut loose from the mothership. Finally, Ovid spotted a bright yellow newsstand shining in the mist like a beacon.

"This is the stop. I know it," he shouted, reeling them back to earth. If they could have articulated thought, they would have felt grateful to their all-knowing leader, but they were beyond thought.

They staggered to their feet and worked their way up to the bus driver.

"*Pare, por favor,*" said their elder brother.

The bus driver glanced over his shoulder. The brakes screeched like a dying animal, and the driver pulled back the door lever.

After the bus growled away, they stared at the paved road opposite the newsstand, curving up the hill into a gray cloud.

"Are you sure?" asked Fallon.

"Completely," Ovid answered, shoving his hands deep into his pockets.

They tucked their gigantic sandwiches under their arms and began to climb. The fog gradually cleared and the sun burned hotter. Olive green hills, dotted here and there by dark green bushes, surrounded them, but there was no sign of the school. The sun climbed higher into the sky as they climbed the hill. They shed their matching sweaters and kept walking. Finally, when the road petered out into a red dirt path that wound under a barbed wire fence, they knew they had either taken a wrong turn or gotten off at the wrong stop.

Looking down at the ground, Terrence began to cry.

"What are you crying about?" Ovid asked, irritated.

"We're lost and we'll never find our way home. We don't even know where we live."

"Mom and Dad will find us," Fallon offered.

"How can they? We don't know where we got off." Terry's nose ran as his tears escalated. "I'm hungry," Fallon said.

They all sat down and unrolled their sandwiches, which consisted of a few slabs of ham between hard rolls that had only gotten harder as the hours had passed. With the first bite, they realized they were famished. They became so absorbed in the gnawing of their sandwiches that the world faded. When they looked up from lunch, a gaunt man stood over them. His face was dark and wide boned. His slanted black eyes regarded them with an expression that combined wariness and barely restrained laughter. He silently motioned for them to follow.

He led them from one cow path to another. Finally, he stopped and waited for them to catch up. He raised his right hand and pointed to what they realized was a soccer field, nestled between gently sloping hills. They could just see the roof of their school beyond the next swell. By now, heat rippled up from the field, and as they stared, another movement distinguished itself. Reddish brown tarantulas dotted the field, slowly raising their hairy legs and planting them in the olive grass like disembodied hands on a piano.

They looked at the man in fear. His jerked his chin up slightly, the lines around his eyes softened, and he pointed them forward with his lips. They stepped toward the field, working their way delicately through the tarantulas, which turned out to be harmless. By the time they remembered to turn back and thank the man, whom they ever after referred to as the Tarantula Man, he had vanished.

# 6

# BREAD AND CIRCUS

F allon awoke in a panic. Had she missed her stop? The bus reflected only the interior. She sprang from her seat and lurched up the aisle gripping one headrest after the other.

"Have we passed Kingston?"

"What?" said the bus driver. "No, no, next stop, in about fifteen minutes."

At the Harriman stop, as she stretched her legs over the worn linoleum and pondered the junk food in the vending machines, Chile superimposed itself so that she now inhabited two times simultaneously. She had not allowed herself to review that period in her life for a long time. In the first year after the family returned from Chile, she had craved the very things she'd formerly found strange, olive and brown countryside, misty mornings, tarantulas, and she somnambulated through school. But at boarding school, those memories nauseated her, and she fended them off whenever they arose.

Now, like a phalanx of inexorable ants, memories colonized her mind.

At first, they found Chile drab, the hills too brown, the dirt too red, the trees too short. Tall iron fences and cinder block walls with broken glass mortared along the top surrounded every house in their development. At the end of the street stood a recently abandoned farmhouse, with stucco walls, curved doors, and a tile roof. Narcissus still bloomed along the front walk.

Every weekend, Walter and Eustacia took them out to explore the city and surrounding countryside. All the tiny differences lifted them up and set them afloat like a boat without an anchor, the only comfort in sight - the warmth of the Chilean people: a tiny penguin paced the fish counter at the Persion market, fish were sold with their heads still attached, thread was spooled on long cardboard cylinders, roofs were tiled in red, and stinging caterpillars fell from trees. The names of the streets and rivers—El Alameda, La Barnachea, El Mapocho, El Arrayan - flavored their every move.

Their parents fed them food they had never eaten before: stewed peaches, bread toasted over gas flames, live sea urchins nestled in the ice of a street vendor's cart. The vendor cut the top off a sea urchin, squeezed lemon inside, and carved the red flesh from its spiny case. They swallowed it raw like oysters.

Often the walks were too long, and little Terry lagged behind, sniffling with a foreign virus, and limping because he somehow lost a sock. The plumbing in the house occasionally baptized them with spontaneous jets of water from the kitchen sink or the children's bathroom (*el baño chico*). The mornings were cold and the afternoons hot. One night, when Ovid helped Walter start a kerosene heater, he accidentally swallowed some kerosene as he was siphoning it. He burped kerosene all night, and the house smelled as if plastic toy soldiers had vaporized. Thereafter, when they needed warmth, they built a fire in the fireplace. Some mornings as the tectonic plates shifted beneath them, they awoke to find their beds buzzing across the floor while glasses clinked in cabinets.

Like their mother, Chile was long and skinny, and at the end of the world. The Pacific to the west, the snow-covered Andes to the east, and the high desert Altiplano to the north protected the country from the rest of the world. Its southern tip, Tierra del

Fuego, or Land of Fire, was the last bit of land before Antarctica. At some places, Chile was so thin they could almost touch the Andes from the ocean, the way their mother could almost touch her back through her bellybutton.

*Chile means the land where the earth ends, children,* Eustacia told them in her not quite present way. *Come out and see the stars. We are almost the same distance below the equator now as we were above the equator in New York. See how the constellations are different? There is Centaurus and the Southern Cross. We can't see them from our home. And from here we can't see Polaris.* As she looked up at the sky, the tiny brown mole beneath her right eye might have been their north star. *When it's winter here, it's summer there, and when it's summer there, it's winter here. Everything is opposite and upside down. Even the cyclones spin in a different direction.*

At the international school, where classes were taught in English, but Spanish was spoken in the breezeways, their history teachers proudly shared that Chile's history was the most stable in South America because of its geographical isolation: "In Chile, we all speak the same language, *Castellano, not Spanish.* The indigenous Araucanians mixed with the Spanish long ago, and to symbolize that, the Araucanian star graces our flag. The blue represents the sky, the white represents the snow of the Andes, and the red is for the blood we spilled gaining our freedom."

One day after school, noticing the cadre of kite flyers on the broad Avenida de Las Condes, Ovid begged a kite from Walter. The thermals in Chile buoyed them higher and sustained them more steadily than he had ever seen before. The three children launched their own kite. At first, they were confused when the Chilean children guided their kites so that they crossed paths with their own kite. To their amazement, the other children's kite strings cut through their own, and it spiraled out of sight. The second time it happened, Ovid ran off to recover it and returned with a black eye, a patch of hair missing, and a valuable piece of information. If you dipped your kite string in glue and rolled it in ground glass, you could use it as a sky knife. From then on it was war.

Slowly, however, the Chilean children made friends with the Kazan children, and the land wrote itself into their souls. The plants spoke to them in a lexicon of leaf and stem. Pursed mouths of color sprang from arid hillsides, rose bushes billowed over high walls, and mimosa leaves folded shyly to the touch. In the backyard, avocado and lemon trees bore fruit. The brown hills became changeable but familiar faces, and the black, snow-capped Andes heightened their dreams.

Even before they came to Chile, they were never sure if Eustacia could tell the difference between the food and its wrapper, and they would surreptitiously remove fragments of plastic from their meals and push them under the seat cushions so as not to offend. But now, Walter took over the job of cooking, and what he lacked in artistry he made up for in quantity and consistency.

The problem was, Fallon thought as these memories marched before her, Eustacia could not distinguish her children from herself. She loved traveling the world, so she assumed they did, too. They had been to Israel, Germany, Italy, Morocco, Greece, England, Switzerland, and many places in between. Wherever they landed, Fallon and her brothers merged to cope. And because their parents were unpredictable, they had grown so adept at reading the tilt of a head or the twitch of a finger they often knew what their parents were thinking before their parents knew it themselves and could deliver the saltshaker before Walter or Eustacia so much as looked up from their first bite.

She had loved feeling like a three-person posse with her two brothers. She missed it. Ovid usually directed their adventures, but it didn't feel that way, since they were one thing. "Welcome to the riverous mountain range!" he would say, making up words like Shakespeare. He quickly learned the names of all the spiders and orchids in Chile and taught them to his younger siblings.

Leader or not, he was more accident-prone than either Fallon or Terry, so the bee attack wasn't really new. Once a Man o' War jellyfish wrapped its poisonous tentacles around his calf, sending him screaming to the hospital. In Chile, as they scrambled up the boulders of Santa Lucia Hill overlooking hundred-foot drops or held mock sword fights in stone caverns at the foot of beach bluffs, raced through museums or built forts and carts, he was the one who broke his arm, knocked precious artifacts to the ground, and cut off the tip of his thumb. Nevertheless, when he bled, they all bled.

Even integrated units fight, though. When verbal sparring escalated to hitting, and hitting escalated to an all-out brawl, their parents only shook their heads as they rolled by, a screaming conglomeration of punching fists and kicking feet. "Sibling rivalry," Walter would say. *Evolution*, Eustacia would reply and turn the page. Sometimes the only thing that stopped their fights was the cactus they rolled up against.

Chile wrought a gradual change on Eustacia. Maybe it was only evident in hindsight. She had always floated in a cloud of internal focus, but in Chile she hardened and tightened as though her bones strained to surface, and her collar bones gasped for air. She devoted long periods of time to close observation of things external to her, with a limitless patience she never exhibited before. She would stand stock-still, and strain her eyes, ears, nose, and skin to comprehend and absorb her subject. One of her projects was to ascertain the exact moment twilight lost its duality. She wanted to know just where light met dark, and what exactly that quality of twilight was that was suddenly so much more alive than the light immediately before it. For one moment of suspended time, evening inhaled, expanding itself with light from the inside. In a blink, it deflated, empty as a bucket waiting to be filled by night.

Once, while Eustacia was practicing her observation, the children looked into the backyard and saw nothing. A tiny flicker of movement distinguished Eustacia from the background. She had blended in with the wall between the trees, like a lizard.

Small changes jiggled the amoebic tissue between the children over the year they lived in Chile. Chile was where Fallon became conscious of the special kinship Ovid and Eustacia had. Ovid and her mother lengthily discussed the physics of motion, the laws of thermodynamics, and supersymmetric string theory. Fallon could follow their thoughts through the first two or three branches, but soon they leapt between entire trees of thought like squirrels on caffeine, sometimes overreaching and crashing to the ground. They would shake their heads slowly, look at each other, and say, "What were we talking about?" and Fallon would remind them of the last thing they had said, and they'd be off again.

The children learned Spanish and reveled in the roundness of its vowels and the rhythm of its multisyllabic words which carried pictures and stories more immediate than English. The arms of the children's amoebic unit stretched to its limit in different directions. Terry played soccer with the kids in the street and became known as "Casca Romana" because of the straight blond bowl-cut hair. Fallon made friends at school and took up running. Ovid dove into the encyclopedia that arrived with the missing luggage and read it from A to Z, staying up late into the night until dark circles formed under his eyes.

Whenever Fallon asked Ovid a simple question, like how a switch on the wall caused the light to go on, his explanations became so long and tedious, delving into electrons and neutrons, and the inventions of Tesla and Edison, that her eyes nearly rolled up in their sockets.

On family weekend treks to Chiloe and Valparaiso, Ovid sat up front, poring over the maps and guidebooks with his parents, urging them on to new places. Fallon, for her part, floated around on an interior island, noting without emotion the concatenation of sights, ornate churches, some stucco, some blue clapboard, some stone, and each with a different kind of bloody, half-starved Christ staked to its cross. She paused before each reliquaries by the door, reading the labels under eye-shaped pieces of paper with unidentifiable globs at the center. This spec of granular brown was the blood of St. Hernando, this yellow fragment was the bone of the child saint, Blessed Laura Vicuña.

One day, on a hot mountain road, bobbing along in their car, the smell of gas infused the cabin. Though their parents told them to ignore it, the smell overpowered them. When they stopped, they discovered a leak in the gas tank. They were hundreds of miles from a gas station. Walter gave the children raisins to eat while he and Eustacia discussed their options. They didn't want to stuff anything into the holes for fear that it would enlarge the holes. As Ovid popped the third raisin into his mouth, his face lit up.

"I've got it! We can plug the holes with raisins. They will stick to the outside and sugar doesn't dissolve in gasoline, so it won't work through."

The only face brighter than Ovid's was Eustacia's. "My brilliant boy. Let's try it."

It worked magnificently, and they returned home safely. In fact, the raisin plugs worked so well that Walter and Eustacia saw no reason to waste money on a new gas tank, which would take months to procure, anyway.

After that, Eustacia invited Ovid to join her quest for the most brilliant invention in the world. They talked through many ideas. No idea was too big or too small: the lightning deflector suit—like a thick wetsuit, or teether-alls for teething babies, whose heads always ended up lolling on their chests. But they wanted to come up with something truly world changing: a telephone watch like Dick Tracy's that could send images, or a car that could part time or reverse molecular charges. Ovid's brain was on fire. Both of them consumed information wherever they could get it, books, magazines, television, lectures. Only Eustacia could match his rapid-fire recitations with recitations of her own.

Once, after a fight with Ovid, in which he twisted Fallon's arm behind her back, wrestled her to the ground and taunted her, she went to her mother, her face red with rage, tears screaming hotly down her face. "I hate him so much!" Eustacia, who had been listening to a ceramic pot outside, looked on her daughter impassively and took her down the street and out to La Avenida de Las Condes. The city was covered with blue rags that day. Blue rags scuttled down the avenue, got caught in windshield wipers, twisted around telephone wires, and blinded pedestrians. It was as though a blue rag factory had blown up.

*Isn't it wonderful?* Eustacia said, spreading her arms wide to encompass the sight.

Fallon caught her breath and looked from her mother to the blue rags in puzzlement, her tears drying.

*Where do they come from?* Eustacia prompted her.

Fallon shrugged her shoulders as her tears cooled on her cheeks.

*You must look for what is good in life. Look for the wonder. Isn't it marvelous to be alive? How did it happen that we came into existence on this blue ball in this vast universe? Such a miracle! You children are so lucky that your parents brought you to this place.*

Ovid had followed them outside and was listening as if there never had been a fight. As Eustacia and Ovid oo-ed and ah-ed over the mystery of the blue rags, amnesia flowed into Fallon's mind as cool as a windless lake, and she found herself temporarily one with Ovid again.

The next morning, not one blue rag could be found. Even the ones that had not been given by the city were gone. Housewives, maids and janitors who reached under the sink and found nothing ran out into the street indignant at the city's injustice.

*Whatever the city brings, it takes back overnight!* Eustacia said, clapping her hands with delight.

That was not all the city tried to take away. One day, when Eustacia was supposed to be cooking a pot of beans and Ovid was supposed to be watering the lawn, they instead dove into a conversation about the Big Bang and black holes. As they talked, they salivated and gesticulated. They drifted away from their posts, down the tiny street on which they lived, and out onto Las Condes. Fallon worriedly followed.

*Did you hear? Scientists picked up a hissing sound on their cosmic recorders. They thought it was pigeon droppings on their antennae at first. But do you know what it turned out to be?* Eustacia rhapsodized.

"Yes! I read that same article!" Ovid said. "In *National Geographic.*"

*It was the leftover sound of the Big Bang!* they exclaimed in unison. Fallon puzzled over how they could possibly tell that this hiss came from the Big Bang, especially since it could so easily be mistaken for pigeon droppings, but Eustacia and Ovid were talking so ecstatically they began to physically leave the ground.

Fallon ran back into the house, rummaged through the utility drawer—such a mess—and grabbed a ball of hemp twine. By the time she caught up to them, they had drifted down the avenue, but still hovered a foot from the ground, talking so fast their hot breath lifted them like hot air balloons.

She tied the string around their ankles, and just in time, because a surprise thermal swept them high into the air. The ball of twine spun so fast in the cage of her fingers that it burned her palms, but she hung on with all her might. Eustacia and Ovid were oblivious. Other children were out, flying their kites, and when they saw Fallon with her magnificent kites, they flew theirs closer. Fallon reached the end of her string and leaned all her weight backward to keep Ovid and Eustacia from flying away. Tears of fear itched the corners of her eyes when Terry popped up behind to lend a hand.

"Look out!" he cried. He pulled his sweater sleeve down over his hand and wrapped the twine around his wrist, jerking it to the side. "The kids are going to cut the string."

When Walter stepped off the bus from work, he found Fallon and Terrence flying Eustacia and Ovid high in the blue sky. They only became aware of his purple face when he reached over their heads, grabbed the twine, and reeled Eustacia and Ovid in, spluttering epithets.

At least, that was how she remembered it. Some things could only happen in the land where the earth ends, Fallon reflected, as she boarded the next bus to Roscoe at 5 a.m. Other things were dreams. Even as an adult she still confused them with reality. But Eustacia was definitely gone. On that they could all agree. What happened next had to be true, she thought just before she fell off to sleep against the cold bus window, because it was the kind of thing that happened all the time.

*Walter, dear,* Eustacia said as soon as her feet touched the ground, *we were having such a lively conversation.*

"They could have been killed!" Walter raged, shaking his finger at Fallon and Terence. Fallon began to cry in earnest and Terry to blubber.

"It is all my fault," Ovid said, stepping protectively in front of his younger siblings.

*What are you talking about?* Eustacia looked in puzzlement from Walter to the children and back again. *Why are you so angry?*

"I'm not angry!" Walter said, turning a deeper shade of purple.

*But you're shouting.*

"I'm just trying to make myself heard!"

*Well,* Eustacia drew herself up tall and cold. *I never. Ovid, children. Let's go. Father is in a most disgraceful state. There can be no good reason for such bad behavior.* She lifted her chin and walked off with the children trailing behind her.

Walter reversed into apologies.

When they got back to the house, the kitchen was on fire and the lawn was drowning. Ovid had left the hose running, and Eustacia had left the beans on the stove. Walter shrugged off his blazer and used it to waft his way through the black smoke billowing from the kitchen door. He wrapped the jacket around the handle of the blazing pot of beans and dumped it outside. He disappeared into the smoke one more time and re-emerged with a charred kitchen cabinet door. The fire was out. Eustacia, still as cool as a statue of the Virgin Mary, stood outside the kitchen, watching Walter with a raised eyebrow. Walter avoided her eyes, as if he were the one responsible for the fire. He wiped his sooty hands on his white shirt and the black marks signaled the end of that episode.

---

The bus pulled up to the Roscoe Diner, a sprawling 1950s, stone-veneer building with a flagstone floor, long counters, vinyl padded seats, and the biggest selection of pies she'd ever seen in glass display cases. At six a.m., it was already open, and she ordered eggs over easy and French toast. Mammoth slices of cream pies had already been cut and placed on plates, ranging from pale green to butterscotch. Oddly, they reminded her of the circus they had attended in Santiago. Delirious after a nearly sleepless night, she continued to straddle both worlds, 1987 Upstate New York, and 1975 Santiago, Chile.

*Children!* Eustacia called to them one day, clapping her hands. *A circus, a circus. Don't you just love a circus?*

Had Eustacia reflected on it, she would have remembered that they had never been to one. A dingy white tent had been erected in a dusty lot on the other side of Las Condes. Now, as the sun fell, the canvas walls glowed soft yellow. People streamed into the tent talking and laughing, and the children took up seats beside their mother. It turned out to be a rather depressing affair, with a tired horse wearing a dirty pink plume being led in circles, and some jugglers whose faces were deeply creased by hardship. The children could almost smell the air of desperation and hopeless fury and soon fell asleep. Eustacia, however, stayed awake, clapping her hands, eyes sparkling.

The children barely remembered going to bed, but the next morning, Eustacia drilled them over breakfast.

*What was your favorite part of the circus?*

The children shrugged and tried to digest the vat of oatmeal Walter had served each one.

"Eat up," he said with an exasperated sigh. "You children look like you're starving to death." He pinched Fallon's thin arm and went back to the kitchen for a frying pan mounded with scrambled eggs and hamburger.

*My favorite part was Mirabel the Chameleon,* Eustacia said, squeezing her knees together and leaning over the table. Fallon and Terry looked at each other and shrugged again. *Don't you remember? Mirabel danced around the ring, and each time she turned, she became a different shape, sometimes a small girl, sometimes an ibis. Then she turned herself into liquid in an old Coke bottle and a man came out and poured her onto the ground, where she turned into fire and burnt a pit from which she rose in fresh clothes. Isn't that marvelous? You could learn a thing or two from her, Fallon, when dealing with Ovid.*

*And Ovid, you should have loved Jaramillo. He was so good at building things, like you. He was tall and thin and danced with poles and sticks, building them into towers which he ascended and descended, rearranging, and dismantling as he went, his face popping up here and there between a whirl of lines.*

"Oh," Ovid moaned, true pain twisting a sigh from him. "I wish I hadn't fallen asleep!"

She squeezed his knee. *Such a mind. You have such enormous potential. You really should do better at school. Even Fallon gets top grades.*

A sliver of disloyal anger pricked her conscience, as the waitress delivered her breakfast to the table. "Even Fallon," she had said, as though Fallon represented the bottom rung of mental acuity. The smell of cooked eggs, vanilla and imitation maple syrup buoyed her mildly. If Ovid was so brilliant, why had he failed college five times.

*Well, my dear, her mother often said, some children are just too smart for school. You are wonderfully competent. Ovid is special. He needs a truly remarkable and unorthodox education.*

"What about me, mother?" Terry had asked that distant day at the breakfast table. "Was there anyone who reminded you of me?"

*Oh yes, there was the little boy who vanished. One minute he was there and the next he was gone. So clever. And you know what?* She clapped her hands. *This is truly best of all. After it was all over, I met the ringmaster. Such a mysterious man. We spoke in Spanish, you know. I've gotten quite good. I don't know what you would do without my Spanish skills, my dears. Anyway, he said he had met you three.*

The children sat up straight and looked at her with wide eyes.

*He is a Mapuche Indian. Did you know they were here before the Spaniards came? He's going to teach me how to vanish. I'm closer than ever to discovering how to rearrange atoms, I just know it! I'm going to take lessons from him.*

"Circus lessons?" Terry piped up. "Like how to juggle and stuff?"

*Sort of.*

"Can I come, too?"

*Oh no, dear. This is just for me. It's part of my research. Sometimes mothers have to do things without their children.*

And that was how their mother began to vanish and reappear on certain afternoons, like the yellow birds and blue rags. But unlike the blue rags, she always returned, until they reached the *Altiplano*.

# 7

# FAMILY PATTERNS

Ovid lay unconscious in the hospital bed, hooked to several IV bags, his eyes swollen shut, his skin yellow. Red welts all over his body were darkening to purple and black. Fallon pulled up a chair, sat down beside him, and took his hand hesitantly. If he were awake, she wasn't sure he'd allow her to touch him. His hand was wide and square. Dirt had worked its way into his fingertips, and calluses roughened the base of each finger, including his thumb. After he had cut the tip of his thumb off, his thumbnail had grown back strangely rounded, as if to protect the tip. He told her it was called a murderer's thumb. In her hot, dry hands, his were just as clammy as they had always been when they were children.

Later that morning, the doctor came around. "He's lucky. Some people sustain organ damage. His skin is a bit more yellow than we'd like, but his numbers are coming up fine."

The afternoon nurse told her he'd been stung 211 times. By the time she was done pulling the stingers out, the bottom of the pan was black with them.

Later in the day, Ovid opened his eyes. His hand twitched in hers, but he didn't pull it away. "Hey," he said softly, and smiled.

He talked with her groggily for an hour, explaining how it was his fault that the bees swarmed him. They were querulous before rain, strong scents stirred them up, and he'd been sweaty from working on the treehouse that was inspired by the blue woman, plus he'd been clumsy. As usual, he went into more detail than she required, and by the end of an hour, he was exhausted and fell back to sleep, so she went back to the family home.

———————

She pushed hard on the door, out of habit, knowing it stuck a bit. The familiar smell of old wood and her father's indefinable scent infused her. She could tell by the quality of the silence that he wasn't home. She checked the driveway to be sure. The old Dodge Dart they'd driven back from Chile, which, Eustacia-charmed on ran forever, was gone. She wasn't all that surprised that she hadn't met Walter at the hospital. He was an awkward man, and he probably felt overwhelmed, but she'd thought she'd at least find him puttering around the house, painting windowsills, or sweeping the back porch. Forty years Fallon's senior, he had retired a few years back.

As she looked around the kitchen, at the hand-hewn beams across the ceiling, the thick-walled but defunct fireplace behind the sagging Formica table, she was surprised that the house felt like home to her, and was still so redolent with memories, longing, and lassitude. At twenty-five, she calculated that she'd only spent about nine sporadic years in that house, the first five, and alternate years between their years abroad, and a few vacations here and there. She'd actually spent more time away from the house than in it, yet no matter where she lived or how long, she referred to Oneonta as home with all the weight that word carried.

She crossed over to the faded 1970s family studio portrait that hung on the unevenly plastered wall. She had forgotten it and its place of honor in the kitchen.

She leaned in close to look at her mother's narrow, intelligent face, frizzy auburn hair, and that mole on her lower lid like a bit of misapplied mascara. Walter sat beside her the proud, but oblivious patriarch, Terry a chubby three-year-old in lederhosen they'd brought back from Germany. Fallon dressed in a ruffled Gunny Sack dress popular at the time, and Ovid, standing behind Eustacia with his hand on her shoulder, looked wistful, even hopeful. Even then, he had circles under his eyes.

She marveled that they survived that first year after Eustacia's death. She didn't know how she'd gotten through. She'd just stopped feeling, she guessed. That worked until she graduated from high school. Then, in college, she nearly had a nervous breakdown. But Ovid descended into the depths and never really stopped descending, cycling up for air now and then, but dropping down again, each time lower.

Though she and Terry had achieved basic functionality at school, Ovid came home from school and begged not to return on a daily basis. He metamorphosed into a ceaseless critic, whose lip curled with disdain at her or Terry's presence. He stayed up until two in the morning watching TV and the circles under his eyes deepened. He sat at the kitchen table after dinner with Walter in a pool of yellow light, holding his head in his hands over his homework, after hours of argument. Despite his intelligence, or maybe because of it, he couldn't complete his homework or concentrate in school. He appeared to have a dangerous bottleneck in his brain that prevented him from translating its expansiveness to paper. Fallon had no such bottleneck. Her brain's capacity matched its portal. All flowed from mind, to paper, to test with minimum drama. No one even asked Terry about his homework. She couldn't remember much of Terry at all that year.

Fallon brought her suitcase into her bedroom behind the kitchen. Before Chile, she had shared a room upstairs with Terry, and in Chile, Terry and Ovid had shared a room. But when she got home, Walter gave her the room behind the kitchen, which had only ever been used for storage. Instinctively, she glanced up at the crack in the door frame. She remembered cowering with Terry behind her locked door while Ovid raged outside. Terry was nine by then, but still quite small, and she just turned thirteen. She wrapped her thin arms around his small body as Ovid threw himself against the door.

The frame cracked, and they watched anxiously for the door to fly open.

That was one of the few fights Walter actually happened upon, and he'd whipped Ovid's backside with a ruler for the first time. She came out of her room an hour later when all was quiet and sought Ovid out in his room. He was lying on his stomach reading a book, and she sat down on his butt in a gesture of reconciliation. He winced and told her to get off, without looking at her, and she realized Walter had bruised him.

Fallon sat, now, on her own bed and opened the drawer to the nightstand. She spied her teen journal crammed beneath junk mail, Chapstick, and pencils. She paused and dug it out. Its pink gingham cover spoke volumes. She opened it slowly. Pencil caricatures of herself and Terry fell out. Terry was a metal-mouthed dwarf with a huge head, and she was a knock-kneed teen with an enormous butt and horsey buck teeth.

It was odd how distinctly she remembered the day she found them. Seeing herself through Ovid's eyes shocked her. Up until then she had floated in that innocent self-love children are born with. But this was worse than a punch. She'd run out of the house into the wooded acres behind and come to a clearing where wild roses bloomed in profusion. Their rich scent filled the humid air. But deep in her ear a worm of doubt squirmed and an oily film of self-hatred oozed from her pores, which she felt to this day.

When Ovid flat out refused to go to school, Walter decided to send him to a boarding school where someone who knew something about teenagers could handle him. They had toured four different schools, and Ovid said that if he went to any school, it would be a small school in Williamstown, Massachusetts. Walter put down a deposit. But on the day he was supposed to go, Ovid wept, raged, and adamantly refused. Fallon had pleaded all along, "Send *me*. Send *me*."

Walter said, "You? You don't need to go away to school. You'll be fine wherever you are."

But Ovid stormed and ranted he would run away or kill himself if Walter sent him. So finally, defeated, Walter came into her bedroom behind the kitchen, and asked her if she wanted to go in his stead.

She said yes instantly. It was so instinctive and thoughtless, she couldn't even call it brave.

The school accepted their unusual request. The very next day, Walter brought her to the small school in the Berkshires and left her there.

Two days later, the admissions counselor asked if she would mind if her brother Ovid joined her.

"Why should I mind?" she asked, unused to having an adult consider her feelings, and unwilling or unable to take on the power that conferred.

Ovid joined her at the boarding school. Later he told her that he felt like Walter was banishing him, so when she went, it changed the conditions. She was able to earn good grades, run for student council, and take on extra-curricular activities, but Ovid's trajectory continued downward. One teacher remarked that Fallon's grades over the years mirrored Ovid's ups and downs. If Ovid's handsome, brooding genius hadn't earned him the devotion of the school director, he probably would have failed high school. As it was, he was held back a year and the two of them graduated together.

Fallon took mental inventory of her room, her red and white poncho from Chile folded at the foot of her bed, and her old stuffed animals. Her bedside lamp was missing. She would need that to read herself to sleep tonight. She found her lamp in Ovid's room, so she took Terry's osters of Aerosmith and Mötley Crüe, bands he'd liked in his junior high years, and which still hung on Terry's wall. She smiled at their permed hair, high waisted Spandex leggings, and bolero leather jackets. Ovid had teased Terry mercilessly about his taste in music. Terry's tastes had changed, so it was odd that these posters were still here.

As she stared at his room, it hit her how strange it must have been for Terry to lose his mother, and only eighteen months later lose his two siblings. She could only imagine the endless chain of silent dinners with Walter. What had he done after they left? How had he felt? She had no idea. When she left home, he was the last thing on her mind.

When Terry turned fourteen, he joined them at boarding school, but they were seniors by then, already looking at college. Though the school had only about a hundred students, seniors didn't have much truck with freshmen, so she didn't remember much about Terry once he got there except for one time they were on the same crew during work program. It was the kind of school that didn't have custodians, so students had work program twice a week to do maintenance and cook, signing up for different kinds of work crews, like wood chopping, brush clearing or kitchen crew. Fallon and Terry ended up on kitchen crew together. She showed him how to knead bread. He was still a small boy that year, with dirty blond hair, glasses, and braces.

As they kneaded the dough, he grew excited. "I'm going to get really good at this," he said. "The best in the school." She felt a mixture of annoyance and shame that he should want to copy such a deficient specimen as she, and that he had to be the best. But other than that, she didn't recall even checking in on him over the year. It now seemed odd.

Over the summer between Terry's freshman and sophomore year, he made a startling physical transformation. He shot up from five-foot, five inches to six-foot, two. He had his braces removed and got contact lenses. His voice dropped and became loud and resonant. She'd smelled pot emanating from his room. What's more, he turned into a wickedly funny storyteller full of bravado. Fallon hardly recognized him.

His sophomore year, Terry was kicked out because he overdosed on prescription drugs he stole from a roommate. His roommate found him unconscious, and when he was unable to wake him, he panicked and told the teachers. Terry had his stomach pumped in the emergency room. It wasn't a suicide attempt, he later told Walter, brushing it off, but an attempt to get high gone wrong. He was the one who always said during family reminiscences, "No, that's not how it was."

The memory of it was all terribly dim. She experienced a near mental breakdown of her own during her freshman year in college. The compartmentalization stopped working, and the strangeness of her mother's death, the dearth of support from Walter, and the hatred and incapacitation of Ovid all came crashing in, causing her delicately restrained low self-esteem to blossom into full-fledged and nearly incapacitating depression. To make matters worse, her inability to acknowledge her pain made her unable to ask for help. Somehow, she finished her assignments and earned decent grades. Failure simply wasn't an option, she reflected, as she unplugged the lamp from Terry's bedside and took it downstairs.

Under the lamp was a black and white photo of Terry that had been wadded up then flattened out. He was seventeen or so, with a square jaw and strong nose. He was looking straight into the camera lens, and his black eyes had a jaded, dead look, much too old and cynical for such a young man.

Terry and Ovid ended up at home together for some indeterminate period. Ovid had gone to art school and failed, attempted architecture school and failed, then another art school and dropped out though he was doing well. She wasn't sure what Terry had done about finishing high school. Maybe a GED.

Somewhere during her college years, she came home to visit. The three of them had some fun driving around at night with the music blaring, smoking pot, playing pool, and drinking beer. She loved reliving the three-person posse feeling.

Ovid always seemed genuinely glad to see her and often invited her to tour his projects. One time, he asked her to come see a project in the upper field. Strung from ground to treetop, where the field met a row of fir trees, thousands of threads of iridescent fishing line fanned out like harps layered over each other and shooting off in different directions, some going thirty feet to the top of a tree, others splayed horizontally and diagonally behind. It was a barely visible sculpture of multiple spider webs, and when the breeze picked up, the strings vibrated into a chorus of insect humming.

Ovid stood with his head back, slight surprise and pleasure loosened his features.

"It's beautiful," she said.

His face immediately darkened, his shoulders hunched, and he shrugged. "But useless."

"What are you talking about? It's a work of art."

"Art is useless."

She'd felt grief for him, for all his pent-up potential and his inability to direct it. If only she could figure out the right thing to say, she might motivate him.

When they got back to the house, Terry was up, making coffee.

"Where were you guys?" he asked.

"Ovid was showing me his sculpture," she said.

"Why didn't you wake me up?"

"I didn't know you wanted to come," she said, and it was true.

Before Eustacia went up in flames, when they had been one thing, she hadn't needed to ask herself who Terry was, because he was she, and she was Ovid. But now that they were separated, she only knew that he was different than she was, and that she didn't understand how. She felt Ovid's feelings, but Terence felt like a stranger, especially since his physical metamorphosis from small boy to the booming giant.

Later, when Ovid ended up living in Washington D.C., Terry went to live and work with him. They'd had a falling out, and Terry dropped off the face of the earth.

The Dodge Dart pulled into the driveway, wheels crackling over gravel, and Fallon went to the kitchen to greet Walter.

"Hey there," he said, his smile genuine. "I just missed you at the hospital."

They exchanged an awkward hug and kiss hello.

"Oh? How is Ovid doing?"

"Better, better. How long you here for?"

"Just until tomorrow. I just wanted to make sure he was okay."

"Stay as long as you like."

"Have you had dinner?" she asked.

"No."

She opened the refrigerator and rummaged around, finding a pan of beef stew Ovid must have made.

"I'll heat something up."

"That would be nice."

Over dinner, she tried to start conversation a number of times by asking him questions. He'd give one or two-word answers. His tone was always light, so she didn't think he was trying to kill conversation. He just didn't know how to converse. Talking to him about the family was out of the question, though he did offer that Terry had called a few months ago and seemed "fine."

He didn't ask her about herself, and when she volunteered information, like, "I finally signed up for the MCATS," he'd say, "That's nice," as if she had been talking about the weather.

After an endless episode of halting conversation, her mind went blank and she couldn't think of anything else to say, as if his condition were contagious. Her spirits sank and her head ached. She didn't believe he was as vacuous as he acted, because why would he have married someone like her mother? How could he be shallow when such profound things had happened to him? Maybe it was a matter of social skills. She couldn't fathom why he never learned to socialize or how he managed to go through life so disconnected. He was like a plant that had been caught under a rock and that had grown pale and crooked, twisting this way and that, looking for the light but never finding it. Between them all, she had grown up in a human desert, and it didn't bode well for her future.

# 8

# A PRETTY BROAD SITUATION

"Hey, pretty woman," Will said as she entered the pub with a jingle of the bell. He was cutting lemon rinds for the bar caddy. A cool mist, heavy with the smell of rotting seaweed, lingered over the seaport harbor, pressing against the windows, obscuring the view of the cobbled square. As soon as she saw Will, her brow smoothed, and she became aware of how tight her jaw was.

"I thought Collin was on today," she said.

"Disappointed?"

"Are you kidding? I hate Tuesdays. Too slow." She closed the door behind her. "I can never think of anything to talk about with Collin. He thinks I'm a snob."

"How was Oneonta?"

"Hard. They said my brother was stung 211 times. But he's okay. Sort of."

Fallon stashed her bag in the cubbyhole behind the bar in silence, and as she tied on her black apron, a yellow leaf on the floor caught her attention. A flesh memory of Christo sprang up in her abdomen, surprisingly hot and sharp. She hadn't heard from him since their last encounter over a month ago. She left several messages, but he didn't reply. The shame of it only increased the burn.

The honeycomb floor tiles came into focus under the leaf. When she returned to the hospital for a second visit, Ovid talked more about the blue woman dancing naked at the edge of the forest. His details were so precise that Fallon could picture her exactly, with her sway back, her childlike breasts, the glittering chain around her waist. He told her he'd checked with the neighbors and determined he had to have been hallucinating, and if he were hallucinating— well how could anyone blame him with a family like theirs?

Why blue? What could this figure mean to him? She knew from the family's brief tour of India, that Kali, the Hindu goddess of time and death, was blue. The Picts were said to have painted themselves blue to make themselves more frightening when they went into battle. She shivered. Was he preparing for some kind of battle? The blue rags in Chile. Maybe the blue woman was a symbol for depression. Maybe she was some kind of Oedipal mother substitute. She could see the blue woman too easily in her own mind's eye. For a second, she could feel the cool comfort of being able to embrace one's own flaws, to give oneself over to shoreless grief, to dance in the arms of one's own blues.

Just as hard had been the conversations about his brilliant plans to build a combination conservatory, water park, and hotel, and he had tried to convince her once again to come home and run the business for him. The bee disaster had filled him with ecstatic purpose. He talked incessantly, and when she could manage to insert a word of practicality, he flipped into bully mode.

She counted out her checks and recorded the numbers in the logbook, a restaurant security measure. The last check number was 10271987.

"Hey, look at that," she said, holding up the check. "Today's date. October 27, 1987. It's a sign," she said, mockingly.

"Of what?" Will asked.

She looked at it and shrugged. "I have no idea. Maybe today is an auspicious day. Or maybe I should play these numbers in the lottery."

"Do you believe in signs? In magic?"

She weighed the checks in her hand. "Not really." However, her fingers still had a sense-memory of the tug of the string when she had flown Ovid and Eustacia like kites. Was it memory, or a dream, or just a story her mother had told? "I mean, I don't *dis*believe in anything. But I'd rather not believe in signs."

"Why not?"

She shrugged again and thought. "It gives you too much control and yet not enough at the same time. You'd have to be constantly on the lookout. If you misunderstood a bad omen, you'd be responsible for everything that followed."

"I never thought of it that way."

"How about you?" she asked.

"How about me, what?"

"Do you believe in all that otherworldly stuff? Like I've been hearing how the planets are lining up in some quadrant or other, and it's supposed to mean the end of the world. They're saying the crash is part of that."

"I don't know. But I do know that you are one interesting person. I mean, it's not even 9:00 a.m., and we're already going all metaphysical."

She fetched the ketchup bottles from the kitchen and began wiping them down vigorously as she debated with herself whether to move home and put her shoulder behind Ovid's ambitions or try to carry on with her own life, here. Truth was, Will was the only thing she liked about this job other than the occasional whirl, and New York overwhelmed her senses on a daily basis. However, Ovid was starting to sound delusional. Then again, maybe the curtains of reality were about to part again like they had when Eustacia combusted. If she stayed the skeptic, she'd miss it. What if the world is driving him mad because he could see a truth others couldn't? All the more reason to go home.

What if she told Will the depth of her worries about Ovid and explained how they stemmed from the bizarre death of their mother? If anyone could wrap their minds around her freakish past, it would be Will. He had turned eighteen in 1968 and was part of that generation that dared to crack open the country's unexamined values and fashion a new, more idealistic society. He told her that when he'd seen the news about Vietnam on the television, he'd known what America was doing was wrong. There was a draft, and there was no way he was going to fight, but neither did he consider himself a pacifist. He was thinking about running away to Canada, but as luck would have it, he got a high lottery number, so he was never called to military duty. The experience had galvanized his political activism. He left home, changed his name, grew his hair long, and started to play guitar. He lived on a commune for a brief stint, but ultimately was disillusioned by the emotional entanglement and bickering.

"What's on your mind?" Will asked after an interval of silence.

"How do you know when to trust yourself?"

"Easy. Follow your gut."

"But what if your gut says ten different things? One part says run away, the other says run right at it, and yet another part says you've got the whole thing wrong and you should be doing something completely different. That ever happen to you?"

"Never. That's how I climbed so high so fast," he chuckled. "Single-minded ambition."

"Or what if you ask your gut, and it's totally mum, no matter how many times you ask?"

"Well, try me. What's the decision you're trying to make?"

"Whether or not I should move back home."

"Another easy one. You shouldn't."

She smiled, then frowned, irked.

"Sorry. I guess I have a vested interest in you sticking around," He chucked her shoulder. "I interrupted you." He pulled out a jar of olives and filled another section in the garnish caddy.

"He's got this grandiose water park idea that's totally unrealistic, but some of his other ideas make sense. He thinks we could grow ginseng on the farm and make a business out of it. I could get out of the city. But another part of me thinks that's the worst thing I could possibly do. And yet another part wonders if I'm turning down a great opportunity just because I lack faith or courage. Ovid obviously thinks the latter."

Will replaced the caddy in silence and mopped the bar with a rag, putting his shoulder into it, making wide circular arcs. She placed the tray of salt and pepper shakers on the bar and began wiping them down.

"Sometimes you just have to take a course of action and see what happens," Will said finally. "Accept the mistakes. Make a correction."

Fallon's stomach clenched. She'd seen for herself how one small, random mistake could change everything—if that's in fact what her mother's death had been.

"He has so much potential," she said. "You should see his greenhouse. If I was there, I could help him set goals, get him on a schedule, help him stay on track. It would make Dad so happy."

"You're not your brother's keeper," Will said, moving to the door and flipping the sign from closed to open. The sun was beginning to burn through the mist.

"I know," she said, a little irritated by his cliché response. "But family has got to mean something."

"Isn't he the one that beat you repeatedly?"

She had forgotten that she told him, and now she regretted it.

"You make it sound worse than it was."

"How so?"

"He was technically a child. It stopped when he reached legal adulthood, and that isn't the sum total of who he is. He can be so tender."

Will shrugged as he restocked the house liquor. "I don't get it. But you wouldn't be the first woman to stand by her man beyond all reason."

"He's not my man," she said, setting the salt and pepper shakers down too hard. Will looked up from his work.

"I'm sorry. Some of the things you've told me make me want to put my fist down his throat."

Fallon finished placing the condiments on the café tables. It hurt her to imagine someone hurting Ovid.

"No one likes to be told what to do," Will continued. "Why do you think your brother would take your advice?"

"Well, it's more like he wants to tell *me* what to do so that I do it *for* him." She waggled her head, smiling ironically.

"Why is it so important that you save him?"

"He's my brother. Once, when we were living in Germany, he threw a tantrum. He was about seven years old. He got so mad he stuck his feet out our third story window and threatened to jump. My mother yanked him back in by his belt, and when his feet hit the floor, the belt snapped. It was made of cardboard." *Never jump until you can fly, dear heart*, Eustacia said. She tucked the broken belt deep into the trash can, underneath the other garbage, so that the incident would be forgotten. "I guess I never stopped being afraid."

A customer walked into the pub and took a seat at the bar. "That's harsh," Will said, patting her shoulder. He went over to take the customer's order. Fallon circled to the waitress station and turned on the computer. She measured coffee into a filter basket, shoved it into the coffee machine, and poured water from the glass carafe into the top. As boiling water growled and spurted through the grinds, the aroma of coffee drifted up into the air. Droplets of water slid down the outside of the glass carafe, hissing on the hot plate.

A woman walked in and took a seat at one of Fallon's tables. Fallon took her order, punched it into the computer, and pushed through the swinging door to the kitchen to see if the order came through.

"Hey, Rodney," she called to the cook, a tall, handsome black man.

"Morning, Hon."

"Got that order okay?"

"Everything's working just fine. Missed you here the other night. The computer stopped sending orders. Got backed up big time."

"I would never let that happen."

"I know you *wouldn't!*"

She went back out to her station and checked on her customer. The next few hours passed slowly, with never more than one or two customers at a time. The lunch crowd was always anemic at the beginning of the week, but it had been almost nonexistent since a little over a week ago, when the market crashed on Black Monday, as it was now called. All sorts of psychics were saying they had predicted it, and astrologers said the planets were lining up for the end of the world. Watching the way the stockbrokers drank every day, she knew it was only a matter of time. And wasn't a crash caused by panic? If people had just kept their money where it was, there would have been no crash. The world appeared to hinge on perception.

The urge to tell Will about her mother's spontaneous combustion, pestered her, but his reaction to Ovid discouraged her. Besides, in her head, the combustion was incorporeal. It wasn't something that had to be reconciled. Putting it into words would make it real or call reality into question—or her sanity, more likely. The event contrasted starkly with what everyone around her understood to be reality. She wouldn't be able to bear the pitying look that she knew would be inevitable. Or worse, the secret eye-roll, his backing away. She looked over at him, serving a few stockbrokers. If she told him, he would be kind. But in his kind way, he'd think she was beyond hope.

---

By three o'clock the pub was empty but for the three stockbrokers at the end of the bar, who nursed their drinks, not ready to end their overly long lunch hour. Will was telling a story about working as a mechanic at a Texaco station in Cotati, California, where the owner kept a mountain lion named Junior as a pet. When he told stories his voice boomed, his arms swept wide, and everyone leaned closer to him and laughed.

"So, I lie on the ground to check out the oil pan, and next thing I know, Junior flops on top of me. He's like 200 pounds. He wraps his paws around me and gives me a nice *squeeze*." Will pantomimed with his burly arms.

"I say, 'Hey, Junior. Get offa me.'

"He just squeezes me a little tighter and bites down on my shoulder, sort of-- gently.

"I give him a little bump and he bites down harder. He's got my whole shoulder in his jaws now, and I'm thinking to myself, this little cat frolic is about to get bloody.

"I holler for Tony—the owner—but he doesn't answer. So, I lie there thinking about what Tony told me about handling Junior.

"He said, 'Don't show fear. Be in charge.'

"I take a deep breath and yell, 'Hey JUNIOR. GET OFFA ME,' and I give him a hard shove at the same time.

"He gets offa me with this offended look," Will laughed, "like, 'Hey man, I was just *playing*.'"

The men all laughed with him, and Will poured them another round. These three were regulars and knew Will well. They always tried to tip him with paper twists of cocaine. Will took the twists out of politeness, but while he still liked the occasional toke of weed, he didn't care for harder drugs. He'd seen firsthand the chaos created. One of their bartenders' entire personality had changed because of too much cocaine. He'd gotten paranoid and temperamental and had to be fired. For her part, Fallon thought her mind was trippy enough without the added confusion of drugs. She got the feeling there were doors in her mind that acid might open that she'd never be able to shut.

She retrieved a cashmere coat that had fallen off one of their stools. The stockbrokers barely acknowledged her as she hung it over the back of a chair. They seemed so selfish to her, so used to money they couldn't imagine being without it. They didn't quite see her as human. She was a thing in their landscape. Or maybe it was the other way around. Maybe she objectified them. She could be so judgmental. She looked at Will enviously. He was comfortable in the world, able to talk to people from any vocation or station.

A middle-aged man in a beige trench coat walked into the bar. The instant she saw him, she had a bad feeling. She scrutinized him as he took a seat at her end of the bar. Deep lines scored his face from his big green eyes to his jaw. He might have been handsome had he been better rested. What was it that bothered her? Maybe the cuffs of his coat, which were gray. He had the air of a homeless person, without the stench. He wasn't the "type" that usually came in here. Was she just prejudiced?

"Can I get you something?" Fallon asked.

"Cuppa coffee, please," he said rapidly.

She turned back to her station, poured a cup, and slid it across the bar to him.

"It's cold today," he said, cupping the coffee with both hands.

"Is it, still?" She looked out the windows and noticed that the sun was already low in the sky.

"I can't get warm."

"Well, this will warm you up. Can I get you something else?"

"Nah," the man hunched over his cup, flicking his eyes toward the brokers and back to his cup. "Thanks. That's all for now."

Dread settled like a lead shawl onto her shoulders as she wiped down the tables and straightened the chairs. After the things she'd seen in her life, she prided herself on open-mindedness. So why did she distrust this man? Just because he looked poor next to the brokers in their $900 suits? But something about him sucked her in, made her feel dizzy.

When he was nearly finished, she approached him with a pot of coffee.

"Shall I top you off?"

"You know what day it is today?"

"Tuesday?"

"October 27. Ten, twenty-seven." Something stirred at the back of her mind. The check numbers. Her neck prickled.

"Yeah?"

"World is coming to an end." He tucked his right hand inside his coat, as if to hug himself for warmth. Fascination and alarm battled within her. He believed the astrologers.

"Feels that way to me, sometimes," she said, hoping to comfort him by validating him, and in that way, ease him toward sanity.

"Oh, it is. I've seen the signs. One-zero, two-seven, one-nine-eight-seven. That's today's date."

The hair bristled along her forearms at the words. She checked her apron. Her last check was today's date, and it turned out to be his check. That was just too weird. If she had read it in a book, she'd have said it was contrived. What if the world really was controlled by disembodied hands, like those hairy brown tarantulas working their way across the soccer field that hot morning so long ago? She glanced at Will, who was in the middle of another story with the brokers. He caught her movement, and his eyes shifted from hers to the man she was waiting on.

"But why is the world ending today, exactly?" she asked. She didn't know if it was a good idea to draw him out or not.

"It's in the numbers."

"What numbers?"

"Black Monday. Black Monday. Don't you remember? It was only last week!"

Will curtailed his story and drifted to the center of the bar.

"2412. That's the number the market dropped to. It's divisible by six. The devil's number." He sounded irritated.

"Today is October 27. 10-27. If you add it up, it spells God. See?" He fished a pen out of his coat and scribbled the digits on a napkin. "One plus two equals three, God's number. This seven is God's number again. One, nine, eight, seven. It all points to six, the devil's number. Today is a day of reckoning. God smites the devil."

Like a car hitting a puddle too fast, Fallon's feet lost their grip on the ground. She connected to his crazed mental leaps disturbingly well. You never know, she thought. He could be right. Anything is possible. The bees attacked Ovid. Her mother spontaneously combusted. *No object is solid.* Who was she to say he was wrong? Her mother's bright eyes stared at the spot on the pillow beside her head where the molecules seethed.

The bell on the door jangled harshly as a young stockbroker in a gray suit and red tie bounced into the pub. He clapped the other brokers on the back. He had the thick build of an ex–football player, a frat boy.

"Bartender! Drinks on the house! Double martini for me. Made my first million today," he said. His meaty face shone under a cropped bristle of red hair. "Those bastards had no clue what I was doing to them!" The seated men rolled their eyes. Fallon circled to their end of the bar to clear their empty plates on her way back to the kitchen.

The man in the raincoat stood up so quickly that he knocked his barstool over. All eyes snapped to him. "I have a clue about what you did, and I'm gonna shove it down your goddamn throat, you greedy piece of shit," he said, pulling out a gun and waving it in the air. "You and your buddies are stealing the hard-earned savings of decent folk like me just to line your pockets! Before you destroy the country, I'm going to destroy you." Silence dropped on them like a bomb.

"Whoa, hold on, fella," Will said. The brokers' eyes snapped to Will, whites flashing, hands gripping the bar. The newcomer's smile wilted. His eyes shifted from the gunman to Will and back again. Fallon's throat swelled shut.

"I thoroughly agree that he's a greedy piece of shit." Will slowly came around the bar as he talked. "The worst kind. Thinks only about himself and none of the human cost." He kept his voice light but eyed the gun as he positioned himself between the gunman and the brokers.

The redhead's eyes widened, then narrowed. "Hey. Whose side are you on? Call the fucking cops, goddamn it, or I'll sue your ass."

The gunman shifted to circumvent Will, jabbing his gun at the redhead. "You don't get it, do you? You're not gonna sue anyone. Your day is done."

No one moved as Will realigned his body to shield them.

Fallon's head began to float as though on the end of a string.

"I get it." Will smiled tightly. "I know why you're pissed off. Look, everyone here knows this guy isn't worth the space he takes on the planet. He's definitely not worth you spending the rest of your life in jail."

"I got nothing to lose. It all ends here. Today. I want him to feel like I do. To be totally powerless. To lose everything because some asshole was gambling on your future."

Will looked the gunman in the eye, lowered his voice, and

stepped imperceptibly closer. "I've been there. Believe me. But this is not the way to go." He reached out his hand.

Fallon held her breath. The gunman looked back at Will. No one moved. The man's eyes watered. He tried to look away, but Will maintained his visual grip on the gunman's gaze.

"This is not happening today," he said, gently placing his hand on the gunman's forearm. The tension went out of the gunman's arm, and he lowered it a notch.

"You're going to let this go and walk out of here," Will continued.

The man's large, creased eyes flickered, as they searched Will's face.

"It's a cruel world, but the sun is still shining out there, man," Will said, tilting his head toward the window.

The young broker twitched toward the door, drawing the gunman's attention re-igniting his rage. Without breaking eye-contact Will turned his head to the side and said over his shoulder, "If you so much as breathe, I'll step out of the way and let this guy have you." The gunman relaxed and looked back at Will.

Will took a breath.

"You got a wife? Kids?"

The gunman nodded.

"How many?"

"A daughter," the gunman's voice rasped.

"They want to see you again. They deserve to see you again. This is not the way."

The gunman deflated, and the gun trembled in his hand. He relinquished it to Will.

"Now go, while you still can," Will said, clapping the man on the shoulder. The man ran out the door with a stifled sob.

Everyone in the bar sat still and listened to the doorbell jingle. Fallon's throat opened, and she took a breath.

The young broker started screaming. "Call the cops. He's getting away. Call the goddamned cops!"

Will looked around the room and went back behind the bar. "There's no problem here, now," he said.

"What?! That guy almost killed me!"

The other brokers jumped to their feet, scrambled into their coats, and shushed their colleague.

Will examined the gun. "It's just a toy. And you better learn to keep your mouth shut. I'm thinking today is not the best day for you to have a drink at this bar."

The young broker began to answer back, but the other three hustled him out the door.

"Wow," Fallon said. "That gun wasn't real?"

Will clicked it open and emptied the bullets into his palm. When he dropped them on the bar, they clattered heavily. "Reality is a pretty broad situation." His hand shook slightly as he pulled it away.

# 9

# A STUDY IN CONTRASTS

"There was a moment today when I really thought my life was over," Fallon told Will. Both of them had been so jittery that they'd gone out together for a few drinks after their shift was over. Now they were back at his apartment, a third-floor walk-up.

"Yeah, everything slowed way down for me."

"The shooter's state of mind sort of infected mine. I was totally muddled," she admitted with embarrassment. After a childhood like hers, she should be able to deal with any experience life threw her. Instead, she froze.

"I may not be the brightest guy on the planet, but—I think that's called radical overidentification"

"Actually, you're one of the brightest guys I know," Fallon said as it occurred to her for the first time. He had the kind of intelligence her family lacked. She had prejudged him as simple and ordinary because he lacked a college education. But he wasn't ordinary at all, just balanced, and balance was anything but simple. Was it possible that all her experience had prepared her for nothing, had simply confused her and complicated her reaction time? "I'm sorry, what were you saying?"

"Maybe you identify with other people so much you sort of lose your own identity," Will said.

"I definitely over-identify with my brother. When that guy started talking about numerology, yeah—I was just lost. But you stayed so centered. How did you do that?"

"I don't know. I meditate a lot. But I've never had a lot of fear, which can be its own kind of problem. They say God protects a fool, but I'm pretty sure there's an expiration date on that status. Lack of fear made me fall off a cliff once."

"You fell off a cliff?"

"Two hundred feet."

"Two hundred feet... how far is that?"

"It's about six times this building."

"What? And you survived? How is that even possible?"

"I fell onto a slope and over a bush. Shattered my forearms, broke my back and my leg. But that slope was the only reason I survived. And maybe the bush."

How much more unbelievable was that than her mother combusting?

She examined his apartment furnishings, the Mexican blankets, three guitars on stands, real paintings on the wall, a small shrine with Buddha and incense, but no family pictures.

He poured white wine into two hand-thrown mugs, and they sat together on a folded futon mattress on the floor. Over the course of the evening Will told her about his life. He remembered little of his childhood. The family dinners consisted of chipped ham on toast in white sauce eaten in a silence broken only by arguments over who had dropped the spoon under the table. His father rarely said a word to him, his mother read all day long, and his siblings got into screaming matches on enough occasions that he'd learned to just detach. He wasn't sure what the point of school was, and when he got bad grades, no one enlightened him.

His love of guitar drew him to New York City in the late seventies. He squatted in an abandoned apartment building in Alphabet City, so called because east of First Avenue, the avenues were named A, B, and C, as if the city had run out of names, or as if the places where poor folks lived didn't deserve names. He'd lived cooperatively with a band of like-minded squatters and turned out to be the only handy one, able to scavenge enough electrical wire to run a line from the streetlamp into the building. In winter, he was the one who knew how to fix the kerosene heaters and properly vent them so they didn't poison people. But kerosene heaters and late-night parties didn't mix well, and a fire destroyed that building along with his Martin guitar. Everyone got out alive, thanks in part to his quick thinking, and he managed to salvage the boot in which he stored his cash.

"I'm impressed," Fallon said, picking at the wax of one of the candles on the coffee table made of a discarded wire spool.

"Don't be. We were violating all kinds of building codes, and it was probably my wiring mistake that caused that fire."

He had stashed enough money in his boot to get a legitimate sublet in a rent-controlled apartment building on the Upper West Side where he installed and soundproofed a recording studio for pennies on the dollar. By the early eighties, however, a lot of buildings went co-op. If you didn't have the money to buy in, the landlords killed the heat, stopped repairs, and hired thugs to hassle you at the front door. He organized a tenant's union, which resulted in his eviction. He'd had to dismantle his recording studio piece by piece.

"Like I said, I've racked up a whole lot of fool points."

"You rejected society's materialism. You carved your own path. You fought for justice."

"I don't mind you thinking well of me, so I'm not going to argue," he said putting his hand along her cheek.

"What do you even like about me?" she asked, allowing herself to rest her cheek in the palm of his hand.

"You compel me. You're a study in contrasts. You're tall with a sturdy bone structure, but you're somehow delicate... like a dragonfly. You're fragile, but brave. You're shy, but not afraid to talk about strange things. You're insecure, yet smart; complicated yet innocent, super sharp and just a little bit dumb."

Fallon smiled and the candlelight flickered.

"I've had some of the most interesting conversations I've ever had in my life with you."

Fallon kissed his palm, thinking she might be ready to make love to him after all. He rushed on as if he'd thought about this a long time, reminding her the things she'd told him, like being attacked by shepherds in Turkey while visiting the ruins of a crusader castle, or her mother driving down an icy mountain in Yugoslavia without brakes. "My family was empty by comparison, and we are so different, but I feel like we came from the same tribe or were cut from the same cloth. You have this—" he paused searching for the right word, "ocean of grief that I kind of relate to, but you have a smile so bright it absolutely blinds me."

"I don't think anyone has ever summed me up so—"

Will kissed her, and she kissed him back, but that worm wiggled in her ear.

"I don't want to be your damsel in distress, your case study in abnormal psychology."

Will laughed quietly and kissed her again.

She liked the softness of his lips and beard. His arm hair was silky and his skin warm.

"I like helping you, but not because you're helpless. Because you open something up inside me, all these possibilities. There is something of the older, dustier roads of America in you, the real America that I've been missing."

"I didn't know you could be such a poet, Will."

They fell backwards on the futon beginning to disrobe, but Fallon's mind did that annoying thing it always did when she had sex, fluttered from one thought to the next, leaving her body.

Will stopped moving. "Where did you go?

"What do you mean?" She looked up at him in the flickering light, but his face was mostly shadowed.

"I don't know. You just seem—not here."

"No, I am."

Will's touch became platonic. "Maybe we should take more time to get used to each other," he said.

She tried to read his expression in the darkness. Was he rejecting her?

"I'm sorry," she said.

"Don't be. I don't want to make love to you unless you are absolutely, one hundred percent into it. I can wait."

"I feel so…awkward."

"Don't, we're getting to know each other at a new level. No reason to rush. My generation did way too much of that."

"You're not mad?"

"Let's just sleep together. It will be nice. Besides, we both have the morning shift tomorrow."

---

The next day Devon, the manager, walked into the pub and fired Will in front of the entire staff just before they opened. Fallon stopped wiping down the waitress station and stared at Devon in horror, not just at the fact that he was firing such a great employee, but that he was doing it in such a callous way.

"You're firing me?" Will said from behind the bar.

Rodney came out from the kitchen and stood in the doorway listening.

"You failed to report the incident to the police," Devon said. "You insulted customers. It was gross negligence."

"Man, he saved people's *lives*," Rodney said.

"You're *firing* me?" Will repeated.

"It was *gross* negligence," Devon said again as if trying to convince himself. "You let the criminal get away. The partners are apoplectic."

Will looked at Devon a moment in silence seeming to weigh out his possible responses. Something clicked.

"Fuck you, you cocksucker, and fuck your apoplectic partners, too."

Fallon and Rodney gaped. They'd never seen this side of him.

"*Gross* negligence—" the manager talked over him.

"I should have let the guy shoot the place up."

"Are you threatening me?" A hint of hysteria tweaked Devon's voice a few notes higher. "You're lucky we don't sue you."

"Sue me? I should sue *you* for dangerous work conditions."

"You can finish out your shift today, and we'll give you a week's severance pay."

"Finish my—" Will shook his head like someone coming out of a dream. "Take your job and stick it up your ass," he said, slamming the keys to the cash register on the bar.

"Will—" Fallon said, as he went for his jacket.

"No good deed goes unpunished," Will said with a bitter laugh. He grabbed his jacket and stormed out.

"I quit, too," Fallon said.

By the time she'd caught up with Will, he'd already cooled off.

"It's okay," Will said. "I need to do something more worthwhile with my life, anyway."

"I quit out of solidarity."

"Man, you didn't have to do that. That's a good paying job."

"I need to cut the cord, too. I really want to go to medical school. Maybe I could pick up some kind of aid work at the hospital for the time being."

"Let's celebrate. Ever climbed the Statue of Liberty?"

"That's such a dweeby, touristy thing to do," she laughed and hit him.

"I've lived here for nearly fifteen years and never been. Come on, let's go."

They toasted their freedom at the top of Lady Liberty. It was one of those balmy October days when the light is golden, and the breeze is laden with memory. By the end of the day, they were both emotionally exhausted and agreed to spend the night apart but call each other the next morning.

No sooner had Fallon opened the door to her apartment, but the phone rang as if it had been ringing all day. She could tell it was bad news again before she even touched the receiver.

"It's Ovid," Walter said. "He's taken a turn for the worse. Please come home at once. I don't know what to do."

# 10

# COMBUSTION

Giant x's crisscrossed the façade of the Port Authority Bus Terminal Even without the disaster awaiting her, exiting NYC was difficult in its own right. Hugging purse and duffle bag, she had to find the right booth, stand in line, decode the arrival-departure board, locate the right gate, and line up the connection from bus to bus, each step a hot-dog-cigarette-urine smelling game of dodge and dart between people while pickpockets and con artists sized her up. It was only slightly easier because she had done this four days ago. This time, her bag was bigger, she'd quit her job, sublet her apartment, and didn't know when she would return.

The ground hadn't stopped tilting since she'd gotten the phone call. Fear billowed and redoubled itself, as if missing her stop would send her off the edge of the world.

"Hey, lady, got a quarter?" a filthy woman at the entrance to the terminal called out. She sat on a sleeping bag and held up a used paper cup.

"I'm sorry," Fallon said sincerely, looking her in the eye. Though she didn't give, she tried to at least acknowledge the humanity of this woman in need, fearing that someday she might end up being one of them.

"God bless," the homeless woman replied, smiling. The blessing helped her —as if the spirit of her eternal homelessness had spoken.

She caught the first bus in good time, and as it pulled out of the station, she thought of Will's face, his proud nose, the beginnings of wrinkles around his agate blue eyes, his hand reaching out to the shooter, self-possessed and calm. That feeling of safety she felt with him, hitherto so easy to overlook, took on substance now. This was a new feeling in her life. What was it? Admiration? No. Admiration was a dark and glittering thing, a crinkled piece of the night sky, a wild creature, both pursuer and pursued, darting out of the underbrush, and disappearing again. Respect. Yes. When she said the word, *respect* to herself, warmth expanded inside her and reverberated with rightness. Respect was a house you could move into, a post and beam house, uncluttered, spacious, and warmed by a wood-fire stove. From inside that house, her feelings for Christo felt delusional. Yet here she was hurtling away from Will at seventy miles an hour. Why?

Ovid needed her. She felt important, rushing toward him, and strangely alive rather than afraid, though her neck muscles seemed to have fused with her spine.

---

The blue woman was singing alone in a minor key, lilac on black velvet, willow fronds over dark water, filling Ovid with sadness that he never wanted to stop feeling. He would be Odysseus, lashing himself to the mast to hear the impossible, a voice that spoke of hunger fulfilled by its own hungering. Her voice notched down to a low hum, a purr. How strange. More like pistons than purring. That's what it was. He was driving his mother's car, the one they drove home from Chile, 12,000 miles. It was humming to him. He ran his hand over the faux wood trim of the dash. It didn't look large from the outside, but from behind the delicate steering wheel, the Neanderthal dash was vast. The grass spinning by, outside the window burned unnaturally green, and horned steers bobbled their heads on suburban lawns. When he rounded the corner, their skulls were empty as dried gourds. But he was driving the car, leaving that mindless world behind. The shocks were spongy, and the odometer had broken at 350,000 miles, but Eustacia-charmed, the car kept going. It had countless and perhaps infinite miles on it. Round and round the wheels went, the pistons churning, the motor humming, a floating, boating movement that set the story in motion again, in that pedantic, childish voice he knew so well, the voice of his mother, the voice of the story itself, telling itself into existence, as it had always done, on and off, since she had left him. It wove together all the loose ends leading up to her liberation. It polished all the details caught like flies in amber, until they shone like a sunset, so he would never forget, so he could trace out the path she'd left for him, like Hansel meting out those shining white stones. He would decipher the code, or decode the cipher, really zero in as it were:

Over the course of their stay in Chile, their precious mother—origin to them all—became literally brilliant. Her skin took on a lamp-lit tone. She returned from her circus lessons incandescent.

*Oh, my children,* she would sometimes say upon her return, *I can hardly wait to share with you what I have learned. It is larger than all of us.* Other times, skimming just above the ground like a paper lantern rising from candle heat, she would say, *I never knew it could be this way. When it comes like this, you must obey the call no matter the consequence. No matter.*

But whenever her children tried to get her to take them to the lessons or share her newly acquired knowledge, she would shake her head and say, *You must wait for the right time and place.*

"But, Mother, you've always shared before," her favorite son would whine.

*There are some things a mother cannot share.*

One day she made an important announcement.

*Children!* She clapped her hands. *It is time to go home. We will drive! It will be an adventure. No family has ever done this.*

So it was, and so it came to be that they drove all the way up the Pan American Highway in their Dodge Dart sedan, stopping to cook their meals by day on a table that hooked onto the back of the Dart's trunk, and sleeping under the stars by night.

They began their journey on a road not marked on any map that passed from Chile into Bolivia, a road through the fabled *Altiplano,* a desert plateau so high that the altitude made gringos sick, a road their Illustrious Mother had learned about from the circus master. Strange goings on had been reported there. The ancient Nasca people had carved mile long spiders, monkeys, and airplanes into the plain. No one knew how they could plan and execute such drawings from the ground, nor why. Some preferred to believe aliens had visited them rather than that they were so advanced, while others speculated that they had ridden the thermals in giant fiber kites, using the pictures as maps of their territories.

*Just wait, children. You'll see. We are going to a magical place where the ground is so high it touches the sky. The air is thinner there, so I will be able to demonstrate to you the greatest mystery man has ever achieved. It will change you forever.*

The children were eager to learn the mystery she would impart and eager to go home. The family drove north and stopped at all the military checkpoints above Santiago, but once they drove off the map, there were no boundaries or checkpoints to tell them when they passed from one country into another. That was how they forgot to say goodbye to their beloved country, never knowing how they would miss it until they got all the way home.

As they climbed the mountains, the landscape shed its vegetation until only a few low shrubs crouched near the ground. Higher still, the ground produced nothing but stones. The air thinned and the tightness in their lungs engendered a certain queasiness of stomach and dryness of mouth. As the road deteriorated, it churned up boulders and spat out streams. All at once, the road leveled out, and they found themselves at the edge of an expansive, sandy plateau rimmed by perfectly conical volcanoes. The road before them dissolved into two sets of deep tire tracks in the sand. Walter turned off the engine and the wind sucked up its rumble. All five of them looked blankly through the front windshield at the greatest expanse of nothingness they had ever seen. The sky was gray and the sun cold as gruel. The colors of the desert might have been named vagueness or loss.

"Who did you say told you about this road?" Walter asked.

The wind rocked the car.

*Nothing is what it seems,* the Wise One said, her eyes avidly eating the landscape.

---

Something was different about the humming noise. It bothered him. He listened more closely. It didn't sound like the car, it sounded like —my God—bees. One ricocheted off his brow. He jerked himself upright and found himself sitting in bed. Why was he still in bed? What time was it? He looked around. There was something odd about his bedroom. His bed wasn't against the wall, and the windows were steel framed without mullions. The hospital. That's where he was. The memory returned like an avalanche. The bees had betrayed him. He wanted to set the hive on fire. Then he wanted to apologize. He had fucked up. He couldn't get anything right. And now they wouldn't let him out. He remembered that nurse—what a stupid, ignorant bitch— had insisted he hold still for that shot. She didn't even know what it was. He hadn't meant to hurt her. He had just meant to push her away. She had fallen over backwards. Clumsy cunt. She probably did it on purpose to make his action into a federal offense. She wasn't hurt, but she acted like he was a criminal. Doubt washed through him. Maybe she *was* hurt. He hadn't meant to hurt her. Fatigue bloated his mind and waterlogged his legs. He fell back into his pillows, and the story hummed itself to life again.

---

When Fallon had picked up the phone, Walter explained that while Ovid's organs were recovering from the venom, he had attacked a nurse. They were holding him for psychiatric evaluation. They thought the steroids had triggered a psychotic episode of some kind.

He had been babbling at high speed and didn't recognize his own father.

"I don't know what to do," Walter said. "Maybe you can talk some sense into him."

Walter never knew what to do.

Now, as the Greyhound bus wound its way through the capillary veins of Upstate New York, Fallon noticed that her teeth were clenched, and her shoulder muscles numb. She stretched her neck and kneaded her jaw and neck muscles.

Ovid hadn't been violent with her since she was fourteen, so this was dire news. She always feared he would be violent against himself, not others. Once, when they were arguing as usual, he advanced on her, raising his voice, and she shouted back at him, giving as good as she got. She backed up instinctively and knocked a glass jug into the table leg. It shattered and she felt the sting of a cut. She yelped and fell to the floor, grasping her toe so hard that all she could see was that a thick slice of skin had been cut clean off, and tiny beads of blood specked the severed flesh. When she released her grip, the toe gushed blood. Ovid paled, his voice instantly downshifting to soft. He knelt before her, shushed, and comforted her. He helped her hop upstairs to the bathroom and took the bandages and antiseptic down from the medicine cabinet, crooning to her comfortingly all the while. Ever since that day, she had known he would never kill her.

But now, on the bus, finding her jaw locked and her neck muscles clenched again, she realized this revelation sprang from its antithesis: on some level, she'd always been afraid he would. She shook her head.

What would Ovid pull her into this time? She caught her ghostly reflection in the bus window as they went through an underpass. She couldn't help but flinch at the sight of her pale, plain face. She couldn't see the beauty others claimed to find. However, she had always seen Ovid's beauty.

She remembered how he seized her by the waist once in high school and squeezed, saying, "Is it wrong for a brother to find his sister beautiful?" He discarded her just as quickly as he grabbed her.

One minute he might pick a fight with her over some inconsequential thing, like whether yams were the same as sweet potatoes, excoriating her for her ignorance, and the next minute he would be peeling apple slices and feeding them to her one by one. She had always been a vivid dreamer, but in high school her dreams ramped up into technicolor violence. She had incestuous dreams she was too horrified to articulate to herself, other times she dreamed of a murderous child with enormous teeth killing babies, and still other times she dreamed that zombies had caught up to her and her only hope was that they would kill her before they bit her so she wouldn't become one of them.

This bee attack was like her mother's combustion, yet in reverse. Instead of all the pieces flying apart, the bees, like insane clusters of molecules, flew together and injected themselves into him. Ovid was in danger of imploding, and she had to figure out how to keep him together. She didn't know what would happen to her if she lost him. She massaged her rigid neck muscles, but they only bunched harder.

Outside the window, the humpback curve of a particular hill, patched with red, yellow, and brown, moved by. Now she recognized a particular gas station with the winged horse sign. They were within a half hour of Oneonta. The bus engine hummed, filling her ears, and suddenly she didn't want to get off. The deep rumbling sound cradled her like a nurse-mother's ample breast. As soon as she relaxed into that churning lullaby, the story of her childhood began to tell itself to her in a sing-song voice, not her own, weaving a web like a spider, cleverly, assiduously, spiraling in on itself:

The Intrepid Explorers, facing a vast nothingness, resolved not to turn back. Instead, they launched the car onto the sand at top speed. Within a few feet, the car stopped, blocked by the mound between the tracks, and the wheels spun uselessly.

Their brilliant mother and handsome father placed stones behind the wheels and got back in the car. Their father gunned the engine. The wheels spat out the rocks, the car lurched forward ten feet and stopped, blocked by the sandy center again.

Father and young god Ovid got out to push. Mother flipped her legs over the hump and wiggled into the driver's seat. The car lurched forward twenty feet and stuck again. They continued working their way forward a hundred feet or so in this manner, before Mother finally shut off the engine. Silence rushed in, followed by wind. Now they couldn't go back even if they wanted to, and they couldn't go forward either.

Walter came around to the driver's side. "What should we do?"

*Something will come to us,* she replied.

"I'll walk to those hills. There might be a village," Walter said pointing to low brown hills to the left of the volcanos. "I'm sure it's only a few miles." He kissed Mother on the cheek.

They watched him walk away. Vastness diminished his movement, and distance erased his height, until at last, he was only a tiny blue dash against the gray, barely discernible, blinking up and down, his movement indistinguishable from imagination.

As soon as darkness fell, the desert cooled. Mother got out of the car to set up the camp stove. The wind kept blowing the flame out, and her thin body wasn't up to the task of shielding the flame, so the children locked arms around the stove while she lit it. They heated up some coca leaf tea, which was supposed to cure altitude sickness. Inside, Mother spread sleeping bags all around, filling the car with the downy scent of wet dogs. They sat in silence while the wind rocked the car like a cradle. Mother pulled out Plato's "Allegory of the Cave" to pass the time and teach them the truth beyond shadows. Brilliant Ovid leaned forward and listened with his whole body, interrupting her excitedly now and then to discuss an idea, but the words lulled Fallon and little Terence to sleep.

The wind outside rushed over the massive plain, diminishing their tiny car, whispering indecipherably into their ears, and eventually everyone dozed.

*Oh look!* Mother cried in the darkness. The children sat up, the air in the car warm with down and farts, tiny feathers sticking to their hair.

"What is it?" Ovid asked.

*The mystery. Oh, children, the mystery!*

She wiped their condensed breath off the windshield and pointed out into the absolute darkness of the desert. At first the children saw nothing. Then, far off, a bright orb or light appeared and moved horizontally in a perfectly straight line, then disappeared. The children gasped. "What is it?

Another light appeared above and dropped straight down.

"It must be Dad," Terrence said. "Coming toward us with a light."

*No, no. It's much too high and too large.*

"And anyway, that's north. Dad went off to the west, idiot" said Ovid.

"What's over there?" asked Fallon, trying to remember.

*Nothing. Nothing but volcanoes.*

"Could it be a truck driving down the volcanoes?" asked Fallon.

"No, the road would be going diagonally," Ovid said.

Farther to the right, another light moved from east to west, again in a straight line.

"Helicopters ?" said Fallon.

"Why would helicopters be flying out here at night?" said Terence.

*There have been reports of spaceships,* Mother said. *I have marked the spot they appeared on the windshield, my dears. We'll check in the morning. Perhaps we've forgotten what was there.*

They watched the lights in silence and drifted back to sleep.

Later, the cabin light speared a hole in the darkness, and frigid air blasted in. The slam of the car door returned them to darkness. Walter was back, teeth chattering. His hands were too cold to close around the cup of tea Mother poured from the thermos. She piled a sleeping bag around him, and they whispered. It had taken him hours to reach the hills. There *had* been a village, but no one owned a truck. Large trucks came through daily. They would have to wait. Mother told him about the lights: had he seen them? He had, but he didn't know what they were. There was no village in that direction.

They never did find out what the lights were, Fallon reflected as the bus pulled into the Oneonta station. That mystery had been eclipsed by a much greater one.

It was a giant puzzle, and Ovid couldn't get the pieces to fit. He kept putting them together, and they would almost fit, but one piece would overlap, irrefutably proving that he'd put it together all wrong. The misaligned? edges dug into him, stirred up his blood, made him sick to his stomach. His mind worked feverishly to rearrange the pieces, but those jagged? edges kept turning up like splinters, more painful than their size would suggest. Then the bees buzzed madly, darting at him, hitting him scoldingly in the head. "Dummkopf, dummkopf," they kept saying. How could he have gotten it so wrong when he was so sure he had it right and when his mind had been working so fast, and so brilliantly? The buzzing was a circular saw. "You always fuck things up," Terry yelled, throwing down a circular saw, and stomping out of the room.

Ovid tossed and turned in bed, waving the bees away. His hand hit something. An intravenous stand rattled. That was odd, he thought, he didn't know he owned an intravenous stand. Strangers were constantly walking into his home, poking, and prodding him, asking him inane questions, pulling him away from his thoughts. Why couldn't they leave him alone?

He was forgetting something, something essential, something that made it all work. It was right there at the edge of his mind; he was just about to see it, but some idiot would come into his room and interrupt him, causing him to lose the scent. Maybe he was in Bolivia. There was one man in particular with a worried air, who kept returning repeatedly to interrogate him. Another man kept coming in and accusing him of being a spy because he had entered Bolivia without an exit stamp from Chile. It wasn't his fault. His parents had chosen the road. He didn't know they needed an exit stamp. He should have known. He was smart enough to know. They kept asking him where his mother was. He didn't know, he didn't *know*. If he knew, he would tell them. If he knew, he would have followed her.

The sun was rising over the *Altiplano*. He awoke in the front seat of the car with his head on his mother's shoulder. The pieces all fell into place. Thank God, he was back. She was back. He was right here, where he had always wanted to be. Their breath had frozen along the bottom of the windows.

*Look! Look!* she said, her face shining, faintly orange. The black mole on her lower lash looked almost like a tear.

He looked out, and the sun was an orange disk on the horizon between two volcanoes.

*Look the sun full in the face as it rises!* she said.

"No!" Walter cried, his hand clumsily falling over Ovid's eyes. "It will blind you!"

*Tish, tosh!* Eustacia replied. *How can the world be dark with the sun forever burned in their eyes?*

Ovid shook Walter's hand from his eyes and let the sun sear his retinas, sear a hole in the rods and cones at the back of his eyes, sear a hot glowing hole in his heart.

It would be all right now. His mother was back, and they were on the road, where they belonged. The next day passed quietly. The sun rose up into the sky, warming the land. The winds were gentle. There was nothing for miles and miles, no animals, no birds, no people, no cars, just silent volcanoes, and distant sun. He wandered with his younger brother and sister. Something was different about their mother. She was buzzing slightly inside, like the bees. Out of the corner of his eye, he watched her. She was talking to herself, playing an inaudible tune with her fingers as she sat on a camp stool, and every once in a while she would rise to a crouching position, hold the stool to her butt, and scoot a few more feet away from the car, as if they might not notice her moving away.

"What are you doing?" he asked, but she waved him away.

*Watch from a distance, my dear, I'll show you the cipher of ciphers.* Dread filled him. He couldn't breathe.

Off in the distance a cloud of sand spun up from the ground. It was a truck driving toward them, but it drove away. No other trucks came their way that day. Walter prepared dinner for them. The scrape of his spoon against the aluminum pan sending chills down Ovid's back. The camp stove's flame guttered with the breeze like his mind. That scraping sound was so loud, Ovid thought. Why was it so loud? It was getting louder and louder, taking over his thoughts. It was coming, that terrible moment when his mother took flight.

"No!" he cried. His sudden intake of breath choked him.

She had taken off already. When he looked up, she was a blur of silver molecules dancing a furious reel, spinning so fast they cut a hole in the space like a circular saw cutting the very fabric of the universe, and that scraping sound, echoing and reverberating, felt like it would split his head open. In one all all-absorbing intake of breath, one apocalyptic inhalation she sliced through the universe, stepped through, and vanished. Space knit itself back together as soon as she passed, and it was as if she had never been.

He coughed and stumbled forward. "Wait for me!"

"You idiot, that's not how it happened," Terry yelled. Where was he? He couldn't see him. He stumbled out of bed, and a woman caught him, one hand clasping his tightly, the other clasping his elbow. His vision cleared, and the woman turned into Fallon.

"Did it really happen?" he asked, tears streaming down his face. "Did she?"

"It happened," Fallon said. She had known he was reliving their mother's apotheosis the instant she had entered the hospital room. He was talking and crying in his sleep, his brows furrowed, his hands restive. As she touched the tears from his face, she relived it, a flash of fire, a searing instant, an instantaneous transformation, and spontaneous oxidation. There was no cry, no pain, as her mother ate oxygen, oxygen ate her. In one stroke of fire Eustacia achieved complete material disintegration.

"Why didn't she wait?" Ovid asked Fallon now, gripping her arms, his eyes turning vivid green within their bloodshot whites. "Why didn't she tell me . . . ?"

"I don't know," Fallon said, pushing him back into bed. "Maybe she didn't do it on purpose. Maybe things accidentally orchestrated themselves to this end."

"No," Ovid said, shaking her loose and jumping to his feet again. He paced the small hospital room, head ducked, fingers crooked and calculating, trying to sort it out. "She said we had to wait for the right time and place. She did it. She figured out how to rearrange the charges to pass through. She left me—"

"Maybe the earth tipped slightly, or a cold front moved in." Fallon kept talking, though she didn't know if it would be more comforting to believe the earth was such a random place that something like this could happen, or to believe that their mother left them on purpose.

"Maybe you made it happen," Ovid said, his face contorting into hatred. "You never loved her like I did. You thought she talked too much. You thought she lied. I was more her child than anyone else. No one understood her like I did, and there will never be another person on this earth who understood me like she did."

"I understand," Fallon said.

"The fuck you do," he pushed her away, an insolent smile marring his beautiful face.

"No, I don't mean I understand you. I understand what—"

"You understand fuck all."

"Look, there's no need to—"

"Just get the fuck out of here," he said.

Fallon stumbled backwards into the hospital hallway, rage competing with sorrow. She ran down the hall past the nurses' station, past the elevators, and onto the staircase. But running couldn't blot out the memory of how they'd stood at the empty spot where their mother once was. Fire breathes, feeds on substance, fire is light, explosion, and white ash, softer than a caress that catches the wind and flies.

Fallon found herself standing on the sidewalk outside the hospital, on busy Main Street, staring at a soggy tissue tangled with wet leaves in the sewer grate. Cars splashed by in both directions. Suddenly, she longed for Terrence.

## WALTER'S TOAD

Walter hung up the phone. He knew that Fallon was on her way. Should be home by morning. She was a good girl. She would be able to talk to Ovid and straighten him out. She was catching the first bus out of the city. He walked outside to the back porch to see if the toad was still there.

Sure enough, the toad squatted on the cool cement behind the shovels leaning against the stone wall. Bracing his hand on his knee, Walter crouched and, with one arthritic finger, gently stroked the toad's right side. The toad bloated on the right as Walter stroked, as if his finger were inflating it. Walter smiled and switched to stroking it on the opposite side, watching him deflate on the right side and bloat on the left as he stroked it. Such direct communication. So simple.

In the years after Eustacia had left them, they had resumed the duties of the living in Oneonta. He would wake, dreaming of Stonehenge and small obelisks, only to find one or another of his children standing next to his head, staring at him silently. He stared in turn at their knees, annoyed that no matter how much he fed the children, those knees still bulged beyond the breadth of their thighs.

"Don't you feed these kids?" his colleagues joked when they

poked their heads through the door to his office, where the children obediently congregated after school to do their homework. These aloof not-so-little strangers always stood around, knobby-kneed, looking at him as if he were supposed to do something for them. But what was it? He fed them, he reeled them in when they got out of hand, he made sure they went to school. What else did they expect? Naturally, they expected their mother, but he could no more deliver her than he could pull a rabbit out of a hat. They stared at him with eyes as dark as his own fathers' eyes. How had his father's eyes—those ouzo-doused vats of charcoal, those mazes of disappointment with the human race—shown up in his children's heads? He'd never said a harsh word to those children except when he was supposed to, like when they were misbehaving. What was wrong with them?

He stroked the toad on the right side again, watching it inflate. The toad's gold and black eyes closed as if it genuinely enjoyed the caress. Walter straightened with a sigh and a grunt of pain and picked up the broom as he did every night. Starting at one end, he swept the porch in measured strokes. The sweeping sound, this ritual stroking of the earth, soothed him.

Eustacia would have told him everything was all right. She would have said that Ovid was too much of a genius for the world to understand, that all he needed was encouragement. Ovid had stumbled into adolescence with blue rings under his eyes from staying up all night watching TV. He complained bitterly about going to school. Walter forced him to go. There had been threats, tears, rage—even pushing matches, he was ashamed to admit. Ovid would come home sometimes with black eyes or a limp from fistfights. Walter would have liked to let him skip school entirely, but that just wasn't done. How would Ovid ever make his way in the world? The teachers sent notes home about Ovid's untapped potential, encouraging him to do his homework. Walter would sit with him at the kitchen table and try to get him to write his papers, but they would end up shouting at each other. Each time he would promise himself he wouldn't lose his temper, he found himself shouting again.

Ovid missed his mother, of course. Their family had a terrible time entering Bolivia after she vanished. A huge truck had come along and towed them to a village where the pavement started. The border guards detained them and questioned him and all three children, accusing them of being spies because they came into the country over this unmarked route. And where was his wife? He had had to lie, saying she flew home ahead of them. Eventually, with the children exhausted, frightened, and despairing, the border guards stamped their passports and let them go.

He stopped sweeping to pick up a spray of silvery green lichen. He examined it minutely. Lichen was a beautiful thing. Two and sometimes three different organisms lived together symbiotically. When conditions were too extreme, lichen could shut down and wait until things got better, and then go on living. How many times had he wished to be able to do that? Lichen was one of the oldest living species on the planet. How was spontaneous combustion any less likely than lichen?

He looked up to see what had dislodged the lichen from the locust tree that dwarfed the house. An entire flock of turkeys blinked down at him . He was surprised they were so quiet, and that he hadn't startled them off their perch with his sweeping, the way he had so easily dislodged his own children. All except Ovid, of course.

He had researched spontaneous combustion. It wasn't well documented, but there had been other cases where people had burned up without setting their surroundings on fire, as if it were a different kind of flame. He found a news article about a man who survived it—he lost his hand and part of his groin. In *Bleak House*, one of the many books he had to read to the children before bed, Old Krook had spontaneously combusted, but it was because he was so full of alcohol. Eustacia didn't drink. The human body was made of carbon, hydrogen, and oxygen. Gasoline was just hydrogen, carbon—and oxygen made it combust. Couldn't things in the body get mixed up once in a while? It seemed entirely possible. He was surprised it didn't happen more often, really.

He wasn't so sure it had been spontaneous, though. She had talked about vanishing acts and about showing them an amazing discovery when they reached the *Altiplano*. He knew the story of the event that she had wanted him to believe, and he did his best to oblige her. So full of light, she had always been full of discoveries. From the minute he'd first seen her in college, talking avidly with physics classmates while expressions played across her face like a rapid river, and her black mole highlighted her lower lash like a jester's tear, he knew he must marry her. She was more alive than anyone he had ever met. He had such a hard time kindling a spark of his own that he hoped he could warm himself against her fire.

He looked up at the stars, dimly poking through the clouds. The Incas named the shapes of the dark space between the stars rather than the constellations of stars themselves, as the Greeks did. That was how he felt about Eustacia's death. He loved the shape of her in his mind, which even included the shape of her absence.

Not so for Ovid, he supposed. For him, the shape of her death was a ragged hole that sucked everything into it. Well, it was understandable. Eustacia had been his mother. They were cut from the same cloth.

Now they were grown. Fallon was a good girl. She had at least finished college and got a job, not much of one, but it was more than he could say for Ovid. Eustacia had always said that Ovid couldn't be easily satisfied because he was meant for greater things, but he sometimes wondered if Ovid's intelligence was a curse. Add to that, he was so clumsy. He was always injuring himself. He had too many hobbies. Why was he messing about with those damn bees, anyhow?

Terry called once a year to fill him in. He was living in Los Angeles, manufacturing and selling "100% natural diet pills." He had changed his name to Cosmo, which Walter found vaguely offensive. Of the three children, Cosmo-Terry had been secretive. He kept to himself. And when he'd grown up, he developed a swagger. All show, Walter thought, shaking his head and tsking, but he supposed salesmen needed that sort of personality.

"Diet pills are like gold here, Dad. It's really great stuff," Terry had said in an offhanded, Marlboro man voice, as new to Terry as the name Cosmo.

"That's great, Terry," Walter said.

"Cosmo. I'm Cosmo, now."

"Cos—"

"To tell you the truth," Terry talked over him, "I felt kind of bad selling the shit I used to sell. This stuff is really good for you. Your metabolism starts jammin' to a serotonin orchestra. And it's *all legal.*"

Walter sighed as he entered the kitchen and poured red wine into a small green glass. He ambled to his chair in the living room and turned on the evening news. He smiled bitterly. "The evening noose."

He should have told his children about their name, Kazan. It was Greek. Why had he never done that? His father had been a refugee from the political turmoil between the world wars. He had run his cheese shop in Astoria, Queens, while Germany looted Greece, Jews were deported from Salonika, and famine sucked hundreds upon thousands inside out.

As a boy, Walter had never breathed freely until his father left their one-bedroom apartment above the cheese shop to argue with his fellow Greek cronies and berate the world for its injustice.

"I'm going! I'm going! And don't ask me where," his father would shout in his thick accent, slamming the door behind him. His mother would cringe and bend lower over the deep cast-iron sink she was scrubbing, her head almost disappearing beneath the rim, her silence perpetual. She was American born, with a weak chin and eyes so pale they were almost white. His father had married her to straighten out the noses of his progeny and then had blamed her for their American-ness ever since.

After his father slammed the door and his mother nervously dried her hands and went downstairs to mind the cash register, the shadows in their apartment would grow deliciously cool and quiet. He would sink into the dusty velveteen chair in the corner of their crowded dining room and lose himself in a book until his father came in and smacked him on the back of the head, admonishing him to go down and help his mother.

As soon as Walter was old enough to live on his own, he got out of the city, finding the quiet of Upstate New York heady relief. His father disowned him, and he was too ashamed to go back and check on his mother.

In college, he had designed beautiful new housing developments that he thought would wipe clean the past and make his parents happy. He hadn't realized how soulless they would be, how those developments would be the antithesis of everything he really loved: toads, lichen, traveling abroad with a brilliant, eccentric woman, and turkeys perched in a locust tree over an old stone house. His whole life had been a failure, then, he thought, settling into despair like a favorite bathrobe with a hole at the elbow.

It was too late, now, to do anything about it. He could at least tell Fallon about her Greek heritage, he thought, watching the moving pictures on the television screen, and listening to the newscaster's cadence rise and fall like a roller coaster, predictably unpredictable. He nodded slightly, and his eyelids drooped. He would tell her when she got home, he thought, if the right moment arrived.

He sighed again. He had done the best he could with his children, but in the end, human nature was far more mysterious to him than his wife's vanishing.

# 12

# OVID UNTETHERED

F*allon!* Eustacia's voice echoed in the still morning air, startling her awake.

Fallon's eyes flashed open. The air reverberated with the aftershock of a sharply spoken word recently silenced. She was disoriented but wide awake. She looked around. A sliver of morning sun slanted orange through the gap like a hot finger tilting her chin up. She was in her old room at the back of the house, behind the massive kitchen chimney. She jumped out of bed, her heart beating hard. Whatever had awakened her, her heart wouldn't stop drumming the alarm: "Go to Ovid, go to Ovid, go to Ovid, *now.*"

His mind was buzzing again. How had she done it, flipped the charges so that the electrons didn't repel each other but stood aside so she could pass between? His mind buzzed around the problem, circling faster. At first it felt good, but then it went too fast, like a fever. He wished that someone would close the door in order to slow down the buzzing so he could catch the tail of the equation. *Why didn't you wait for me, Mom? Why didn't you tell me how to do it?* Fallon didn't understand. She wasn't smart enough. She said it was an accident. It was no accident. If only he could slow his mind just a fraction. It had to go fast enough to make sense of it, fast enough to put all the pieces together at the same time, so that he could figure it out, but not so fast that it would spin off kilter.

The blue woman was standing in the doorway. His mind stopped when he saw her. She stood there, leaning against the frame. Silent. Smiling. Flirting. Her blue belly peeked out beneath her midriff shirt. The glittering chain around her waist fell down the path to paradise, disappearing inside silky pantaloons.

"You came," he said, reaching out to her. She slinked over to the bed and took his hand. He could smell the envelope of grass-scented air she walked in. The nearness of her flesh stirred his loins. From his angle beneath her, he could see up her shirt to the underside of her bare breasts. Oh, to cup her breasts in his hand, his mouth.

"Fallon said it was an accident, but it wasn't, was it?"

The blue woman shook her head and smiled, her eyes strangely light against her blue skin, a strand of her dreadlocked hair falling into her face. She tugged at his hand. He sat up and ran his hands up her side, under her shirt, but she stopped him before he could touch her breasts. She shook her head and pulled at him again, smiling, playful.

"It's not about belief. It's about truth," Ovid told her. "My mother figured it out, didn't she?"

The blue woman nodded.

"If I could just figure it out, I could follow . . ."

The blue woman nodded again, collapsed her body poutingly, then smiling, pulled him forward.

---

Back at the house, Fallon stood in the center of her room, frozen with indecision. It was only half past six. Should she wait until Walter was up? Make breakfast, then go together? Was she being melodramatic? Ovid was in the hospital. People were looking after him. He was medicated. They probably wouldn't even let her see him this early. The pounding of her blood wouldn't allow her to stay still. She grabbed up her father's car keys, flew out the door, and gunned the engine.

---

"You're going to show me, aren't you, Blue?" Ovid said.

She nodded eagerly and pulled him onward.

He followed her down the hall. There was a bluish light coming from the windows. Blue put her finger to her lips and dropped to her knees. He did likewise, and they crawled past the nurse's station. They pushed through the door to the stairway, and Blue pulled him up a flight. She stopped and turned around, and he slid his hand up her leg, now miraculously bare under silky pantaloons, right into her hot, slippery twat, the smell of grassy fields surrounding him, but she pulled herself away and ran ahead of him up the stairs, giggling. He ran after her, riding the curve, flight after flight, until she pushed open the door to the roof, and the *Altiplano* stretched before them, a vast robe of gray sands, the sun rising orange on the horizon between snow-peaked volcanoes, winds traveling for thousands of miles to greet them. She danced, her arms overhead, hands flicking flamenco-style against the burning backdrop of the rising sun, shaping letters, numbers, some kind of silver calligraphy. He could almost read it. She was dancing the alphabet backwards, and—why hadn't he noticed this before—the backwards alphabet spelled out words, the answer to the cipher:

*Zyx w vut srq ponml kjih gfed cba*

The words warmed around the edges, took shape:

*Ztik wr vut srix pomond jill get by*

Resolved into focus:

*Stick your foot slick upon kill get by*

Made sense:

*Seize protons with skill to get through*

Instructions. Yes, that was how it was done, that was how you separated the electrons, just grab them between their silver interstices and—

Something nagged at him, a buzzing sound that brought him back to the rooftop. The rooftop? How did he get to the rooftop? Where was the *Altiplano?* He looked down at the tarred roof, and that buzzing sound was someone calling him, reminding him of something he didn't want—

"Ovid!" he thought he heard someone scream.

Blue, that goddess, grabbed his hands, her grip like steel, and pulled. She ran in a circle, and he stumbled after. The buzzing went away as he fell into step. They ran faster and faster, becoming a silver ring, a spinning wheel, faster than light, faster than thought.

"Ovid!" he thought he heard again. But their speed thinned and distorted the sound, raking it out of his mind. He was spinning so fast now that Blue became one with him as a vortex sucked them in. Finally, he understood. If you spin fast enough, faster than the atoms spin, you could do it.

Out of wild nowhere, silver far interstices of space, between ancient molecules, his storm began to rise. All along it had been possible. Eustacia could have told him how to do it. Which means she had left him by choice. Betrayed him. A cry rose up from the desert floor, the stone depth, the tangled labyrinth. A cry rose up from inside him at such a steadily accelerating decibel that every atom of his body shot screaming toward the sky. It was a never-ending cry, an outraged and joyous cry, the cry of a man who had finally cracked the code, passed the test, and aced the exam that all along his mother had set for him, knowing that his atomic call could summon the force to part the fabric of life and step through.

He flew. That was what it felt like to break through, flying and falling and buzzing so fast that he was dispersing into a million silver specks and joining his universal mother.

———

Fallon drove to the hospital full speed and came screeching to a halt at the edge of the parking lot, transfixed by the sight of Ovid on the hospital roof. He ran full tilt at the short wall that rimmed the hospital's flat roof, and she gasped, but he just jumped onto the wall.

The sun was up, having just let go of the horizon, and it was directly behind him so she could barely make out what he was doing. He was walking on the ledge, teetering, crouching, hopping, gesticulating. She jumped out of the car, leaving the door wide open.

"Ovid!" she screamed. "Ovid!" She waved her arms at him, but he didn't notice her. Even shielding her eyes, she couldn't see him clearly between the stabbing rays of sun. But she recognized the posture, the gait, the way he held his hands. Was there someone up there with him? Something flickered in and out of the light behind him. She called and called, but he didn't listen.

She couldn't say what happened next. She was caught up in a roaring wind, a cry so loud that it twisted her intestines by the roots and splintered her nerve filaments, a shriek that thrust a flexible metal blade between her scalp and her skull. She covered her eyes.

What happened? She wasn't sure. She had an image of him on the ground, running in circles over the blacktop in a rage just as he had run over their mother's remains on the *Altiplano*. As he ran, his fists became stones, the stones jumped, and the ground trembled. His grief toppled, his anger cracked, and his tears split the blacktop hot and hissing. He threw himself at the ground so hard that he became the ground, went into the ground, spread himself out and upon and through and beneath the ground, because only the ground knew how to handle so much rage and grief, only the earth could receive it and send it down, down through the rocks, through its molten center, until all that was left was liquid metal. And Ovid no more.

But Fallon, who had seen this before in the opposite direction, who ran to the spot where Ovid had once been—who ran in circles over the cracked blacktop searching for some entry for herself— Fallon remained just a body above the stones. Just the body of one who had lost herself, to find herself, to lose herself again.

Fallon stopped breathing—or realized that she had stopped and tried to breathe again, finding the air so long gone it scraped her lungs like sand when it returned. Then she ran.

She ran from the parking lot, down the street, past houses, fields, and trees, out into open space. She flew over rock and walls, ditches, and streams. Branches beat her face and briars tore her legs, but still she ran, until she too might disperse, ran until the air ripped her lungs with fire, ran herself to exhaustion, ran until she dropped, senseless and heaving onto the quilted forest floor between tree roots, waiting for her own apotheosis. But she remained accursedly solid. Above ground. Whole, yet halved.

A world of fatigue dropped on her and crushed her to sleep.

## 13

# FUGUE

In the days that followed, Fallon sat on the gray bank of a long black river, looking at the people walking on the other side. Her side of the river was the land of the dead. The people on the other side were far away and no taller than her thumb. Their muted voices pushed through cotton. Policemen, lawyers, and morticians came and went, talking and sitting, but the river carried off their words. She sent words over the river toward them in boats made of leaves, hoping her words would stop theirs from crossing.

Walter came to talk to her as she lay on her bed in her original childhood room, the one she had shared with Ovid and Terry. She tried to focus on the shapes Walter's lips were taking, but she couldn't make out what he was saying. She felt vaguely sorry for him but wanted to slap him at the same time. Nausea sloshed somewhere far away. She nodded her head to make him leave.

It was unseasonably warm, and it rained and rained and rained. When it didn't rain, the air itself swelled to the point that it was hard to walk through, so she lay down most of the time. But her bedspread absorbed the water from the air and stuck to her skin. The rain saturated the cells of her skin, bloating it. She wanted to scrape it off with her nails to get down to the bone-clean quick of it all, the hard, white, mindless core. Silence. She craved silence but then found it horribly long and boring, so she had to get up and move.

Days passed in jumbled images with no connective tissue. She tried to watch TV, but the words moved too quickly, and she couldn't follow the pictures. She tried reading, but her mind slipped off the words like water off plastic. She stared at a chunk of chicken on the end of her fork and thought how much it looked like wood. It tasted like wood. No saliva formed when she chewed. How strange the word "fork" was. Such an absurd sound. Fork. Fork. Fork. No logical connection to the object.

*No object is solid,* said Eustacia's voice. But that wasn't the issue. The issue was that every object was too solid, too grubby, too grimy, too sticky, too full of every thought and feeling that anyone had ever invested in it. At the furthest edge of her vision, Ovid's tools sat in their boxes, the oil of his hands still fragrant upon them. But she couldn't think of that now.

And still it rained. Endless rain. Rainingly endless. Doors swelled so that they were hard to open and close. The air was laden with water, more like July than October, and it saturated even the floor so that it grew dark in patches where the varnish was thin. Rugs, walls, and woodwork filled beyond capacity with water and wept. One morning she woke up to find her right hand was swollen like a rubber glove filled with water. She could barely move her fingers. When she reached for a coffee cup, she knocked it over. When she reached for a doorknob, she jammed her fingers.

Another day, she found herself standing in front of Eustacia's green Dodge Dart. Her body remembered how to drive, though she didn't. She took the car out in the rain. For a time, it *was* comforting, as it sailed and bobbed over hill and vale. But then, through the blurry windshield, just outside of town, something black reached up from the road ahead of her. She slowed her car. There it was again, a black hand reaching up out of the asphalt and disappearing. She applied the brakes. She wasn't imagining it. The world really was like this. Something was coming to take her. She was ready.

She pulled over and got out of the car. No one else was around.

Shielding her face from the rain, she darted into the road. But it was only a dead crow. The wind was blowing one of its wings into the air. Its black feathers fanned upwards and out, then fell back to the earth.

Sanity was a cliff, she suddenly realized, from which she was almost ready to jump, to be free, to be free of logic, of reason, of responsibility, to be free of the exhausting possibility that there was a right way to put the puzzle pieces back together that she just wasn't seeing.

At home, more people from the hospital came to talk to her. Nobody on that side of the river knew what it was like to be on her side of the river. Christo would know; with his psychotic mother and schizophrenic brother, didn't he live on this side? He would never call. And Will? The river was too wide to even think about Will. Will belonged too firmly on the side of the living.

The rain finally stopped one day. It was November. The sky was still overcast. She went out to what was left of Ovid's vegetable garden and lay down. The wet of the cold earth soaked into her clothes. How tenderly he had staked the tomato plants, now gray, hairy stalks. How thoughtfully he had mixed the compost. The sweet smell of leaf rot surrounded her. The broken beehives lay abandoned at the edge of the garden. She looked up at the sky and could not tell if the dim ball in the gray sky was sun or moon. The moon might be a nice place to live, so far away, so quiet, a great big zero in the sky, a cipher to climb into and feel nothing.

A tiny movement on the ground caught her eye. One ant maneuvered a dead spider over its head into an anthill. All its brothers and sisters streamed around it, carrying grains of sand out, bits of food in, endlessly building and cleaning and storing, as they had built and cleaned and stored for thousands of years. They were all ants, the townspeople, the hospital workers, herself, her father, all working tirelessly, buying and selling, building and destroying. The whole noisy planet was humming and spinning, a ball of dirt and water hanging in space with no top and no bottom, no beginning and no end. Exhausting.

# 14

# EMERGING

Staring at the bark of the sycamore tree, Fallon's feet touched ground for the first time since the unnamable event. That was how she knew she had crossed the river back to life. The sycamore tree, with its puzzle-work bark of gray, green, and brown, towered over her. *Be like me. Just be. Like me.* Its crooked, bushy branches arched skyward and dipped earthward, like a mother reaching down to pick up a child. Weeks of rain had combed all the leaves from its branches, but it stood there more beautiful for its bareness.

Beauty hurt, so she waded back to the shores of death.

Some immeasurable time later, she found herself on the life side of the river again, washing a cup at the kitchen sink. The warm, soapy sponge circled the mouth of the cup and infused her with calm. It was as if her body had a will to life all its own. That's when she heard a voice in her head say distinctly, "Call Terry." She stopped washing the cup. Whose voice was that? It was gone. But it was enough. Her mind became clinical. She watched herself look up Terry's number in the family phone book. She stood outside herself as she dialed, noting how vast the blank space inside her was. After two rings, an ear-splitting tone sounded, and an automated voice spoke: "This number has been disconnected. No further information is available."

The library was a place of information, her brain told her. But the library was overwhelming. All those books, all those names. It would be easier to drive to California. The simple physicality of it. Just putting one foot in front of the other. Her mind began to tick off items she would need to assemble for the trip.

However, as she stood in the middle of the basement, staring at the layer of dust and crumbled cement that covered the moldy suitcases she'd pulled out around her, she was sucked back to the death side of the river and went to bed.

A few days later, the insistent sound of voices rising and falling woke her, an indefatigable argument. The 6 o'clock news.

She followed the sound to the living room, where Walter sat in his usual chair, long legs crossed, boots neatly polished and tied, one hand resting in a bowl of Spanish peanuts. The news anchor was saying something about a "Miracle Mud Baby."

"You're up," he said. "Feeling better?" He looked grayer. Older.

"What's going on?" she asked, looking at the footage on TV of a sheriff holding a muddy child in his arms. The camera had cut off the top of his face. He spread his jacket on the top of his squad car and sat the child upon it, her back to the camera. Her muddy arms reached out to him reflexively, and he picked her back up.

"There was another tornado in Oklahoma." Walter said. "Ripped this child right out of her mother's arms as she hid in the closet. But this sheriff found the child face down in the mud a hundred feet away, unharmed. They're calling it a miracle." The word hit her stomach like tainted food.

"I want to go find Terry," she said in a monotone, not taking her eyes off the TV.

"Yes. That's what I've been saying. I didn't think you heard me." He also kept his eyes on the TV.

She pulled her eyes from the TV screen to scan his face. It was blank. He was still handsome even in old age, with his blue eyes, hawkish nose, and broad brow, hardly wrinkled. He could have been dictating a grocery list. Nothing seemed to surprise him. For a second, she was overtaken by a wild urge to shake him, but an answering blankness inside of her extinguished the urge.

"Can I take the Dodge Dart?"

"Of course." Eyes still on the TV.

"What will you do without a car?"

"There's the Colt. You will need to take the Dodge Dart to a mechanic to check it out."

She was about to return to the kitchen but hung back and peered at him.

Her wobbly legs felt almost solid on the ground.

"Dad, how . . . are you?"

"Me?" He pulled his eyes from the TV to look at her briefly, then off into space. "I don't know. I'm—puzzled."

"Puzzled?" she held the word out from her, like a dirty sock pinched between her thumb and index finger.

"Yes," he said. He leaned forward in his chair, clasped his hands, and stared at the ground in front of him. "Life is something that happens to you. Why would anyone ever give it up?"

She returned to the kitchen. A few yellow leaves clung to a black branch outside the deep-set window. Christo. Here was a feeling she could withstand, the darkness of their embrace, the stark roundness of their mutual loss.

The phone rang. She jumped. She waited to let the answering machine pick up. When the tone beeped, it was Will's voice. Her heart surged painfully, as if it was trying to pass a small stone through a valve. He was like that sheriff on the news. For a second, she felt like the muddy baby on the roof of the car, and she could feel the sheriff's arms under hers as he responded to her gesture and picked her up, a reflex mapped in his DNA.

As Will's voice sounded on the machine, Walter said, "Oh, there's that fellow again. He's called a few times. Said he was a friend of yours."

She listened to the message. She didn't move. His voice was so warm. It made her feel her blood flowing, her terrible, toxic blood that carried so many messages through her arteries. He sounded sad, caring, hopeful. She remembered the look on his face when he'd faced the shooter. He cared even for a potential murderer.

His voice paused in the middle of his message, letting the tape recorder spin a moment in silence as if he knew she was standing right there. Her heart twitched painfully again at the thought that she would lose him forever if she didn't pick up. She reached for the phone, but wordless resistance held her fast, louder than blood, louder than thought.

"Take care," he said, and hung up, and she could almost feel the cord that attached them ripping.

Her father went out to the porch to sweep. The screen door slapped shut behind him. The methodical swish of the broom brought the rational part of her brain back. She would need warm clothes and cool clothes for crossing the country, as well as a sleeping bag, some plastic dishes, a few pots and pans, water, a first aid kit, and spare gas for the drive through the desert. She began to assemble cooking gear. She could drop the Dodge Dart off at the mechanic in town, and Walter could pick her up.

She went out to the porch to ask him if he would. That's when she realized the sweeping sound had stopped. He was sitting on the pavement at the far end of the porch, next to the tools. He was leaning over, his hands clasped between his knees, head bowed.

"Dad?" she said, going over to him, placing her hand on his shoulder. He looked up at her, his eyes red-rimmed, watery.

"What happened?"

"It's gone," he said.

"What's gone?"

"The toad that used to sit behind the shovels."

---

Over the next week she developed a curious, if obsessive, energy, planning her moves down to the smallest detail to maximize efficiency. To heat a cup of coffee, she had to wash the dirty cup first so as not to make more dishes. Then she'd rush to finish other dishes while it was heating. But when the soapy sponge was in her hand, she couldn't stop washing the dishes until they were done. Then the coffee was cold. While she reheated the coffee, she would take a load of laundry to the basement, but in the basement, she found her sleeping bag, and when she brought it back upstairs, the coffee was cold again. So the week went, but it got her through, and all the while she thought deeply about Terry, about reclaiming the boy who had always been left behind, the boy who always said, "No, that's not how it was," and tapped his foot impatiently.

---

One morning she woke up with a ray of sun warming her brow like a loving hand. When she opened her eyes, she found Will at her bedside, and the ray of sun actually *was* his hand.

"Hey, sleepy-head," he said quietly. "I've been sitting with your father for a few hours, waiting for you to wake up. I hope you don't mind."

She would have been alarmed, but the warmth in his dark blue eyes surrounded her, made her muscles relax. She rose and hugged him, and he, smelling of fresh hay, pulled her tight. The body connection was a revelation, a startling contrast that re-exposed the tissue paper illusion of her love for Christo.

Of their own accord, tears spilled from her eyes over his shoulder, out of his line of sight, dampening his wool shirt. She hadn't known this kind of connection was possible.

# 15

# CHOOSING THE ROAD

That night and for the rest of the week before she left, they slept together romantically, but without having sex. No one had ever offered her intimacy and space simultaneously, and trust grew.

"I hope I'm not disappointing you," she had said as they got into bed together the third night.

"I'm happy to be here," was all he said.

She smiled, stroked his face, and kissed his neck.

They pulled her mother's car into the barn because it was getting cold. For days, Will crawled over, under, around, and through the car, checking, rebuilding, and replacing parts. He was stumped by a particular problem he'd found in the carburetor. The hood of the Dodge Dart gaped over them like a crocodile's jaw as he explained that the carburetor's job was to mix just the right amount of gas with air to create a tiny explosion to move the pistons. Fallon wasn't really following his explanation. Instead, she was noticing how nice it was that the cold made his breath visible, and that his breath contained tiny particles of him that were now becoming part of the barn, part of the car, and how his voice vibrated in her sternum and radiated warmth through her chest like a hot drink on a cold day. Her entire life, she had been hiding in a cave, and the few men she had slept with had done nothing more than bash the entrance. Will was the first man who had ever, quietly, patiently, lured her out.

When she tuned back into his lecture, he was showing her how to check the oil.

"Give it a try," he said, lowering the dipstick back into the oil well.

"What?" she asked.

He reached under the lip of the grill for a rag.

"Curious," he said, as he pulled a small yellow scroll from a niche. It was tightly rolled notebook paper. Something was written on the pages. With a tightening of her stomach, she recognized the scrawl, more like horizontal lines with occasional bumps, illegible to most people. It was her mother's. She had studied it as a child, carefully matching the incomprehensible squiggles with the comprehensible ones, until she could decipher it at a decent pace.

She pulled the scroll from Will's grease-stained hands.

As she unwound the paper, it cracked and flaked.

*Nothing is impossible.*
*"Nothing" is impossible.*

Inside Fallon, something shifted. The second page was a dictionary definition:

*Cipher: 1. a secret or disguised way of writing; a code. 2. a zero;*
*Ciphery: 1. the practice of sorcery using a cipher; 2. an enchantment*
*with zero or nothing; 3. a mystery.*

The third page read:

*Billions of years of molecules sorted themselves into egg-like*
[indecipherable word] *that translate the rough materials of life*

[more words she couldn't make out]—*algorithms we are still trying to decipher*

"Wow," Will said, "I'm too stupid to make heads or tails of that."

"Do I look like the kind of woman who would date an idiot?"

"Now that you mention it, no," he gave her a squeeze. "Go on."

She read aloud:

*Einstein said, "Logic will take you from A to B, but imagination will take you everywhere."*

Further down on the same page, with a few words scratched out and inserted above:

*It took billions of years for cells to make the eye—for creation*
[something] *the ability to see itself.*
*Can you see me? Can you see me?*

Seized by some savage emotion, Fallon let the notes curl shut, and shoved the scroll at Will. "I can't read these. Not now." A wave of heat rippled through her.

Over the next hour and a half, in fits and starts, watching his face for signs that he thought she was crazy, Fallon told Will how obsessed her mother had been with quantum physics, genius, and making a great discovery. Between sips of strong coffee as they sat on cinder blocks beside the car, with vapor rising from their mouths like smoke signals, she mustered the courage to tell him how her mother had spontaneously combusted.

"What do you mean? Like she literally went up in flames?"

She searched his face apprehensively. "Yes."

"Whoa. That's—"

"Crazy?"

"Yeah, but I'm not saying you're crazy. It's just wild. I've heard of a lot of ways of going, but not that way."

"But you believe me?"

"Of course, I believe you."

She rushed on to tell him. How Ovid had never gotten over it. How she had never been able to trust her perception since then.

Will put his hand on her knee. "Have you ever read Carlos Castaneda?"

She shook her head.

"Castaneda claimed he apprenticed to a Native American shaman he called Don Juan," Will explained. "Don Juan supposedly taught him to see the energy of the universe directly by taking hallucinogenic plants. The idea was that hallucinations, rather than being illusions produced by the mind, were messages from the plant spirits helping us to see what is really there."

As they talked, they left the barn and stood under the sycamore trees.

The sun had warmed somewhat, and their breath was no longer visible. Fallon brushed the green and brown camouflage bark. Sycamores were said to be the places of vision, the twin guards of the gates of the house of the sun god, Ra.

"If you told me you could turn yourself into a bird at night and fly," Fallon gestured to the sky, "I'd think you were delusional. In America, you would be."

"Look—I'm not saying I believe Castaneda's version of events. But this is not quite the same as telling me you can fly. If you did tell me that, incidentally, I'd assume that on some level it was true for you… but I wouldn't believe you could literally leave the ground unless I saw it myself. What I'm saying, though, is that the idea of 'reality' and 'sanity" is a matter of debate. You are looking head-on at something most people don't have the courage to tackle. That makes you brave," he cupped her face with one hand, admiration in his eyes, "not crazy."

His open-mindedness filled her with corresponding admiration. She leaned into his body, folding her arms like wings in front of her, matching thigh to thigh, pelvis to pelvis, cheek to shoulder, and he curved around her in answer. They stood in silence. A crow, perched on a high branch, cawed down in irritation at them, telling them to move along.

"Am I doing the right thing, going to find Terry?"

"Definitely."

"How can I believe myself when I have seen others deceive themselves? I have been wrong so many times, about people, about jobs, about the choices I've made."

"Just breathe. Just listen." He gave her an affectionate shake.

"But which voice do I listen to?"

"The voice that isn't afraid. The voice that shows you how to take care of yourself without doing harm to others."

"But I *have* harmed others. I didn't stop Ovid—"

"You can't do it alone. You know that story about the blind men all feeling the elephant? One is feeling the tail and says it's long and thin, the other one is feeling the ear and saying it's wide and flat? Part of how we know what is real is by sharing our perceptions. Let me go on this trip with you. Together we'll find real." He looked as if he had surprised himself. He had certainly surprised her.

He twined his forearms with hers and pulled her into his chest.

"I've put some money by. I've crossed the country a million times. Let's find your brother together."

"I don't know," she said, untwining her arms, but still holding his hands.

"A burden shared is lighter," he smiled ruefully.

"I don't want to hurt you. You've been so good to me." His grip loosened slightly.

"Close your eyes," he said. She closed them. "What do you feel, inside?"

She felt a jumble of sensations, her beating heart, tension in her neck and shoulders, uneven breath rattling into and out of her lungs, the crow cawing from above.

"Underneath all the worry and fear, look to that older, wiser part of yourself, the part that has always been there."

"I can't feel anything. My mind is buzzing all over the place."

"Notice that. Accept it but let yourself sink into the trunk. Let the branches of your mind toss all over the place but feel your feet on the ground."

That's what she had told Ovid. Funny she had to be reminded.

She breathed. The feel of her back against the tree calmed her. She sank down inside, the breath filling her from head to toe, warming her thighs and calves. When she breathed out, she sank down under the shifting leaves of self, into the ground. Her shoulders warmed, molded around the trunk, and there, underneath it all, just as he had said, was an older, wiser, warmer self. The answer was simple. When she opened her eyes, they felt clean and clear.

"I need to do this alone."

"Okay, then." He smiled, but she could see the disappointment, feel a door closing between them.

"But," she said, "Could you—would you, stay here until I get back?"

"Here?"

"Dad could use a little help around the house. And a little company."

"How long do you think you'll be gone?"

"I don't know. Depends on what I find. But I figure I need at least a week of travel both ways. I've got enough money to last about a month."

His brow wrinkled, thinking about it. He shrugged. "This is as good a place to mark time as any." He paused and thought some more and shrugged again. "I've got no plans, anyway. Sure. I'll stick around if he wants. If *you* want."

"I want," she kissed him. "Having you here would anchor me. Give me a reason to come back. It would mean a lot to me to know my Dad is okay."

"That's a good enough reason for me, as long as you call and check in, regularly."

"Absolutely," she said and smiled, though it made her nervous.

"And if you change your mind, I could come whenever you want."

She leaned into his lips and they kissed, smoothly, warmly, sweetly.

In the distance, fog rose from low blue hills, sending a message far easier to read than her mother's handwriting or Ovid's moods. White birch trees glowed against the dark woods behind them. She was made of the same matter as the hills, the trees, and the crow. They were all simply different arrangements of carbon, oxygen, mineral, and water molecules. Did anyone tell the trees how to grow? Did anyone teach the crow to caw?

# 16

# THE CIPHERY

W hen she asked Walter how he felt about Will sticking around until she returned, her father had responded with surprising cheer. Will talked of renting an apartment in town, but Walter said he'd rather have Will in the house; there was plenty of room. Though the house had once been elegant in its time, with its thick stone walls, high ceilings, and large windows, now it leaned and leaked. Will quickly secured a part-time job at one of the many bars downtown, which left plenty of time for whatever repair jobs Walter wanted him to do.

Fallon picked a random date to leave. But as it approached, a white-of-the-eyes panic germinated. She found more and more things to do before going: pay bills, water plants, sort the spice drawer. She was contemplating a complete overhaul of the basement when she caught on to what she was doing. As her list of excuses thinned, a child-part of herself kicked up a ruckus. "I won't go. You can't make me," it insisted.

However, the impetus to find Terry was equally strong. She stared at a family portrait. Eight-year-old Terry looked at the camera with a slightly sardonic expression far too old for his face, like he was an actor in a bad play who—having momentarily caught an audience member's eye—was acknowledging just how stupid he thought his lines were. She had never noticed that before.

Maybe he knew something about Eustacia's vanishing act that she didn't. Maybe he could tell her where she went wrong with Ovid, so she would never make that kind of mistake again. Before Eustacia's apotheosis, she had walked between her brothers feeling complete —or at least — not separate. Wasn't that the same thing?

It was three o'clock in the afternoon when she finally dragged that inner child kicking and screaming, to the front door, almost forgetting to take leave of Walter, who sat at the kitchen table.

When she approached to hug him, he didn't get up, so the hug made an awkward triangle. "Go get him, girlie," he said, over her shoulder, patting her vaguely on the back. "Drive safe."

Will accompanied her out to the car.

"Have you got everything?" he asked, looking down at the neatly packed trunk. She had a tent, camp stove, sleeping bag, crates of dry food and dishes, and some emergency gear. She consulted her list and nodded, looking up at him wordlessly.

"You sure you want to do this alone?"

She nodded, trying to swallow the unreasonable fear rising within.

"Do you understand?" she asked.

"I'm working on it." His voice was modulated to sound casual, but she caught hints that he felt otherwise.

"You're not hurt?"

"Should I be?"

"You know it's not about you. It's not about us."

"Glad to know you think of this," he waved his hand back and forth between them, "as *us*."

She hugged him, inhaling his solid, hay-scented warmth, and a chasm wrenched itself wide inside of her. Why was she leaving the first safe haven she had ever had, the only shore on an otherwise shoreless lake of grief?

"I'm not sure I understand why I'm doing this, either, but I'm trying to trust that voice you helped me find." Beneath the chasm, in an ancient grotto, a maternal figure she'd never known until a few days ago had to be obeyed.

Will nodded and pressed a plastic card into her hand. "This is a prepaid phone card. Call me any time you want. The pin number is 9455, the letters of my name. Any time. Day or night. Leave a message if I'm not there. Keep your feet on the ground."

"That's going to be hard while driving," she said, smiling.

As she headed southwest on Interstate 88, the tentative safety she'd found with Will dissipated and was replaced by the floaty feeling that had gotten her through so many different countries, lulled by the turning wheels and humming engine. The map was spread out on the seat beside her with her handwritten notes sitting on top of it listing the route names she and Will had plotted out. Eustacia's notes curled in the cavernous darkness of the glove compartment. She would deal with them later.

She didn't know if she would find Terry at the end of this trip. She was fairly sure he didn't want to be found. She couldn't reconcile the small boy with whom she'd searched for four-leaf clovers on the lawn in Chile with the arrogant teenager he later became. Who would he be now? How would he react to her terrible news? The jaded look of those deep-set, heavy-lidded eyes, that slack mouth seemed to say, "I told you so."

Unbidden, a memory arose. Sitting on the iron fence that surrounded the house in Santiago, when he was eight, they spoke frankly about their parents. Terry had said, much to her surprise, "I don't know if I love them."

"Of course, you love them," she had said. "You have to. They're our parents."

He shook his head and said nothing. What could an eight and eleven-year-olds know about love? It was a strange conversation for them to be having so young. Maybe he'd stopped believing the family mythology at a much earlier age than she'd realized. Maybe she remembered it wrong. Maybe she had said it to him, and he had agreed.

Maybe finding Terry was just an excuse to get away from it all, even Will. His arms held a kind of danger, the danger of loss, the danger of being discovered, of not being present enough to love or be loved. Deep down, she was numb. Maybe the truth was that she could not stand to be anywhere, so she returned to the one place she felt most safe, the place that was no place at all. Driving was a way to go somewhere without really going anywhere, a way of moving while standing still. As she drove, time unhinged, moving fast and slow simultaneously. The landscape changed from hills to exhaust filled suburbs, to narrow valleys of towering redolent pine. The car was a machine that would carry her through what her own body could not.

The sun went down. Night-driving suited her. All she could see were the white dashes in front of her and a small circle of road illuminated by headlights, a world small enough to manage. The rest was darkness and engine purr.

She drove into a deep fog. Sometimes it thinned, and other times it was so thick she could barely see a yard in front of her. She slowed down to 45 miles an hour but kept moving. The roads were empty, and the only sounds were the hum of the motor, muted now, and of her turning wheels shaped by the things she passed—the choppy swish of skunk cabbage, the mineral buzz of cut rock walls, the flopping of closely planted trees. Her mind was as blank as the fog.

A small green sign just before a bridge read, "Nameless River." That was funny. They had named it "Nameless." That would have been a good name for her. Nameless Kazan, daughter of Eustacia. Sister to Ovid.

She and Will had looked up the word "cipher" in the dictionary. The first two definitions were just as Eustacia had noted: a zero, a code, but the third was: "a person or thing of no importance, especially a person who does the bidding of others and seems to have no will of their own." She herself was a cipher. Even when she was living in New York City, she had been living in the epilogue of Eustacia's story.

She wasn't sure how long her mother's words had been snaking through her mind.

Eustacia must have tucked the notes into the car when they went on that final trip. How had they managed to survive this long? *Nothing is impossible.* In other words, all things are possible, so Eustacia parted the curtains of physicality and stepped through—to what? To another plane of existence? To nothingness? To the state of zero? But she also wrote, *"Nothing" was impossible.* The second sentence contradicted the first. It wasn't possible for Eustacia to become nothing. *Molecules sorted themselves into egg-like*—what was it?

Keeping her eye on the road, she reached over to the glove compartment. She had to take her eye off the road for a second to snap it open and find the scroll. Looking up, she swerved to bring the car back in the lane and dumped the scroll in her lap. She gripped the delicate wheel between both hands and took a deep breath. She reached for the dome light and snapped in on. God bless Will for replacing the bulb.

It was 1:00 a.m. She had been driving for . . . she tapped the hours out with her fingers on the wheel . . . ten hours. Bracing the wheel with her knees, she unraveled the scroll. Yellowed bits of paper flaked away around the edges, and—dartingly—she read, . . . *molecules sorted themselves into egg-like*—what was that word? She squinted, swerved, corrected—*membranes*—*molecules sorted themselves into egg-like membranes that translate the rough materials of life into electrical impulses, algorithms we are still trying to decipher.*

Fallon looked up at the red taillights far ahead of her at the top of a rise. They looked like the eyes of an enormous giant, its long arms forming the lanes of the road.

> *Cipher: 1. a secret or disguised way of writing; a code. 2. a zero;*
> *Ciphery: 1. the practice of sorcery using a cipher; 2. an enchantment*
> *with zero or nothing; 3. a mystery.*

Had Eustacia distractedly left these notes here while communing with the carburetor? Or had she stashed them here for them to find after she vanished to provide some kind of hidden message, a cipher? They didn't provide a key to the mystery. If anything, they only enlarged it. That was probably what she wanted.

Fallon couldn't put all the pieces of the story together in the right order. If she could just tell the story of her life in the right order it would lead her out of the labyrinth of pain, but she had too many different voices, too many different selves, to figure out which voice was hers. Each voice told a different part of the story. When she tried to speak, Eustacia spoke, or Ovid, or Walter or Terry.

She threw the notes down into the footwell in anger. Thinking better of it, she leaned forward to find them again, tearing her eyes from the road, swerving slightly. She giggled nervously. She should stop the car to read these notes, but she couldn't bear to stop. The only way she could read them was to keep moving.

> *It took billions of years for cells to make the eye—for creation to develop the ability to see itself.*
> *Can you see me? Can you see me?*

God, Eustacia was such a narcissist. Fallon checked the rearview mirror. The road behind her was empty. She yanked the mirror toward herself so that she could see her own eyes. Her face was pale green, illuminated by dashboard lights. The smell of swamp filled the car.

A parent was supposed to see who her child was and hold a mirror up to her so she could see for herself, so she could learn who she was. Instead, the mirror Eustacia held up had no room for Fallon in it. To Eustacia, Fallon was only Eustacia's extension, a pale reflection, a less exact copy. Fallon's entire job was to honor and admire Eustacia, to reflect Eustacia back to herself. How could a child in this situation develop any sense of self—or of anyone else's self, for that matter? No wonder she felt nothing deep down. She was literally driving with no hindsight. She had been suckling at the teat of a great ocean that threatened to drown her.

She straightened the rearview mirror, stretched her torso, pulling herself out of her hips, and leaned forward into the wheel, feeling how steely her neck muscles were. Her mouth was sealed shut with bitter dried saliva. If Fallon had gone to the authorities to complain of child abuse, they would have laughed. "Your parents clothed you, fed you, bathed you, took you all over the world, gave you a life of privilege, and you complain? You are the narcissist," they would have said.

That was part of the problem: she couldn't admit to herself how much pain she was in because there was no apparent cause.

Why was she thinking about this? Why wasn't she thinking about Ovid? Why wasn't she grieving?

The hyper-rational part of her brain, which had guided her to pack her bags and which sat outside of her, wryly taking notes on her state of mind, now waved the image of Ovid in front of her to see if she could feel anything about it. Nothing. She might as well have been waving a plastic cup in front of her eyes.

She was approaching a large city. Was that Pittsburgh? Down to her right, a hump of dusty, rose-colored fog came into view, speckled with lights. The smell of diesel and oil filled her nostrils. That shelf of blackness behind it must be a mountain. Then again, it could have been sky. She plunged into a tunnel, and the tires made a high, whirring sound as they rolled over the yellow brick, the amber lights on the ceiling of the tunnel sped above her, and her own car exhaust sedated her. Then she shot into blackness again, driving through the tangled spaghetti of overpasses, underpasses, on-ramps, and off-ramps.

One summer she had taken an internship in Pittsburgh, copying death certificates from the 1880s and 1900s for one of her professors. The certificates were too brittle to photocopy, so she had to copy them by hand. Most of the immigrants and laborers died at thirty of "exhaustion." The only people she came across who lived to be seventy had "gentleman" listed on the occupation line. Leafing through the yellow, elegantly scripted forms, she had seen entire families arrive, get sick, and die. First the children, next the father, and a few pages later, the mother.

When she had walked the streets of Pittsburgh that summer, now a city of soaring glass buildings, she could see the sooty streets of its steel-mill past superimposed over it. Even if you forgot—deliberately blotted out —your past, it was still there, building the present, she thought as the city reeled away from her into the fog.

She crossed several rivers. But she wasn't really seeing them. The Allegheny? The Monongahela?

She glanced down at the fragile note in her lap. Here was one she hadn't seen before.

> *unravel to ingest the sun.*
> *I touch the untouchable,*
>
> *do you feel it?*
> *My heart, the philosopher's stone,*
> *drums everlasting.*

Eustacia's heart was stone, all right, thought Fallon, and yet she seethed with life. She had indeed swallowed the sun, and she lived forever in her family's memory.

A light flashed across Fallon's rearview mirror. A white car was advancing on her fast, lights nearly blinding her. She tilted the mirror up to reduce the glare. How did the mirror still show her the image of the head beams when it was tilted to the ceiling?

Something dark called her back to her chain-linked thoughts. Fallon listened harder to herself than she had ever listened to herself before. She could do that now, with Will on her side.

She looked at Eustacia's notes again.

*Einstein said,*

> *"Logic will take you from A to B,*
> *but imagination will take you everywhere."*

And on a different page was written,

> *It is easier to see illusion than it is to see reality.*
> *For me there is no difference.*

That was a dangerous game to play, Fallon reflected.

Underneath all the instruction and wonder, Eustacia had sent her unspoken messages, all askew. *You drain me,* in a high, sing-song voice. *You breathe too much air.* It was a lullaby—*you occupy too much space. Too-oo-oo much!* Yes. That was it. The headlights of the white car behind her stabbed her eyes from her side view mirror, before it sped past her, rocking her car in its wake. Or was it the revelation that rocked her?

She had never heard the unspoken theme song of her life until this moment. Eustacia had never said it. She just emitted it, wordlessly. All her life, Fallon had found safety in wordlessness, in movement rather than thought, in intuition rather than rationality. Rationality was an annoying fiction, as she had been excited to learn in a college class on deconstruction. Words were lies. But the danger of a wordless message is that you can't identify it. You can't report it. You can't restrain it or reject it because it wasn't even said. It was held up to you as a mirror showing you your face. It was inside you. And ask any rape victim if there wasn't a difference between the words *inside* and *outside*. No, the state of wordlessness was no escape, and rendered no defense against a wordless attack.

The white car pulled in front of her and, infuriatingly, slowed down.

Fallon stomped on the gas in a sudden rage and pulled into the passing lane. The white car she was passing sped up, as if competing with her. She floored it, watching the speedometer hit 80, then 90. She kept it there until the white car shrank in her rearview mirror.

The only way to stop a wordless message is to stop breathing. Which she did sometimes, without even thinking about it. Her body just stopped breathing. It had stopped, now. She tried to open her lungs to breathe, but the muscles around them had turned into the wooden slats of a barrel bound together by iron bands. She recognized this feeling. She'd felt it off and on her entire young adult life. All would be fine, and then, for no apparent reason, she couldn't draw a free breath. She would have to force her lungs to open all day long. "Open," she'd say, "open," so that she could breathe, "open, open, open" all day long until her chest muscles grew sore.

That was how bad it got.

Sometimes she could recall the phantom thought that had

triggered the closure, but most of the time she couldn't. Now she knew it was the wordless theme song of her life that triggered it. It felt like someone had rolled the stone of numbness away from the tomb and underneath was anger.

Fallon's lungs opened with the revelation, and she took an expansive breath of air.

She felt like a country besieged by war. She had lived in Israel between the Six-Day War and the Yom Kippur War, when air raid sirens sounded at noon each day to remind people of the Holocaust. When she was five, her mother had taken her to visit the concentration camp where life-size, black-and-white pictures of children stared back at her from inside ovens. Wasn't that proof of how dangerous it was not to distinguish between imagination and reality?

Here, now, driving, she was finally fitting words to amorphous feelings, giving them handles that could help her move them out of her way. She would call Will and tell him what she had discovered.

Cement dividers marked by orange barrels with black and white stripes had been placed strategically to divert traffic from one lane to another. "Lane Change" a sign said, with two crooked arrows running parallel to each other.

"I'll say," Fallon muttered.

She was glad Ovid had died. She gasped. Yes, glad. Not glad that he was gone, that he'd thrown away his life, but glad that she finally had the proof that his problems were real, not self-created or imaginary. She was not the monster. Eustacia was. A hard sob cracked her chest open. She hit the power window button, and all four windows opened, blasting her with cold air. Her map flew up into her face, blinded her, and somersaulted into the back seat, where it miraculously landed on the back dash. She grunted with rage, a sound her throat had never made before, as tears split her hot cheeks. She *had* to free herself both of Ovid and her mother. They had been defining her life for too long.

She seized her mother's notes and thrust them out the window. She craned her neck, looking back. They were gone. For a minute she was deliciously, dizzyingly, terrifyingly free.

She spotted an exit ramp and took it a little too fast. She leaned into the curve. That guardrail was a little too close. She hit the brakes. Would she make it? Or roll over and over and over? One tiny flick of the wrist and it could all be over. What a relief. To finally let it all go to Hell.

She made it off the ramp, slowed the car and pulled onto the shoulder. She was shaking all over. Was she really about to kill herself? Longing for Will seized her, but at the same time, she was glad he hadn't seen this.

She rolled up the windows. She should stop and sleep, but she was wide awake.

Maybe she should look for road signs. There was one up ahead. She squinted. "Menentia." Menentia? That was the name of a town? A cross between the words *mental* and *dementia*. A faint smile cracked her dry lips. What state was she in? She was in Menentia.

There was a service station beyond the sign. She pulled into the parking lot, turned off the car, got out, and opened the rear door. A wide expanse of dark field rolled out to either side of her, and on the far side of the parking lot, a truck engine droned. When she knelt on the seat to reach for the map, she found that most of her mother's notes had flown back into the car. She laughed, and the laughter loosened the way to tears. She sat down and gave herself over to them. They weren't self-pitying tears; they were tears of recognition, of relief, of grief, amusement, and wonder at the grand design of life that had returned the notes to her. When she finished crying, she noticed that dawn had slid up behind her into the sky. Gray light spread backwards from her past to her present. The car ticked randomly as the sun hit and warmed it. That inner mother, who had been hidden so long in the grotto deep underground, had taken her seat above ground inside her. She had made some kind of progress in the last twelve hours but only just begun to unravel the knot.

She took a deep breath and smoothed one of Eustacia's notes out on her thigh.

*No one has ever seen the particles.*

*Yet scientists make predictions based on the idea*
*and prove them over and over again.*
*This idea, this fiction, is the building block of life*
*Just so, magicians lie to set the mind free,*
*to reveal the invisible magic at the root of existence.*

There. Eustacia had said it. She lied. To set the mind free. But what did that really mean? Perhaps Terry would know if she ever found him.

# 17

# SHOWDOWN IN DODGE CITY

The flashing sign as she neared St. Louis read, "Air Quality Good Today: Breathe Easy." Her itchy lungs didn't agree with their definition of good. Then she was in Missouri.

A few hours later and a hundred miles from Kansas City, the land alternated between brown, harvested fields, and hay-bale-dotted pastures with a few horses and cows. The road cut through shallow swells, of striated earth, tan sandstone on top, an olive layer below, and a red layer underneath it all.

The highway afforded a view of the landscape she rarely got when Walter and Eustacia drove. They scoffed at the notion of highway travel. It was too American, too homogenized, with the same food chains, the same signs, the same gas stations. The real America could only be found on the back roads, they contended.

She pulled over at a rest stop in Kansas around five o'clock, unfolded herself from the car, and stumbled to the industrial restroom.

She called home to check in, as she promised Will, hoping Walter wouldn't answer. As luck would have it, he didn't.

"How's it going?" Will asked.

"I'm standing in front of a bronze plaque about 'Historical Kansas' and it talks about General Custer and Hap Arnold."

"I know who Custer was, but Hap Arnold?"

"It says he was commander of the U.S. Air Force in World War II who dropped colored cards here for target practice and developed a bomb chute."

"Weird."

"I know. Of all the things they could have chosen to commemorate—"

"Like the fact that the name Kansas comes from the tribe of Indians who used to live there?"

"No kidding. Really?"

"Yeah."

"And wasn't Custer an Indian killer?"

"The worst kind. Native Americans would be telling a different story on that plaque," said Will.

"See? How can I ever figure out who I am if it's not possible to get a grip on reality?"

"Hey. Like I said, reality is a pretty broad situation. If you get input from a lot of different angles, you're going to get to something that's close enough."

"I've been thinking a lot about my mother." All her recent revelations spilled like a waterfall. He listened and talked her through some ways to cope, and she held fast to the chord of connection she felt to him.

"I miss you," he said, finally.

"I miss you, too," she said, but when she said it, an ocean of need opened up and with it, panic. "Enough about me,. How about you?"

"Nothing much to report, here. Your Dad's energy is low, but that's to be expected. He's stumbling through. We're getting the house buttoned up for winter."

"Say hello for me."

After they said their goodbyes, she hung up and sat in the driver's seat and unfolded the map. She brushed her hand back and forth a few times over the wide space between where she started and where she was now. One thousand miles. She saw the old Fallon, whose brother had just committed suicide, as if through the end of a drinking glass, foggy and far away, someone else entirely. She closed her eyes and slept, waking a few hours later, surprisingly refreshed.

With a tentative sense of freedom and a fledgling urge to explore, she rolled into Dodge City, KS, at dusk.

The strip consisted of a feed mill with a silo and conveyer belts, a few taco places built to look like adobe houses, and a few metal Quonset huts by the railroad tracks. She turned onto Wyatt Earp Boulevard and passed the Silver Spur Steak House and the Cowboy Supply Store, which advertised an "Annie Oakley Free Cologne Sample."

She booked a room at a motel called Get InnTo Dodge—as opposed to getting out of Dodge. A boy, possibly Native American, in a T-shirt that almost reached his knees, dragged his eyes away from the television in the lobby long enough to check her in. After a shower and a change of clothes in the carpeted and deodorized room, she stepped out to explore the town on foot.

Under the flickering parking lot lights, she rummaged in the car trunk for a coat to ward off the November chill. Her hands brushed against Ovid's black, fringed suede jacket wrapped in a dry-cleaning bag. She had thrown it in at the last minute when she saw there was extra room in the trunk. She didn't know why. Ovid had bought it on impulse one day for himself, immediately regretted the decision, and gave it to her. She had never worn it. But this felt like the perfect place for it. In a fit of daring, she shook it out of the bag and swung it on. With a gust of leather-scented air, its weight settled comfortably on her shoulders. Here, she could be someone new.

The town had retained some of its history, with brick buildings and wooden sidewalks. A bronze statue of a longhorn steer commemorated the town's past as the destination of dusty longhorn cattle drives from Texas. Nothing much was open. Her mind was clear enough to need the clouding of a drink. She settled on the Gunsmoke Lounge. She descended the stairs and pushed into the cave-like darkness. Men in cowboy hats and jean jackets lined the bar. She instantly regretted her decision. The murmur of country music and men's voices fell off a bit, and she felt, rather than saw, the eyes turn from the bar toward her. Backing out would be more humiliating than staying. She took a deep breath and the maleness of her coat embraced her. She was as tall as a man, so she would become one. The fringe of Ovid's jacket rapped like falling rain, against her forearms and across her back as she advanced. There was only one woman at the bar, at the far end, and Fallon headed in that direction.

The men's eyes followed her as she passed them, drilling her with looks of desire so hard they were indistinguishable from hatred. She summoned her gray curtains, a kind of self-blinding. Their eyes continued to strip away the clothes on her breasts, her thighs, her face. She made herself transparent, a blue-veined heart beating delicately inside a basket of lucent bones. But their stares only burned. She pressed herself harder until she was nothing but air.

The only woman in the room spun around on her barstool and laughed as Fallon passed her, the dying spin of her barstool matching Fallon's passage. The woman was short with solid, stocky curves. A black rope of dyed and braided hair fell over her red-clad shoulder. Her laugh rasped from years of hardship, whiskey, and cigarettes.

Once Fallon took her seat, shoulder-to-shoulder with the men, she became one of them, she hoped. The conversation in the bar had returned to full volume. They were already forgetting her, she told herself. She creased a ten-dollar bill and held it up between her first and middle fingers, motioning to the bartender.

"I like your jacket, honey," the woman rasped, now standing behind her, smiling widely, hands on hips. A brilliant red angora sweater wrapped her hard body and her black jeans were tucked into fringed, high heel cowboy boots. Sexy at sixty, in a gritty way.

"Thanks."

The bartender hadn't acknowledged Fallon yet.

"Where'd you get it? Your man?"

Fallon waved her bill at the bartender again and looked at the woman more closely. As she took a seat next to Fallon, the long-curved ash of the cigarette between her yellow-stained fingers dropped onto the bar.

"The name's Barbara," she said, holding out her hand. After a moment's hesitation, Fallon shook it limply. "Boys call me Bobby. Sure, ain't no Barbie. What's your name, honey?"

"Fallon."

"Fallo-*what?*" She thrust her head forward like a chicken.

Someone laughed across the room as Fallon repeated her name.

Bobby laced her fingers together and stretched. "I *like* that. Unusual. You from another country, or something?"

"Back east." Another bark of laughter erupted from another dark corner. It couldn't be about her.

"Like I said," Bobby chuckled. "Another country."

"Can I get a Molson?" Fallon called, hating the uncertainty in her voice. Why did it come out sounding so young? She had lower registers. The solemn-faced bartender nodded without looking up as he pulled a draft for the man in front of him.

"It won't work, you know," said Bobby.

"What won't work?"

"Your disappearing act." Her face had wrinkles deep enough to measure with a ruler and black arching pencil lines instead of eyebrows. Her hot breath cut through the cool currents of Fallon's being, making her woozy. The murmur of conversation rose and fell in waves, country music barely audible beneath it.

"When I was married, I thought I could fix all my problems that way."

Fallon considered brushing her off, but some other instinct was drawing her in. They were the only two women in the bar.

"I don't know what you mean," Fallon said as the bartender took her bill and set the green bottle down before her without a glance. The beer foamed up to the lip of the bottle. She wrapped her fingers around the neck reflexively.

"I think you do," Bobby said and pulled a bent cigarette out of an embroidered cigarette clutch with a gold clasp. Squinting one eye to keep out the smoke, she flicked a gold lighter and lit it.

"I'm quite certain I don't." The twinge of anger that edged Fallon's words felt like strength.

"You think you can fix what's wrong with your man by changing yourself."

Fallon considered this and took a sip of beer. "He wasn't my man," she muttered into the bottle opening. "He was my brother . . . and he's dead," she added, hoping to shock her.

"Good for you. You kill the son of a bitch?"

Fallon's face flared with unexpected heat.

"Relax. I was only joking. A good girl like you? What'd he die of?"

Fallon wanted to say, "None of your business," but she didn't have the nerve. She took another sip of beer too fast. It went down her windpipe, and she sputtered.

"Whoa, Nellie," Bobby said, patting her on the back. "Take it easy, there."

Fallon wished she had thrown caution to the dogs and ordered something stronger.

"You're just like me," Bobby grinned, showing strong yellow teeth worn across the top into flat ridges. Fallon gazed into the darkness of the woman's laughing mouth. Small pieces of lipstick-stained skin speckled the rim of her grin-taut lips. Her dark eyes shone with a slightly crazed yet knowing light. Fallon knew better than to engage with her, but she was always drawn to "crazy" people. They said what they really thought. They provided a mirror.

"How am I like you?"

"When you walked in, those animals eyed you, made you prey. Instead of turning around like you should have, you tried to hide inside your jacket, but they undressed you with just a glance. I saw," she waggled her finger at Fallon as her voice careened teasingly, each gesture exaggerated. "You tried to disappear."

Heat flashed through Fallon. How had this woman known what she was thinking? The murmur crested and ebbed, the music whined.

"They didn't turn me into anything. I did it myself."

"That's what every woman tells herself. Let me ask you something. When you're trapped, pinned against the wall, no possibility of kicking or spitting, what's the best way to get out of being raped?"

"You mean if you can't fight?" Fallon asked.

"Yeah."

She thought of that time she'd relaxed her neck to prepare for Ovid's fist. She scraped at the wet label around the neck of her beer as the men's voices swelled.

"Act like you want it," Bobby answered her own question. "That's what women do. It's not rape if you asked for it, right? But it won't work," Bobby darted her head at Fallon like a cobra, her words sharp and angry. "You can't fix the devil with a smile." Just as quickly, she pulled back and smiled. "And I can see plain as that pretty nose on your face that you got a devil in your life."

Fallon wondered, her mother? Ovid? Christo?

"See, girl, you got to draw the *line*. Put some *teeth* in that vagina."

"What?" Fallon's head reared back, eyes wide.

"Never mind. You're too pure to understand. That's the problem with you. You're afraid to get dirty. You want to figure it all out in your head before it happens, so you don't make any mistakes. Good girls don't make mistakes. You know what you should have done to those men when you walked in the door?"

"What?"

"Poked their eyes out!"

Fallon smiled and scraped at the label. It was coming off in her hands in little rolled-up bits.

"I'm serious, honey. This is the best advice a body's ever given you. See, they don't do that to me. 'Cause I call 'em on it. *Haven't you ever seen a lady before, you dumb ass? Quit your gapin' before I smack you sideways to Sunday.*"

"But how do you know what they're thinking? What if they had a hard day, what if they're just spacing out?"

"I knew what you were thinking, right?"

"You can't go off all half-cocked on assumptions," Fallon said, feeling herself come back together.

"Girl, you've got to do *just* that. Your life depends on it. Come over here," she said as she swung away from the bar and gestured toward a dark booth in the corner.

"Owen!" Bobby shouted over her shoulder, pointing toward the booth with her lit cigarette. "Get me and this little girl a drink. Something good this time! None of that European shit you gave 'er."

Owen, the solemn-faced, nodded with just a hint of a smile at one corner of his mouth. At the far end of the bar, as another customer's story reached its apex, the teller sprang out of his seat and his companions nodded and laughed.

"Come on," Bobby gestured again, standing up. "Got to tell you a story." Fallon stood up, momentarily disoriented by the way she towered, reed-like and wavering, over the older woman, unsure of whether she was following of her own free will, or like a cipher, was simply doing Bobby's bidding.

They slid sideways into a battered booth with red vinyl seats slit here and there where white stuffing came out. They faced each other. Bobby pulled the ashtray toward herself and a little puff of ash spilled out as she stubbed out her cigarette.

"Oh, you can always recognize a battered wife. They look at things too hard. They speak too deliberate. Even when they're relaxed, they're thinking about what that other person meant when they said hello in that particular way, 'cause you never know when a *hello* is gonna become a *hullabaloo.* Don't worry. Takes one to know one."

A husk of attempted laughter constricted Fallon's throat, neither affirming nor denying. Uncomfortably hot, she shrugged the jacket off her shoulders without pulling her arms out, wearing it like a shawl.

"Not so long ago and a lifetime away," Bobby began, warming to the tale, "I married a dead man. Oh, at first, I thought he was pure life, the answer to my everything, all fire and energy. I'd been knocked about by my brothers, my father. I was sick of farm life, sick of heavy lifting and hauling, sick of the muck, sick of animals dying in shit. But I was strong." She curled her arms and contracted her biceps sensually. "Still am. I pulled my weight—more than my weight on that farm." She pulled another cigarette out of her clutch and lit it, relishing the drag as if it were the first in a long while.

Owen came over and slid two glasses of what looked like bourbon, neat, at them.

"You're a doll," Bobby told him. Owen's face didn't so much as flicker. "Drink up, honey."

Fallon took a tentative sip. It was sweet-hot lava to her throat. A terrible thirst for cool water seized her, but she didn't want to yell out to the retreating bartender. She took another sip of lava. The floor unmoored itself, or was it her? What if this was some kind of con, and the drink was drugged? She glanced around her. No one else was looking at her. She was being paranoid. Then again, nothing was impossible.

"At first, I'da done anything for my husband. But he was always trying to control me. Not big things. Didn't try to beat me or nothing. It was just a bunch of itty-bitty baby things. That's worse 'cause it slinks up on you, so you're not aware of the effects right away. First, it's little criticisms about every dang thing: the soap's not in the right place, why didn't you pick up the mail, don't chop wood like this, do it like that—and me, working a farm all my life, you know? Then it's not listening when you speak, the eyes glaze over, the silent chewing of your good food. Then it's no idea that comes from your lips is right—an automatic no before he's even heard it, you know?"

Fallon nodded, gripping her glass.

"I know you *do.*" She patted Fallon's hand with the one holding the cigarette, a long ash hanging on to its ember heart past all probability. The smoke curled under Fallon's nose.

Fallon pulled her hand back, her smile a grimace.

"As I was saying, my husband was just a walking dead man. He had to be satisfied every night, and it was the same way over and over. Not about me and him at all. And let me tell you, I'm no slouch in the sack. But all that's wasted on him, 'cause he don't see nothing besides himself. No imagination.

"And money. Oooo money!" she hooted. "I can't spend a dime

that's right, and he's spending all mine. She lowered her voice conspiratorially, "So I had a little trunk in my basement. I say the basement was *mine* 'cause that house was more mine than his. I swept the floors, stocked the cupboards, fed the stove. The cows and chickens all came running to *me* when I stepped outside.

"Yeah, so I had me a little trunk in my basement," her words gathered momentum. "Nothing major, just a set of silverware, a gold pin passed down from my grandmother—nothing valuable really—gold plated probably, a few lopsided pearls, a chipped emerald ring, some Irish linen.

"Come to find out he's been dippin' into the stuff. We had them Bilco doors to the basement. You know, the slanty kind on the outside? That scallywag was sneaking into his own house and honeyfuggling me—to play poker with the boys!"

Bobby paused as the bartender walked over slowly, placed two new shots in front of them.

"Aw. Ain't he a lover!" she smiled up at him. The corner of his mouth twitched as he took the empty glasses and turned away. Bobby waggled her bottom back and forth on the vinyl bench, shimmying closer to the table and hooking Fallon with her eyes. Smoke curled up around Bobby's head like a snake lover. The men's voices purred behind her.

"So, I'm down in the cellar one day, checking this out, with all them old tools and baskets hanging from above, brushing me with cobwebs, strokin' me gentle, like. Her eyes focused on something interior, and her voice grew contemplative, "And I'm thinking, bad enough he's always criticizing me, bad enough he's got the love making abilities of a toad, now he's stealin' from me?" Cigarette smoke streamed rapidly upwards in a straight line as her words sped up. "He was stealing things that had no value. But the stories. There were stories in those things. My grandmother worked hard, but there wasn't a day she didn't stick that pin in her collar in the morning and take it off at night. All kinds of stuff like that. And I've been putting up with this for fifteen years. Then it hits me." She leaned back. The anger vanished and was replaced by breathy ease. "The man's got no soul. He's all dead inside. This is the only thing he knows." She paused, took a cheek-hollowing drag, and with the smoke trailing out of her mouth around the words, she went on with renewed energy. "And I'm still young yet. So, I say to him when he gets home, 'Harry Garfield, I know you been takin' my stuff. And that's all right. I'm gonna give it to you—under one condition. You got to go down in that cellar and take it all right now, *right now*—and you spend every last dime tonight. Go on, now.' And I pointed at the cellar door. He was all surprised. Too surprised to argue, I guess. And he saw that look in my eye, you know? I've never seen it myself, but I've been told. It's a kind of light.

"So, he went. I knew he'd go, too, because it was becoming only too clear to me that the one thing Harry put first was ownership. And you know what the dumb thing was? You know what it was? If that man had had one ounce of love in his body, I'd have shared it with him happily, what's mine is yours, and all that. But some folks don't get that. Some folks are so small inside that they can't imagine anyone else'd be any different. That's the problem with lying and selfishness."

Bobby pushed back in the booth and smiled at Fallon as if the story were over. Fallon waited. Bobby downed the second shot, took a drag, leaned her head back, and blew the smoke to the ceiling with infinite satisfaction.

"So . . . what happened?" Fallon asked uncertainly.

"I shut the door and took the first vacation of my life. It was grand." Her voice was silky, and she winked through a descending curl of smoke. "Had me a lot of man tail, too."

"And he . . . went away?" A slow fear grew inside Fallon, prickling her scalp.

"No, ya dummy. He was in the cellar! I stuck a shovel through the handles and locked him in!"

A sharp pain in Fallon's shoulders stabbed its way into her consciousness, and she realized she had been leaning forward too far, almost gripping the table edge with her elbows. Her head ached from dehydration. Reality stretched and contracted. All at once, Bobby was two inches tall and far away.

"You shut him inside? But—what happened?"

"Happened?" Bobby nearly shrieked. She laughed so deeply it kicked the tar loose in her lungs, rising into a cough and falling back into laughter. The fillings in her teeth flashed, and the hump of her tongue at the back of her mouth jogged up and down, sucking Fallon into its cave, pulling her past her tonsils, pink and gray as oysters. "Nothing happened! I burnt the house to the ground, that's what. I went on with my life, and it's been a damn nice life, too," Bobby's mouth snapped shut.

"You killed him?" Fallon asked as if she were slow-witted.

"Killed him?" Her voice went quiet. "A man's got to be alive for you to be able to kill him. See, that's what I'm telling you. Someone's been stealing from you for a long time, 'cause he don't know nothing different. I can see it under your skin, shining through. He's a blood sucker."

"How the Hell do you figure that?" Fallon hissed.

"I *know* because you're sitting here talking to me. I *know* because anybody else would have brushed me off. You know what your *problem* is? You know what it *is?* Your *problem* is that while you're busy trying to figure out how to solve the problem in your head, you make the biggest mistake of them all. You don't react to the situation at hand. You don't draw the line." Her lips were drawn back in a grimace as if she'd bitten the line with her own teeth. "You need to stick up for number one. You need to be more like me."

"And kill a man?" Fallon was angry now. She had almost liked this woman. Had wanted to believe she was going to impart some wisdom, had felt protected by her from the men.

"Why not? He was a scallywag. A two-bit criminal. Besides. I didn't kill him. He killed himself. He was dust delivering himself unto dust. All I did was open the door . . . and then," she convulsed with a violent spit of laughter, "closed it."

"But there are laws—" Fear crashed like a tidal wave inside. This woman had burned a man to death and didn't show a hair of remorse. Had she stood outside the doors listening to him scream? Death by fire had to be the worst way to go.

"Laws? *Yes*. That's what I'm trying to tell you. There are laws of *life*. When a horse runs by, you jump on. When a snake rattles, you stomp it. You insult life when you hang back. You destroy the one thing God gave you, and that's you. And this one?" She reached over and tugged on the fringes of Fallon's sleeve, rubbing them almost absent-mindedly between thumb and forefinger. "This one's a user."

"He was sick," Fallon said. "Life dealt him a bad hand." Sweating now, Fallon slipped out of the coat.

"And he made everyone else pay for his hand, didn't he? Especially you. He might be dead, but he's still killing you." She clutched Fallon's arm with the strength of a tree root. "You've got to stop doing that disappearing act, girl. You've got to make up your mind and draw the *line*. On the *outside*. I know, I—"

"No." Fallon's voice came out low and unbreachable. Just as her fear was cresting into a wave that could topple her, something strong and equally old steadied her. She grew utterly calm. Utterly self-possessed. She plucked Bobby's yellow hand off her arm. "Don't touch me."

Bobby drew back. Her face clicked to blank as fast as turning off a TV set. She shrugged her shoulders and laughed. "It's too late," she said, stubbing out her cigarette. "I'm already inside you. Have been since the beginning of time."

Fallon jumped to her feet so fast she knocked her side of the booth backward with a great crash. From all sides, heads snapped in her direction, and conversation stopped, leaving only the tinny whine of country music. Bobby threw her head back and laughed, and others joined in. Fallon staggered to the door, stomach sliding, worlds tumbling.

Once she was outside under the yellow streetlamp, fresh air braced her, and the ground stood firmly under her feet again. The cold plucked up goose bumps all over her skin; she realized she'd forgotten the jacket. She glanced around and got her bearings. She breathed again, expelling Bobby's cigarette smoke from her lungs. Her head cleared, but her mouth was tacky. A lump ached at the back of her throat, as if she'd swallowed a tiny, blue-veined heart that had gotten stuck on the way down or was trying to claw its way back up. She would leave the coat behind, but as soon as this thought hit, fury billowed into a tower of smoke.

She turned around and strode back into the bar, past all the men, who whirled around in their chairs. She walked right up to Bobby, who was just raising the jacket admiringly and slipping one arm into it.

"Give me my goddamned jacket." She raked the jacket out Bobby's hands, which remained raised along with an eyebrow in mocking reply.

"Now that's more like it, sister," Bobby said, putting her hands on her hips.

"I'm not your fucking sister," Fallon said as she turned about face.

As she stood in the lamplight outside the door, she grabbed the jacket by the shoulders. "Fuck you, too Ovid," she said, and threw it into the trash can.

# 18

# ONE THING ABOUT THE ANGLO

A metal cart rattled over the pavement. A fist rapped against a door.

"Room Service," a muffled voice shouted. A latch sounded followed by murmuring.

She sat up in bed, her heart beating hard. Where was she? It was dark, but a crack of light shone along the bottom of the door and between the window curtains. *Get Inn To Dodge Motel*, that's where she was.

Last night's darkness swelled and rebounded into an urgent need to call Will, but Bobby had shamed her into feeling like she was overly dependent on men. Maybe Will was yet another man she had let in too quickly, too thoroughly. She would complete the task she'd set herself. Even though he was another man, finding Terry would recover a long-lost piece of herself. She hurled the covers aside, hopped out of bed, dressed, wadded yesterday's clothes into her bag, and got back on the road.

After a half-hour of flat brown fields and gentle slopes rolling by, her thoughts turned to her conversation with barbarous Bobby. A darker form of herself rose, cobra-style, inside her. Bobby had been right about one thing, she hated to admit. Sometimes she let people take advantage of her in the most profound way. She'd almost gotten raped after a late shift at the pub last winter. She didn't like to think about it.

His name was George Baker. He was a regular, a middle-aged, slightly overweight Wall Street broker with a trimmed gray mustache. One late winter night he had come in an hour or so before closing. The restaurant was dead, and she was on duty with Collin, the Viet Nam vet she could never talk to.

Baker sauntered up to her at the waitress station, stopped a fraction of an inch too close, shifted his weight to one hip, and looked her up and down in such a clichéd rendition of a movie come-on that she couldn't take him seriously. He was an inch shorter than she. "You know," he said. "It's Texas Independence Day."

Hostility grabbed the back of her neck. She didn't like his too-soft face and his too-red lips peeking out from under that mustache. She didn't like his business suit. He looked a little like a paunchy James Mason in the movie *Lolita*. But she was ashamed of her judgmental nature and did her best to quell it.

He bored her for the rest of the night talking about the fall of the Alamo as if it had been a victory, a battle fought by noble Anglo Saxons for a just cause. He sprinkled his story liberally with aphorisms like, "The thing about the Anglo is that no matter how many times you knock him down, he'll stand back up."

Looking at the brown fields spinning away outside her window, she realized she had overruled her instincts with George just the way she had overruled them with Bobby. Why did she chase down purse snatchers on the one hand but allow men into her life like Christo and George Baker? Why did she listen to every oddball with a twisted tale?

Maybe because she was overly obsessed with being good. Ever since seventh grade, when she decided she could no longer settle differences with a fist to the face, she had been trying to be good. If she couldn't excel at being smart, like Ovid, she could excel at this. She had constructed a few rules to keep her out of trouble. Rule one was that it was wrong to pass judgment the way Ovid did. She would find something to respect in each person she met.

As if baiting her, George devolved into blatant sexism. "Women are so perverse," he said. "They're not as smart as men. They don't know what they want."

Finally taking the bait, she retorted, "That's because women are taught not to ask for what we want." She found his claims more fascinating than offensive.

She had started rebelling against gender roles as early as second grade. One windy fall day, the whole class was playing its usual boy-chase-girl game under the tall spire of a giant spruce tree. When a boy caught a girl, he'd kiss her and let her go or take her captive at the base of the spruce tree. That day, as she was being chased, she had a flash of insight. If she allowed herself to be caught, she could overhear their plans. She stopped mid-scream and whirled around to face the boy chasing her. He stopped in his tracks and stared at her. Uncertain what to do, he pawed the ground with the white tip of his Converse sneakers and ran off to join the others. It was that simple. If you stopped running, they stopped chasing. Maybe that's what she was doing with George, refusing to play the boy-chase-girl game the world had foisted off on her by neither accepting nor spurning George, but by trying to relate to him as one human peer to another.

Fallon opened her hands on the steering wheel and arched her fingers backwards like wings as she tried to make sense of what she allowed to happen next.

At the end of her shift, George manipulated her into sharing a cab, wheedled his way up five flights to her apartment.

It was early morning by then, and she was desperate to get rid of him because she had a double shift the next day.

He sat at her kitchen table and asked for a cup of tea. He spread his knees and said, "Come over here."

Despite the arrogance of his command, she thought if she humored him, he might leave. She stood before him. He rose to his feet.

"Kiss me."

She looked at his too red lips, stupefied. "No."

"See, that's the difference between a man and a boy. A man can take no for an answer," he said, and sat back down.

"Look, I'm not into this at all. You'd better go," she finally told him.

"I can't." He shrugged his shoulders, arms and eyes wide.

"Why not?" she asked, alarmed.

"Because the Staten Island Ferry closes at 1:00 a.m."

Why had she fallen for that? Fallon wondered, gripping the wheel. He was a Wall Street broker. His whole life consisted of sales pitches and con jobs. Why hadn't she just said, "Tough. Get a hotel room." But for her, getting a hotel room was not in the realm of possibilities, so she did unto him as she would want others to do unto her. She offered him the couch.

He waited for her to get into her own bed and crept to her bedside in the semidarkness. He placed his hands on her arms and tried to kiss her. She pushed him back. She told him to stop.

"Stop what?" he asked. His belly protruded from his polka-dot boxer shorts.

"Stop trying to kiss me," she said.

"I wasn't trying to kiss you," he said.

Behind him, the air-shaft window faced a brick wall, the darkness illuminated by dim light.

"How can you say that?" she exclaimed, hitting the quilted bed with both hands.

"Well, did I succeed?" he asked like a teacher.

"No."

"Then I didn't do it," he said.

She had been so astounded by this blatant lie and total absence of logic that a piece of reality came loose inside her mind, as if it were expanding and twisting to allow black to become white and yet remain black at the same time.

She knew she had behaved like an idiot by letting him in. She knew that some would say she deserved what she got because she offered a strange man a bed for the night. He was only acting out the ancient code of conduct between a man and a woman. She was the one trying to change the rules of the game.

She should have kicked him in the balls and thrown him down the stairs. She was taller and more fit than he was. She could have overpowered him. That's what Bobby would have done; what Bobby had counseled her to do.

Instead, she'd endured his advances all night long.

The last time he came to her bedside, his face close to hers, his lips seeking hers, she finally slammed both hands into his chest and pushed him back.

"George," she spoke in taut monotone, shaking with rage, "I would rather kill or be killed than be raped. Do you have any idea what it's like?" Her voice stabbed him, drilling the words into his brain. "To have someone forcefully enter you? To have your own body used as a weapon against you?" she paused, breathed. "I could never get clean of it. I'd rather be dead. And if it came to that, killing would be easy."

He froze and sank into deep silence in the darkness. She couldn't see his eyes, but the dim gray light from the air shaft shone obliquely on his chin.

"I'm shocked that you would think that of me," he said quietly. He backed up on the bed.

"You've been forcing yourself on me all night."

"But why did you invite me up here?" He sounded truly amazed.

"I didn't!" She slammed her hands again, but the softness of the bed erased the impact.

"You have such terrible thoughts—" he said, musingly.

"Because *you* put them there," she cut him off.

"But—" Now his voice warmed to the drama; the game was back on. "I'm stunned. I would never rape you."

"What do you think you are doing now?" She hit the bed again. "It's just like the fucking Alamo. Those bastards weren't noble independence fighters! They were rapists, stealing the land from the Mexicans by force. They got what they fucking deserved. Even the American government wouldn't come to their rescue."

"Look," he said, suddenly pitiful, "I was fired today. My wife wants a divorce. I can't sleep . . . Just stay up with me or let me sleep in your bed." He plucked at her covers like a child. "Please?"

She gave up, exhausted. The truth was that if she got to sleep now and put off the errands she had planned to run in the morning, she could get four hours of rest before her shift.

"Just talk to me until I fall asleep," he wheedled.

"I have nothing to say to you," she sighed.

"Please?"

"All right," she said, "I'll read to you." She had no idea where that had come from.

"Okay," he said, sulkily. She darted out of bed to get her book of folktales, and he sidled over and got under her covers. Within minutes after she started reading, George's breath deepened. She kept reading. He began to snore lightly. She read on. He continued to snore. She stopped. Deft as a moth, she flitted into the bathroom, locked the door, and spent the remaining few hours till dawn with her head resting on the toilet seat watching a spider in the corner patiently weave its web.

When she came out at 8 a.m., George was already dressed, his dark full-length coat on, a respectable businessman again.

"You should have kicked me out," he said with an ironic smile before he left.

Fallon hit the steering wheel. Maybe to survive Ovid's verbal and physical onslaughts, she had had to shut her body down, and that's why she blew by all her instincts. She had so much rage inside her that she was afraid she would become Bobby if she let it out, and like Bobby, she would burn an entire block to the ground with her rage. She beat the steering wheel again.

A man in a car passed her, honking and shaking his finger at her.

"Fuck off, you giant prick," she shouted, as she jabbed her middle finger into the air at him.

The man in the car shook his head and wagged his finger again. She gave him both fingers, alternating them up and down like pistons. He shook his head again in disgust, shrugged his shoulders, and sped off.

That's when she noticed smoke billowing from the hood of her car. Her forearms prickled, and the top of her head burned as her hair stood up. She was in the middle of nowhere, and her car was on fire. Cursing, she pulled over, jumped out of the car, and yanked the hood open, keeping up a steady stream of epithets.

It turned out to be steam. Like instant karma, the car was overheating. When she started the car again, she discovered the reason why: three tiny holes in her radiator. Nausea washed through her as she looked up and down the flat, empty road. She was at least an hour away from Dodge City. She wanted to fling herself at the ground like Ovid and throw a temper tantrum, but anger had already gotten her into enough trouble.

She took a shaky breath and reviewed her options. She could hitch a ride back to Dodge City, but beside the danger of getting into a car with a stranger, she couldn't bear the thought of retracing her steps and running into Bobby again. She could flag someone down and ask that person to call a tow truck when he or she got to the next phone booth. But again, that plan could result in hours of delay. The next big town, Taos, was at least 300 miles away. With no phones in sight, she was prey to any pervert who came along. She got back into the car and thought. She had water in the trunk. If she waited for the engine to cool, she could refill the radiator and get to the next town. But she hated the whole idea of figuring out whether she was being conned or not, forking over a huge chunk of her travel money, and staying in one place for as long as it took to fix her car.

She got out of the car, her mind spinning. The sun was weak, but warm. She sat down in the scrubby grass beside the road and pressed her palms to the ground. She took a few deep breaths, as Will had taught her to do. Her mind slowed a notch. She lay down and breathed again, feeling the solidity of the earth beneath her, letting her mind soar with the blue sky. Molecules sorted themselves into egg-like membranes," Eustacia's words rose. Surely, she had something in her trunk that could help her. She had extra gas, extra water, a shovel, bread, cereal, milk, and eggs. She needed something sticky, something she could plug the holes with. She breathed again, smelling pine and dry earth. She sat up and looked at the road, searching for tar patches. Ovid had once used raisins to plug the gas tank hole. Gas interacted with raisins and hardened it. She had a few raisins in the cereal box. Could she do something like that? No, the water pressure would blow off any patch. How about putting raisins and gas inside? That was risky. She could clog the whole thing. Then she'd have to get a whole new radiator. Who knew what she'd muck up with that concoction? She lay back down, twining the grass around her fingers, breathing deeply again. That's when a scrap of memory surfaced about eggs in the radiator. What was it she'd heard? You put eggs in the radiator when it was cool and run the engine. When the water got hot enough, it cooked the eggs, and as it sprayed from the holes, the eggs formed clots. It was worth a shot.

She gave the car another half hour to cool and unscrewed the metal radiator cap. She cracked two eggs inside and refilled it with water, then started up the engine. After running it for a half hour, to her amazement, the leaks were plugged.

Joy blasted through her. She had kept her wits about her, had found her inner wisdom, and had solved her problem alone. She could go on.

As she drove, high on her new sense of competence, the story of her near rape replayed itself with different theme music. No longer was she a stupid little victim. She was the crafty victor. After all, hadn't she won in the end? When things got bad, it was her connection to her body that reminded her that she could not permit someone to rape her. A lot of women would have had sex with him and regretted it in the morning. They wouldn't even have called it rape. But she saw it for what it was, and instead of Bobby's violence, she used words to stop him. In the end, he responded to her truth with his own. He admitted that he was just trying to distract himself from two terrible losses. Like Scheherazade she spun a tale to trick the oppressor, and she saved herself. Her way.

She took a deep breath, and her lungs expanded to accept all that she needed from the air.

In the next town she came to, she found a pay phone and called home. Neither Will nor Walter answered. She left a message that she was near New Mexico and doing fine. She checked the water level of the radiator, and it was holding, so she continued the trip.

The sun was already going down when she passed the road sign "Welcome to New Mexico, Land of Enchantment." As if on cue, lightning flashed and lit up the clouds on the horizon, lavender, blue, and crocus white. One cloud was a cup of copper light, drawing her forward like the Holy Grail. When the color faded, darkness fell. An owl flew up from the roadside, spreading its wings over the windshield, blessing her. She ducked and slowed down, noticing a sign for Clayton Lake State Park. As she turned down a dirt road into the park, her headlights picked up a huge jackrabbit turned ghostly. She followed the twist and turns in the road. The main office was dark and locked up. She wove between what looked like low shrubs, past a few tents, to an empty site, and almost pulled the Dodge Dart straight into the lake. She stopped just in time.

In the silence that blossomed when she cut the motor, she pulled a mat, sleeping bag, and pillow onto the ground. She was too tired to set up a tent. With the car lights off, the sky above, like a celestial band, jammed on stars. She sat on her blanket watching the lightning flashes reflected in the lake. The Big Dipper shone up at her from deep under the black water.

# 19

# THE CRY OF THE LOST

She woke up in Chile, and the garbage can was singing. It looked like Chile, anyway, with its gray and red dirt and scrubby plants. An animal in the garbage was crying plaintively, in a language spoken by both humans and animals, about profound loneliness and fear. The horizon was blue, but the land was still dark. Dew had wet her face, and her nose was cold. As she rubbed her nose, she remembered that a family of raccoons had sniffed her face in the darkness. She was at Clayton Lake State Park in New Mexico. She fumbled for her flashlight and staggered over to the can. Bright eyes gleamed up at her and disappeared behind the black plastic bag. Fallon bounced the flashlight beam around the perimeter of the camp and picked up two sets of amber eyes reflecting back at her, the parents, apparently, waiting for their child. As cute as they were, raccoons could be carriers of rabies, so she tipped the can over slowly with her foot. The raccoon pup ran over to the other two and sat down in the protective curve of a parental tail. All three of them sat watching her. She curled back into her sleeping bag, down-scented air puffing up around her.

As the sun rose, it ignited the orange sandstone arms that cradled the olive-green lake. Again, the similarity to Chile struck her. The landscape was clad in the same colors Chile had written into her sense memory so long ago. She basked for a moment in the new story her life was telling, a life she was just beginning to author. She had been thrown a few curve balls, but she had hit them out of the park. She had encountered a witch who offered her power, and she repelled her. She had fooled the giant, had gotten stranded in the valley of the shadow of death, and had concocted her own creative solution to save herself. She was the hero in her own journey.

As she cooked oatmeal on a one-burner Primus stove, she fantasized a new future. When she found Terry and laid the memory of Ovid to rest, she would return to the East Coast, the family whole again and grateful to her. With Will at her side, she would apply to medical school. She could do it. She was smarter than her family thought. Even better, she'd turn her slight resistance to academics into an asset. She would see more than the cold facts on the page; she would astound her teachers with an intuition honed on the rocks of life. She would become the best student they had ever seen, with almost magical insight. They would admire her, she would win awards, she would—

A green dragonfly mounted by a blue one crashed into her forehead, bringing her back to earth. The pair wobbled off over the lake and smacked the water a few times before flying on. Fallon watched. Thousands of dragonflies zipped to and fro. She was sweating. She dipped her feet in the water and sat for some time with her mind as empty as her oatmeal bowl.

Before she left camp, she checked the radiator water level. It was just a hair lower. She checked the map. Taos was less than 200 miles away. She'd get it fixed there. It was supposed to be a pretty cool town with a lot of alternative types, people more like herself, who she'd be able to trust.

Later that morning, as she drove up into the Cimarron Canyon, the cascading mountains reminded her yet again of Chile. Joy for life soared inside her as the Dodge Dart climbed the twisting mountain road. Perhaps this was where she belonged, the land of enchantment. At the top of the canyon, she passed signs for Angel

Fire and Eagle Nest. The latter was the name of the school they had gone to in Santiago. How strange that she had come full circle like this.

Cresting the mountain well past noon, she was lost in a balloon of joy when a cloud of steam from the hood punctured it. The balloon collapsed and skittered to the corner of her mind, slack and obscene. Adrenaline singed the tops of her forearms. The road, so magical only a moment ago, teetered and spilled in front of her. There was no shoulder, so she couldn't stop. She slowed down, hoping to cool the engine. She glanced at the open map in the seat beside her. She was about forty miles from Taos, more than a day's walk. She had no idea whether the descent into Taos was populated or not. She knew she should stop, but fear gripped her in full thrall, prompting her to keep the car moving.

As if two more plugs blew out, the steam tripled, almost blinding her. She shook violently. She tried to breathe, but the steel bands were back, squeezing her lungs. She should stop. No matter where she was, she should stop. Peering through the steam, she looked for a place to pull over. The road wound downwards steeply, with sharp turns. There was no place to stop that wouldn't expose her to the possibility of a collision. Her uncle had nearly been killed in just that kind of accident. Now black smoke billowed from the engine, and the smell of burning oil and some strange sweetness filled her nostrils and prickled the back of her throat. She put the car in neutral and coasted. When she reached the bottom of Taos Valley, the car went dead, and the engine trouble light flashed on. You think? She slapped the dashboard and coasted to a stop off to the side of the road.

"Goddamn it!" she said as she got out of the car. "Goddamn it!" She yanked up the hood, and escaping steam almost burned her. How could she have been so stupid? She should have stopped at any of the towns she had passed. Her anger doubled and tripled on itself: she was angry that she had been so stupid, angry that she was so ashamed, and angry that she was so angry.

She had literally been on top of the world, and now she was at the bottom. There were no buildings in sight. She had no idea how far she was from Taos. Her sole access to power, freedom, and maybe even life was this car, which she had just killed. Even in plain sunlight, shame became a flesh-and-blood being that darted out of the bushes and took possession of her. She looked over her shoulder reflexively, knowing nothing was there, as darkness washed through her.

It was hot in the Taos Valley. She sat down in a bit of shade and considered her options. She had some water in the trunk. She could walk. Who knew how long it would take, but she'd get to Taos eventually and find a tow truck. She hated to leave the car, though; it felt like a lifeline. She could hitch a ride. The thought frightened her, and the road was empty. She waited a half hour, but no one came by. When a car passed, going in the opposite direction, it was full of young men, laughing and hooting. She leaned back into the shadows so they wouldn't see her.

She had finally made up her mind that walking was better than sitting and doing nothing, when a battered pickup truck passed her slowly, heading toward Taos. She looked in the cab and debated whether to wave the man down. She didn't, but he pulled over about twenty yards down the road. He could be danger, or he could be salvation. For a second, no one emerged as the roar of the engine dissolved in the breeze. The sun couldn't even bounce off the oxidized red paint. Finally, an elderly man stepped carefully from the driver's side. He looked to be about her height, neither fat nor thin. A breeze picked up, full of the sweetly complex smell of wild sage.

"You okay, there?" he called. She appreciated that he didn't move toward her, as if he knew what it meant to be a woman stranded on the road.

"Yeah," she called, sounding sheepish and hating herself for it. "I think I cooked my engine," she said, through a breathy laugh. Why was she laughing? This car was her lifeline, which she had destroyed out of stupidity. She could no more buy a new car than she could win the lottery.

He bowed his head slightly, looking at his feet for a moment. "Mind if I take a look?"

He reminded her of an older version of Will. Something about his manner engendered trust. Of course, appearances could be deceiving and reality debatable, but she thought he was worth taking a chance on.

"Sure," she shrugged.

He hesitated. "I've got one of those car phones if you want to use it."

She'd heard about those. But it could be a trick. It could be a gun. He could be luring her closer to the cab so that he could shove her in it. She had to consider that possibility, no matter how unlikely. Especially when unlikely.

"No," she shrugged. "That's okay."

He looked ordinary enough walking toward her. His face had that craggy, sun-aged look. His belly was flat behind the smudged shirt tucked into a pair of belted jeans.

"How do you do?" he said, offering his hand with a smile. "The name's Jacob Sweet." He gripped her hand in a firm yet impersonal way, his callouses scratching her palm slightly as he withdrew.

"Let's have a look, shall we?" he nodded at the car.

She handed him the keys. It wasn't like he could steal it. When he turned to get into the car, a wispy ponytail at the back of his neck marked him as either a redneck or a hippie. It was ironic that two such politically opposed groups could be hard to tell apart at first glance.

He turned the key, and the car did nothing. Totally dead.

"Yup, I smell that burning oil. Mind if I look under the hood?" he asked as he climbed slowly out of the car.

She nodded. "I don't know how I could have been so stupid. I knew there was a radiator leak. I thought I had fixed it, but . . ."

He felt along the rim of the hood for the latch, muttering, "Now where is that thing? Old car, huh? What is it, 1974?"

"Something like that. Belonged to my parents. It's bewitched. Just keeps going—until I killed it."

"That little thing up there," he nodded over his shoulder at his truck, "is 1975. My wife says it's got a spirit. Don't know if I believe a mechanical object can have a spirit."

"Well, why not," she said listlessly, half to herself.

He chuckled. "Why not, indeed?" He yanked up the hood. "Oh yeah. Smell that kinda sharp, sweet smell? That's the coolant. That means the head is probably cracked, and the coolant leaked into the oil."

"Can it be fixed?"

"Well, it could be fixed, but it's major. Depends on how long you drove after it overheated. Might be the engine needs to be replaced."

She laughed falsely again. "I can't believe it."

"Well, don't beat yourself up about it. Everything happens for a reason, you know."

She snorted angrily, thinking what an oddball magnet she was. "You really believe that?" she challenged irritably.

He smiled as he fished a handkerchief out of his back pocket and looked out at the silver green scrub rambling down from the road below them, "I do," he said. He wiped beads of sweat from his brow with the handkerchief and wiped his hands on it. "But the reason doesn't always have to do with you," he said, winking at her. "Where you headed?"

"Oh," she sighed. "God. I don't know. LA. Looking for my brother."

"Well, looks like you're not meant to find him just yet. I don't suppose you have any relatives around here?"

"No."

He was silent as he carefully replaced the hood prop and lowered the hood itself, gently pressing on it until the catch snapped. "Tell you what, why don't you come home and have dinner with me and my wife, Kaela. She'd be glad for the company, sane company, that is," he laughed, somewhat apologetically. "I run a kind of halfway house for 'those who are in danger of being lost to this world' as the story line goes. You ever heard the story of La Loba?"

Fallon shook her head.

"Remind me to tell it to you sometime. Anyway, Kaela and I have an adopted son, Sammy, who has Down syndrome, and we've got two other lost ones who have been living with us for about two years. They can be a strange crew, but they're harmless. Beautiful in their own way. You'll see. After dinner, we'll figure something out. My friend Od couldn't tell you what planet he's on, but he can magic an engine back to life with paper clips and prunes."

"That's very kind of you," she hesitated, "but I don't know."

"It's up to you. I'll call the police and a tow truck, and they can follow us home," he said, as if he knew she'd need some kind of guarantee of safety.

She considered for a moment that he could call some redneck freak friend with a cop uniform, and that this could be an elaborate setup.

"Tell you what, why don't you use this phone to call your family, tell them where you are, and give them my particulars."

She decided to take Jacob up on his offer. It would save her a lot of money. Will wasn't home, but she left a detailed message about where he could reach her that included Jacob's name and license plate number.

———

Jostling along in his truck and mesmerized by the roar of the engine, she calmed down enough to notice the thriving tourist center of Taos, the tree-filled plaza surrounded by adobe buildings sporting balconies crammed with café tables and flowers. There were shops filled with dream catchers, and sandwich boards on sidewalks advertising psychic readings and vision quests. They turned north and headed toward the low, dark mountains that scalloped the edge of a red plain dotted with sage. Periodically, Ovid's voice told her what an idiot she was, but she was able to quiet his voice when Jacob spoke.

"So where in LA does your brother live?" Jacob asked. His eyes grew small behind wrinkles when he smiled.

"I don't really know," she said simply.

He glanced at her quickly to see if she was serious.

"He's dropped out of communication. I don't even have a working phone number."

"I see," Jacob nodded, looking ahead at the road.

"There has been a death in the family, and he doesn't know, yet."

"I'm sorry for your loss." Jacob glanced over at her again.

"Thank you. I had two brothers. Now I only have one."

"It is terrible to lose a person so young," he said.

At the moment, Fallon had no feelings about it. What was wrong with her?

"Our family is so broken. I just want to find Terry and see if I can put some of it back together."

"Were you close once?"

Fallon felt puzzled. She had never asked herself that question. So much of her worry had been about Ovid.

"I don't know. Not really. I guess he and Ovid did more things together before we went to high school. I wasn't the best sister. I'm three and a half years older than he is, so when he was five, I was nine, and I just didn't want to play with him anymore." At Jacob's prompting, she recounted her fragmented memories of him.

One particular fight under a gnarly apple tree in Oneonta stood out. She couldn't remember what they were fighting about. It was one of those sibling things: it's your turn to do the dishes, you cheated, you've got your facts wrong, whatever. She had him by the collar at arm's length, and he was so angry he was swinging at her, but he was so much smaller than she was that his arms didn't reach. As she looked at his face, red and scrunched at the end of her fist, a question, full-fledged, leapt into her mind: "What am I doing?" Everything stopped. She could see her own face at the end of Ovid's fist. It was pitiful that she was beating up on a boy who couldn't even reach her to punch her back. She dropped him, apologized, and walked away. She sat on the grassy bank ashamed. She had read *A Wrinkle in Time* that summer and had been moved by how Meg's love for her younger brother had saved him from evil. Terry came and sat beside her on the bank.

"I realized," she told Terry, "that I am doing to you what Ovid has always done to me. I don't want to pass that along. I promise you I will never hit you again." And to her knowledge she hadn't. She was proud of that memory. It made her feel like a good sister.

Seized by uncharacteristic loquacity, she told Jacob a string of memories, like sitting on the lawn with Terry in Chile, looking for four-leaf clovers. She found them all the time. He wanted to find them, too. In that one day, she had found four. She was touched when he asked her to teach him how to find them. But after a few minutes, he exclaimed, "I can't find any," yanked at the grass and threw the blades back down.

"Just keep looking. When you see four leaves together that turn out to be a mistake, it means you're about to find a real one. I don't know why it works that way." But he didn't have the knack.

She'd spent little time with him the year they overlapped in high school, but when she went to college, she had been so involved in trying to maintain her own sanity, she hadn't paid much attention when the report of his expulsion from school came. As she talked to Jacob, she realized she'd been a terrible sister, almost as narcissistic as her mother.

She vaguely remembered coming back home from college one Christmas vacation. Walter told her that Ovid and Terry were having fights, and Terry was smoking and drinking a lot. He asked her to speak with him to see if she could figure out what was troubling him. She used the Socratic method with Terry, questioning him closely, trying to get him to explore the root causes of his fights with Ovid and his drug use. She sat across the dinner table from questioning Terry, and he answered. Maybe she had been confrontational or made some assertions about his character and motivation. It was odd how murky her memory was. It was only five years ago. She thought she was being observant, hard-hitting, truth-seeking—she thought she was seeing his self-deceptions and asked him questions that would make him see them, too. Ovid who had been silently listening, interrupted and dressed her down. Ovid accused her of being arrogant, ignorant, intrusive, self-aggrandizing, and he insisted she leave Terry alone. He said she was trying to step out of the natural hierarchy. She didn't remember

Terry taking a side in that fight. He just faded into the background as she and Ovid picked up verbal swords and went into full combat.

"Terry is a mystery to me, really," Fallon said. "I don't think I knew who he was as a boy, and when he grew up, I knew him even less. He bluffed a lot. To act stronger and less caring than he actually was."

"So, what did you say you were hoping to gain by finding him?"

"I don't know," Fallon said, surprised that she had thought so little about it. "I've sort of been on autopilot. I just need to find him. He needs to know that Ovid is—dead."

"Makes sense."

Jacob slowed down, shifted to low gear, and turned left onto a dirt road just past a small, flat building that said "Herb's" in lime-green letters.

"I'm sorry if I sounded hostile back there when you said everything happens for a reason," Fallon said.

"You didn't sound hostile. You were honest. I like that in a person."

They passed a sign for "Arroyo Hondo" (deep valley) and followed a dirt road along a rocky stream.

"I had a friend, once, who miscarried. People told her everything happens for a reason, and it made it sound like she had brought it on herself," Fallon explained.

"Yeah, I can see how she would feel that way," Jacob nodded, smiling. "Once I was cleaning up the shed, and I pulled a board away from the wall. A spider fell to the ground, leaving her egg sac behind. She scrambled to get back to them, but I moved the board with the egg sac still stuck to it. It occurred to me that life is like that. Sometimes huge forces beyond our ken act on us. We don't know the reason why these things happen, and sometimes the reasons have nothing to do with us. But there's always a reason."

They passed a few shacks that were a mixture of adobe, tin, and board.

"When you put it that way . . . " Fallon said.

"I believe that we are part of a larger design that we can't fully understand," Jacob said, looking out at the red dirt that resembled a hot scalp between parted hair. "I don't think the universe is punishing us when bad things happen. I think we do best, though, when we seek to be in harmony."

"I'll buy that," Fallon said. He'd said just the right thing, and it flicked a switch inside of her that suffused her with warmth for this man, the kind that would last forever.

At an indeterminate place in the shrubs that lined the road, he turned left onto a stony driveway and pulled up to a round adobe house that blended into the land. White teepees gleamed in the upper brush, pale yellow hills humped beyond blue, boney peaks she later found out were called Sangre de Cristo, Blood of Christ.

"Home again, home again, jiggity jig," Jacob said.

# BREAKDOWN

"Welcome to Buffalo Hill."

The compound had been a famous commune once, Jacob told her. In fact, shortly after he had met and married Kaela, he scrapped law school to come and live here for a few years when it was still running. The film makers of *Easy Rider* wanted to film it here, but the commune turned them down, so the filmmakers ended up constructing a replica. The commune died out eventually, and the few that stayed behind were busy selling off plots of land piece by piece to support their junk habit when Jacob and Kaela bought it. Now they ran it as a bed and breakfast and sort of halfway house.

Next to the front door, a man hunched over something, baring his reddish, stubbly head to the world. Various patches of gardens surrounded the house, some obviously vegetable patches that had finished their growing season and been turned under, others still grew spinach and herbs. Two red hibiscus shrubs bloomed on either side of the door. Ivy climbed a trellis over the door.

"Hallo," the man shouted out cheerfully, grinning widely, his voice cracking with delight. His eyes had the curved look that comes with Down syndrome.

"Hello, Sammy," Jacob called as he stepped out of the truck.

"Hallo," Sammy called again.

Jacob introduced Fallon, and Sammy hailed her again.

"Hello," she said back. "What—"

"Hallo!" he shouted again.

"Hi, what—"

"Hallo!" he grinned still wider. Jacob chuckled.

"What have you got there?" she finally got out.

"A stick," Sammy said, holding it up joyfully. It was marred by unintelligible hack marks.

"He generally works on those until there is nothing left. But if you stop him at the right time, they can be quite beautiful." Jacob pointed to the neat rows of hieroglyphically carved sticks pressed into the adobe surrounding the kitchen window. "Sammy, do you know where Odin and Teal are?"

"In the tree, Od is," he laughed then looked confused. "Teal is . . ." He brightened, "I *never* know where Teal is."

"Well, this lady's car broke down. I'm gonna need Od to take a look at it. He's gonna need your help."

"Oh, I fix cars good!" Sammy said.

Fallon looked doubtfully at Jacob.

"Don't worry," Jacob said, turning away from the house and gesturing for her to follow. "He's just the helper. Passes Od and me tools. The real magic worker is in that tree over there," he pointed halfway down the driveway to what she guessed was a willow tree with a large trunk and tiny green leaves surrounded by sweet waving grass. She followed Jacob to the base of the tree.

"Od," Jacob called up into the branches, "I want you to come down here and meet Fallon."

Fallon saw nothing in the darkness of the branches until the trunk appeared to move up high. Two blue eyes burned down at her, strangely light through the shadows.

"You man or beast?" demanded a voice from the shadows.

Fallon smiled. "I'm definitely not a man, and if there are only two choices, that must make me a beast."

Jacob smiled at her answer and looked at the ground.

"All right, then." Od jumped down and sized her up. He was a slender man just about her height with long, brown hair about the same color as her hair, capped by a blue bandana. He picked up her wrist and held it next to his own, comparing. Viking runes similar to the hatch marks on Sammy's sticks tattooed his forearm. Two lines of gray streaked his beard.

"Are you sure you're not one of those brainwashed zombie servants of the plutocracy?" he said, turning his head to the side and fixing her with his right eye. His eyes were blue with white rings like the spiral eyes children draw to indicate that someone is dizzy from being hit on the head.

Fallon's reality did one of its usual shifts to accommodate his reality.

"I only talk to beasts. Those who are in danger of being lost to this world," he added.

"Fallon was definitely a little bit lost when I found her," Jacob said.

"Then she's lucky, because La Loba will teach her something of the soul," Od answered without skipping a beat.

"La Loba is a folktale figure from this region" Jacob explained.

"She has many names," said Od. "La Loba, Wolf Woman, La Huesera, Bone Woman. She collects bones of lost creatures and sings them back to life."

"Thank you," Jacob said. "I wanted Fallon to hear that story. Now Od, Fallon's car is gonna need some major engine work. Think you can handle that for her?"

"What do you need a car for? Do you know a car puts a pound of carbon monoxide into the air for every gallon it burns?"

"Well, I—" Fallon tried to defend herself.

"Do you know how much a *pound* of vapor is?"

"I know. I—"

"Have you seen Teal," Jacob broke in gently, "since you've been on raven watch?"

"Raven watch?" Fallon questioned.

Jacob put his arm around Od's narrow shoulders and hugged him. "Odin is the Norse god who brought writing to his people. He is served by two ravens, Hugin and Munin, thought and memory. Sometimes my friend here is the god and sometimes he's the raven. So where did you say Teal was?"

"She's around," Od said softly, looking at the horizon. "I saw her following the cat again over the mesa. I think she went to the hot springs."

"Come on in and meet Kaela," Jacob told Fallon.

Though Kaela was in her early sixties, she looked younger. She was dark skinned, with rich black hair and only a few tinsel streaks here and there. Her features were almost perfectly symmetrical, balanced by delicate internal geometry. Her glossy, straight hair was gathered by a simple barrette at the nape of her neck. When she stretched out her hands in greeting, Fallon noticed that her palms were smooth, pale, and marked by only a few deep lines. She grasped Fallon's hand with both of hers and smiled broadly, her white teeth flashing in contrast to her dark skin.

"Welcome, welcome. I was just starting to prepare dinner. Come. Keep me company."

Fallon took a moment to absorb the large, round living space, all stuccoed. The thick walls had a ledge for sitting all the way around the room. Round timbers supported by posts divided the ceiling like a pie. Woven pillows and rugs dotted the room. A few skylights made the room airy. She followed Kaela into the next round room, the kitchen, with a butcher-block island, an industrial grade iron stove, and two refrigerators.

"Can I help?"

"Please. You can be my sous-chef."

Kaela pulled fresh herbs from one basket and onions from another and placed them on the table along with a knife.

As Fallon chopped cilantro and garlic and their scents billowed around her, she questioned Kaela about their lives at Buffalo Hill.

Kaela's parents, Fallon learned, had come from what she called the "better part" of New Delhi, India, but she had been raised in the United States since the age of ten, so she spoke English with round vowels and good enunciation. It was not quite an American accent, but not quite anything else either. Jacob and Kaela met late in their lives when Jacob quit his dry-cleaning business and—stirred by the revolution of the Sixties— entered law school thinking he could use a law degree to fight for justice. Disillusioned by the law, Jacob joined the commune in the early Seventies. The commune, too, proved disillusioning, but left them both craving a cohesive community. They moved into town, where Kaela, with a degree in counseling, worked for the county mental health office, and Jacob took a job at a home for the mentally disturbed. Finally, when the commune went up for sale, they managed to scrape together enough money to buy it to run as a bed and breakfast, while also making a bid at self-sufficiency.

"Jacob has a stronger mothering instinct than I do," Kaela said, "though mine is not small, by any means." She laughed, and her teeth flashed brilliant as she glanced out a thick-silled window at Jacob shoveling compost into the garden. "I suppose it comes from being raised alone by his mother. We adopted Sammy, and ever since we moved back here, people just come and find us." She removed the lid from a pot of saffron rice and looked up at Fallon as the puff of steam escaped. "Besides hosting the occasional tourist or artist retreat, we take in people who need a home for a while. Some of them disappear as quietly as they appeared." She carefully replaced the lid and turned off the flame. "Od and Teal have been with us for several years now. Od, in American culture would probably be considered schizophrenic, though, and we are helping him manage with medication and therapy. Teal is a wild one. Never speaks, wanders around alone all day. More like a cat than a person."

As Fallon chopped and mixed the ingredients Kaela set before her, she watched Kaela move with a dancer's precision from stove to sink to counter, her gestures light, quick, and fluid.

"I admire that you two have devoted your lives to helping others," Fallon said.

Kaela's brows came together briefly, then smoothed out. "I don't think of it that way...as helping...others." She tipped red, yellow, and brown spices into a bowl and mixed them with cream. "In India, children belong to the whole village. The children run in and out of the house, up and down the street. Every adult is a parent. When they are outside, there are outside parents, and when they are inside, no matter whose house it is, there are inside parents. It's just a way of life. Everyone belongs to everyone," she said, flicking her palms to the ceiling, green bits of herbs flying off her fingertips.

How different that was from the way she had been raised, Fallon thought, where everyone cared for Ovid and Eustacia, and nothing ever came back. Shame immediately pricked her for having such a thought. Of course, Eustacia and Ovid had bestowed many gifts just by doing what they did. Ovid's bees, orchids, and hydroelectric plans. Eustacia taught them about the stars and the atoms. They both had filled her life with wonder, and all she did was resent it. She should be more like Kaela, beautiful, wise, generous . . . *balanced.*

"I heard somewhere that in the Kabbalah, that's the highest form of giving," Fallon said, "where you don't know you are giving, and the receiver doesn't know they are getting."

"I *like* that." Kaela nodded, crinkling her brows in thought as she checked a recipe.

"The lowest form is when you know you are giving, and the receiver knows they are getting. In the middle is when you know you are giving, but the receiver doesn't know they are getting. And you make sure not to tell them, either."

"Is that what you do?"

Fallon snorted, thinking of that Christmas episode with Terry when she had tried to advise him. "More often, you think you are giving this great gift, and the receiver sees it as a pain in the ass. "

Kaela laughed. "Now that happens *all* the time in my family. When my father and mother come to visit and try to give me advice!" She laughed again. "After twenty years here, they sold their business for a good profit and returned to New Delhi. They could never accept American ways. Whenever they come back, they make sure to let me know how profoundly disturbed they are by how American I am. Meanwhile, when I go to town, people still ask me where I'm from. When I tell them I'm American, they say, 'No, but where are you *really* from?'"

"They probably think of it as a compliment. A way of expressing interest in you."

"Yeah, but it feels more like they're saying the only people who could *possibly* be American are white," she chuckled richly. "Don't even talk to me about the Native Americans. Imagine when these invaders ask them what country they came from!"

"My ancestors on my mother's side are pre-Revolutionary American, but I spent most of my childhood in different countries, so I don't feel that American. I have all these European and South American traits."

"There's a term for that, you know."

"Oh?"

It's called 'third culture.' We are a little bit from here and a little bit from somewhere else."

"Or a little bit from nowhere," Fallon said, fatigue momentarily dizzying her. "But having a name for it makes it somewhere, doesn't it?" She brightened.

"Exactly." Kaela cracked the lid on the rice again, and fragrant steam filled the room. "Okay," she said with purpose, brushing her hands together with an all-done gesture. "Would you mind going outside and calling the others to dinner? I'll set the table."

There was a comfortable silence at dinner, and for the first time Fallon didn't feel that she had to make conversation. She knew that she didn't need to explain herself or entertain these people. Od praised the food sincerely, Sammy smiled and babbled occasionally, and Jacob and Kaela exchanged the minor details of managing daily life. All were enveloped in the warm, spicy scents that rose from the food. Teal had not yet returned, but no one seemed perturbed. The sun slipped down without event, and darkness bloomed fragrant and resonant over the land.

Fallon hadn't eaten since dawn, and the food sent her into an ecstatic trance where nothing else existed except the rice and spiced vegetables that went from her plate to her mouth, all the cells of her body crying, *yes,* as if they were instantly absorbing and transforming the food into energy and endorphins. So she was totally unprepared when she looked up by chance into the black space framed by the window and a blue-faced woman appeared and locked eyes with her. The food turned to a cold lump in her mouth, and a sickly, feverish chill ran from her temples down her spine.

Fallon's fork clattered to the plate, and she jumped out of her chair in animal horror. Kaela followed her gaze.

"Oh, that's just Teal," Kaela said, mildly irritated. Teal vanished.

Fallon's mind skittered this way and that, wondering how it could be possible.

"Her favorite thing in the world is to strip naked and rub her body with anything she can find, preferably something blue, hence the name Teal," continued Kaela. "Blue as Kali herself. I don't know why she does it."

Fallon's head spun. She stopped breathing, the ground shifted, and she found herself in that terrible silence after the storm, the pit of nothingness after Ovid flung himself into oblivion.

"Looks like she found herself some blue clay. Now I wonder where she dug that up," Kaela said, looking at Jacob.

"Must have stolen it from a neighbor, or from town, God forbid," said Jacob.

"Od, will you catch her and see if you can get her to shower off? Use the outside stall. I don't want that all over the house," Kaela said.

Od rose silently and slipped outside. Jacob followed.

Noticing that Fallon had not calmed down, Kaela said, "Are you okay, dear?"

Fallon looked at Kaela mutely, her eyes wide and dilated almost to black.

"Od is devoted to her," Kaela said, as if she could calm Fallon with chatter and explanations. "He's the only one who can handle her. She gets pretty angry when I ask her to wash up. But she does make such a mess sometimes. I'm not the neatest person in the world, but Teal knows nothing of boundaries— My dear, what is it? Sit, sit," she patted the table when Fallon didn't move.

"It's just," Fallon's voice faltered, "My brother—before he died —he was talking about seeing a blue woman."

Kaela absorbed this in silence. "What do you mean? When?"

"It feels like a very long time ago. But it was, I don't know, end of October?"

"Only about a month and a half. Where did you say your brother lived?"

"Upstate New York."

Kaela rose from the table and wrapped her arm lightly around Fallon's stiff shoulders.

"Oh, you poor thing! You're shaking! Come, let's go to the living room." She guided Fallon gently to the cool darkness. She lit an oil lamp, which cast a yellow glow around the room. "That's a remarkable coincidence, but that's all it could be, of course. She couldn't have gotten to New York and back without us noticing her absence. Two young women who like to parade around painted blue. That truly is something," Kaela said as she steered Fallon to a comfortable couch, pushed her down, and sat beside her. "Do you want to tell me what happened?"

"I—can't," Fallon said.

"It's okay, you don't have to talk. Just take a deep breath."

Fallon tried to breathe, but the familiar steel bands were back, preventing her lungs from expanding. The air scraped the back of her throat as she tried to inhale.

"He was in one of his depressions again," Fallon choked out, inexplicably compelled to speak. "I always tried to help him, you know?"

"Forgive me, is it your brother you are talking about?"

"Ovid, yes." She remembered the storm-tossed, muddy green of his eyes, his hands clenching upward. "He was so beautiful, you know?" She saw his deep-set eyes, the clean lines of his jaw and neck tendons descending to his jugular knot. "I couldn't pull him out of his depression. But he was so vital. He was always inventing things, new bicycles, small hydroelectric plants that wouldn't require those huge dams that destroy the land." She saw his room with its narrow bed, his clothes in a heap on the floor, the walls covered with topographical maps of the backwoods country in Upstate New York. "He harvested honey, built a greenhouse full of orchids, and baked bread that smelled like heaven. He actually knew that *AC* stands for alternating current," she laughed shakily.

"He was in the hospital because of the bees, but something went wrong, the bee venom or the pills— I couldn't reach him, so I went home. But something woke me up. I knew instantly something was terribly wrong. When I got to the hospital, he was on the roof, dancing on a ledge or—or—running, or something. It seemed like someone was up there with him. I couldn't see. The sun was shining right into my eyes. He was flickering through the light. I screamed for him. I screamed and screamed, but then—" Staring into the dark center of the house, Fallon whispered, "He threw himself at the ground and disappeared."

With a harsh, metallic crack, the door from here flashed wide to there, and she saw it all over again—*but in a new way.*

"Ovid," she had screamed. He had paused briefly and looked her way. The early morning air was cool. She could see her breath. Then he jumped—no—dove, as if leaping from a diving board. She saw it. His beloved body unmoored in space above her. She ran to him as if to catch him. She remembered only a dark shadow passing over her head in complete silence, a silence that went on unnaturally long. Then she heard a sickening sound, like a pumpkin squashing, a pumpkin of flesh and bones, crunching wetly, with finality, behind her. It was over. And she couldn't look, for her brother, her father, her lover, her twin, and herself lay burst and broken on the ground behind her.

"He killed himself," Fallon whispered. Kaela's eyes were huge and dark. Fallon's hands lay on her lap like dead birds, flopped open, belly up.

Teal slipped into the room, laughing low under her breath, and pulling Od by the hand after her. Her face was pink, her hair was black with water, and combed straight back from her brow, curling and dripping around her shoulders. She stopped short as the silence of the room hit her like a blunt instrument. Od's clothes were completely soaked.

Fallon drew a long breath and looked down at her own slumped body. She saw a piece of rice sticking to her skirt, looking like a maggot. Sickened, she moved to flick it off. But it stuck to her. She grabbed it between her thumb and forefinger with a fierce pecking motion. It was lint. She saw another white dot, and another. They were all over. She pinched at one, then another, gathering momentum, up and down her thighs, violent rooster pecks, vicious twists. Her hands picked up speed as if she were trying to pinch the skin off her legs.

Kaela's eyes widened and she reached for Fallon's hands, but Fallon hit her hands away and began to laugh. Fallon's hands moved faster. They became a blur of bone and feather, whirring through the air, and her laughing grew harsh, dissolving into ugly coughing sounds. Tears spilled over her cheeks. Embarrassed, she laughed at her tears and cried at her laughter, imagining how grotesquely ugly and red her face must look. Then she was running again. Dimly, she was aware of Kaela's shadow rising, calling for Jacob, but she didn't care. Her legs pumped pleasurably, elbows slicing the air. She arched her back to pull her torso up out of her hips. Her hands became fins chopping at the tissues of this world, and she was running through space, ripping through the silver screen of sky into the cool, clean life of spirit. Hands grasped at her, trying to draw her to the ground, back into her body, but she slipped out their grasp with a toss of her shoulder. She wrenched free of them, cursed them. Hands grabbed at her legs, though she was pumping them like the trestle of a manual sewing machine. They were slowing her down, weighing her legs with lead. She coiled herself into a ball and jack-knifed her body, sending people flying in all directions. Winds howled from the other side of reality. Her strength compounded, doubled, tripled, and she flung people from her as if they were flies. The rip in the screen of reality gaped at her and she hurled herself at the hole. She was almost through, but arms had closed in on her, wrapped tightly around her from behind, pinned her own arms to her body so that she couldn't move, not one inch.

It was over as suddenly as it had begun, with a thunderclap of silence. Her ears popped with the atmospheric change, and the veins in her forehead bulged upward into the stillness as if her blood were slapping against the barrier of her skull.

Kaela's face came into focus over her. Fallon realized she was still inside the house. Od and Jacob were there, too, pressing her shoulders to the earth. A few strands of Jacob's hair poked up over his bald pate, and Od's eyes were the expressionless spirals of the Milky Way galaxy, widened now with adrenalin. They were all breathing hard and sweating.

"Shh, shh," Kaela panted, her hand cool on Fallon's hot brow. Kaela smoothed the wet hair out of Fallon's eyes, and the strands seemed to pull a twisted, hot mask off Fallon's face, revealing a new, cool face beneath. Fallon's eyes wandered. Someone was sobbing and hiccupping. That woman was standing in the shadows, pressed against one of the log posts, barely recognizable as the blue woman now, with her hair wet, brushed clean, and an old flower-print dress hanging waif-like off her slender shoulder. Teal looked at Fallon quietly, with a mixture of weariness and fascination. Or was it recognition? Fallon's eyes traveled the room and found Sammy, crouched on the clay perimeter bench, hugging his knees to himself and rocking. He was the source of the crying. A string of clear snot extended from his nose to his wet kneecap.

"It's okay," Kaela said. "You're here now. You're safe."

Fallon struggled to find her voice and mentally scanned her sore vocal cords. She didn't remember shouting, but her hot breath abraded her throat as she tried to clear the webs of phlegm that bound her voice.

# WHERE THE BUFFALO ROAM

Whenever Fallon awoke, Teal was standing in the doorway. Her indigo energy swirled the air, crackled like static electricity, and smelled of ozone, like an old electric mixer. Or so it seemed to Fallon, from her high lumpy bed in the hobbit-hole of a room where she hovered between waking and sleeping over the next few days. Fatigue lay atop Fallon like a corpse, sealing her eyes closed. Each time she surfaced into near-consciousness, she remembered having the breakdown, and the shame of it pressed her back down to sleep. Other times she remembered her revelation that Ovid had not dispersed into the ground but had broken himself on it. And that sound. That beautiful body and *that sound.* The thought was too much. When she got out of bed one morning, Teal was nowhere to be seen. Fallon looked out a small round window and shivered. The tile floor was cold to her bare feet.

The huge, kiva-style living room was warmed by a wood stove that emitted the caramel smell of piñon pine. When she stumbled into the sunny kitchen, Kaela and Jacob would accept no apology for the scene she had caused.

"That's nothing compared to what we're used to around here,"

Jacob said, patting her shoulder as he rose from the breakfast table. "Come on, boys, time to get to work."

Od looked at Fallon kindly as he rose. "Teal has taken a liking to you. That's rare. You must be a good person." He spoke with a level of sincerity and simplicity that embarrassed Fallon. He stroked his gray-streaked beard reflectively.

"I try," Fallon said. After the men left, she asked Kaela for a phone and called Will.

"Hey, lovely lady," Will said, "how's it going? I called a few times, but they said you were out."

"More like unconscious."

"You okay?"

As Fallon filled Will in on what had happened from the time the radiator sprang a leak to her breakdown, Will tried to interject, giving her comforting interpretations of what had occurred and advice on how to handle it all. But the more he tried, the more irritated she got. She finally came up with an excuse to get off the phone. She felt uneasy. It wasn't a fight, but only because she hadn't said what she was really feeling, which was, "Back off. Let me tell my story—yes I already figured that out for myself."

"Why don't you go out and get some fresh air," Kaela suggested, noticing Fallon's despondent posture after she hung up. Kaela handed her a blanket from a basket beside the door. "Better bundle up, though. December weather has finally arrived."

Fallon squinted in the sunlight when she went outside. The sight of the green Dodge Dart across the sleeping gardens was not a welcome one. Od, Sammy, and Jacob were leaning under the hood, elbows on the rim, talking.

What if this whole relationship with Will was just another illusion, another misperception, another miscalculation.

Over the next few days, Od, Sammy, and Jacob held conferences over the car. Occasionally all three of them would lean together under the hood. But most often Od could be found pontificating about corporate, fascist America and the crepuscular light of TV materialism. "Consume and submit!" he'd yell. Jacob would chuckle, but Sammy would sometimes be reduced to tears, crying "It's *not* a conspiracy!" Then the three would go back to their conference under the hood.

"It takes us a long time to figure out which way to go," Jacob explained one afternoon, "but you're not in a hurry are you? As a general rule, I try to let these guys reach their own conclusions in their own time. It's a long-cut to any practical accomplishment, but a short-cut to redemption."

As the days passed and she waited for the new head gasket to arrive, Fallon was haunted by Teal, who appeared and disappeared at odd moments. At first it unsettled her. Sometimes Teal would appear behind Fallon as if from nowhere and pick up a stray lock of hair from Fallon's shoulder, then leave. Once she lightly touched Fallon's forearm and raised her finger to her lips, as if to taste Fallon's skin. Other times, Fallon would sense Teal's dark presence on the furthest periphery of her vision, only to turn and find she wasn't there at all.

"I've never seen her attend to anyone like that," Kaela commented one day when Teal was off on one of her expeditions. "She avoids everyone except Od, usually. And even with Od, he's the one who approaches her, not the other way around."

Fallon accompanied Kaela on errands in their battered red truck and helped her pick wild sage to make sage sticks that she sold in town. She'd asked for permission of the local tribal council, and because they trusted Kaela, they had allowed her to.

As they worked together, Kaela told her what she knew about Teal. She believed that Teal had been sexually molested during her childhood. She bore the signs. When Od found her, she was homeless and trading sex for food and shelter. Kaela wasn't sure how or why Od attached himself to Teal. Od himself was open about the fact that he had been sexually molested and beaten by his mentally ill parents. He was brilliant. And it was clear he had appointed himself Teal's caretaker and sometime lover. Teal had acquiesced, but Kaela didn't know if Teal experienced anything like love. She surmised that Teal had some kind of attachment disorder.

On one of their errands, Kaela pointed out the entrance to the Taos Pueblo, an adobe brick village continuously inhabited for a thousand years by the Tiwa-speaking people, descended from the Anasazi who had lived as much as ten thousand years ago in Mesa Verde and Chaco Canyon. The village looked like mud building blocks stacked on top of each other three tiers high, echoing in human form the Sangre de Cristo mountains, and accessed by wood ladders rather than stairs. Kaela explained that around 1540, the Spanish had moved in, and at first the Indians had accepted them. But the growing white population warned of problems to come, so the village elders finally asked the Spanish to move a league away. That was how Taos was built. By 1680, disease, intermarriage, and the encroachment of Catholicism finally spurred the Taos Indians to declare war on the Spanish in order to expel them. They did not succeed. Fallon knew the dismal end of the story.

"American archeologists like to say that the Anasazi mysteriously disappeared," Kaela explained, "but the Taos people will tell you their ancestors had merely migrated to this area when the climate changed. In the late 1900s, after years of economic and social collapse, the Pueblo Indians turned their town into a tourist attraction. Now tourists could go from house to house and shop for hand-crafted items. Would you like to visit?"

"Oh, I don't think I could. I would be too ashamed."

"Ashamed?"

"Because some of my ancestors fought the Native Americans in the east."

Kaela was silent.

"And the irony," Fallon continued, "Is that they were running away from oppressors themselves. You'd think they wouldn't turn around and oppress others, wouldn't you?"

"Even today, if you look up the Anasazi petroglyph, the "Sun Dagger," it will tell you that a white person 'discovered' it."

Fallon snorted with disgust.

"I know. Right?" Kaela told her that the Sun Dagger is a spiral solstice marker and lunar calendar of sorts at Chaco Canyon unlike anything else on the continent. Each arm of the spiral corresponds with the 18.6-year cycle of the moon's orbit position relative to the earth. "It shows how advanced their astronomy was. But one video at the visitor center posited that extraterrestrials might have carved the spiral."

"How bizarre. Why extraterrestrials?"

"Presumably because they thought the Anasazi too primitive to figure it out on their own."

"Wow. To be so blind that you have to come up with an insane explanation for the obvious."

"What they don't understand, because they themselves are so divorced from the land, is that when you live a life so close to the land, you notice these things. That spiral represents decades of observation and mapping." Kaela down shifted as she rattled over a rocky section of the road.

"It's mind boggling how much culture colors perception," Fallon said. "As Will put it, reality is a pretty broad situation."

Kaela laughed. "That's a good one. He's so right."

Fallon wanted to tell Kaela about Eustacia's combustion, but she had a traffic jam of thoughts and blurted out a different question instead. "What do you make of the fact that my brother was talking about a blue woman before he died, and that my car broke down in the exact place where I was bound to run into Teal?"

Kaela drove in silence for a minute. "I don't know what to make of it. A shaman or a psychic would tell you that the universe is sending you a message."

"But do you believe that?"

"I only know that I do not know. It could be as simple as this: Jacob and you are drawn to the same kinds of people, and that's why he stopped for you and you accepted his help. The world may just be a lot smaller and a lot more ordered than we think."

"Why do you think Teal paints herself blue?"

"I think she just likes the feel of the clay on her skin. But it's interesting. Of course, there's the association of blue with sadness. It could be self-expression. In my culture, Kali, the goddess of time, is blue. Many people call her the goddess of death, but only in the sense that time takes all people. She is supposed to free the soul from the ego."

"The Celtic Picts painted themselves blue with woad before going into battle to make themselves frightening," Fallon offered.

"Yes, maybe Teal is protecting herself," Kaela said.

"Maybe Ovid was, too, by conjuring her," Fallon said.

Kaela glanced over at Fallon but said nothing and looked back at the road. She slowed the truck and turned east onto a dirt road ridged like a washboard. It rattled their eyeballs in their sockets and made it too loud to talk.

Against the backdrop of the Taos Pueblo, the story of Eustacia's combustion no longer sounded so crazy. In this part of America, where the saints left parts of themselves for people to keep in fetish boxes, where the land and ancient history was so alive, and where Native Americans still practiced their rituals and lived in staircases that mounted the sky, anything was possible.

This thought prompted another. She didn't need to fear the mismatch she'd felt with Will over the phone. It was a simple matter to call him and tell him what she needed from him, which is exactly what she did when they got back to Buffalo Hill.

"I need you to stop trying to fix things for me when I talk to you."

"I'm not sure what you mean," Will said.

"Well, the last time we talked, you kept interrupting me to give me advice."

"I thought you liked my advice."

"I do, I just wish you would wait until I ask for it. I need to make my own discoveries."

"Makes sense."

Like a person in a game of tug-o-war when the opponent lets go, Fallon was surprised. She thought in silence for a moment. "You're not mad?"

"Why would I be mad?"

She paused again. "I don't know." She had never experienced

an interchange like this before, where she set a boundary and the other person simply respected it without a fight or recrimination.

After they got off the phone, her back was straighter, her bones stronger, and her eyesight clearer. When she breathed, her lungs filled easily with air, and for the first time, she trusted herself.

# SPIDER WEB

As the days passed, Fallon grew accustomed to and even comforted by Teal's attentions. The more time Teal spent with her, the more she floated, as if all she had to do was lift her feet from the ground and she could glide above it like water bugs skate on the skin of a pond. Teal's eyes were large and amber, with the coldness and fidelity of a wolf's gaze. Teal never spoke, but her gestures were eloquent and more than adequate substitutes for words.

One day, Teal came to Fallon with a pot of brown paste she had made by mashing a root. She knelt by the side of Fallon's bed and carefully took Fallon's long white feet into her narrow, tanned hands. Fallon pulled her foot back quickly, but Teal held on, fixing her with her fierce eyes. Fallon relented, and Teal rubbed the paste onto the soles of Fallon's feet.

"I don't know if I like this, Teal."

Just the corner of a smile tightened Teal's mouth. She bent her head so that Fallon couldn't make eye contact with her. The paste turned to a red-orange stain when it was warmed by her skin. Teal took Fallon's palms and rubbed them orange, too, and then pulled her by the hand into the kitchen.

"So, Teal will be blue, and you will be red," said Kaela, looking up from the recipe book she was reading. "What is that? Dock root?"

"I don't know," Fallon said, shrugging her shoulders and laughing uneasily.

"Must be," Kaela said. "What are you up to, Teal?"

Teal ignored Kaela and yanked on Fallon's hand.

"The Navajos use dock root to heal sores," said Kaela. "Maybe she thinks you need healing. But she's painted your hands and feet in the manner of a Hindu bride before a wedding. Is that what you are up to? Have you been looking at some of my books, Teal?"

Teal handed Fallon a small white pot with a black hole at the center, only big enough for a spider. The outside was painted elaborately with black markings, exactly regular. The shape pleased Fallon's palm.

"Oh!" Kaela said with delight, "this is a pot for Spider Grandmother. In some traditions she is the creator of humans, and in others, she brought fire to the people inside a pot just like this. She put some fire in all things, trees, tinder, and rocks, so that the people could make their own fire. Then she threw a coal up into the sky to make the sun. Of course, she also taught humans how to weave. The Pueblo call her 'Thought Woman,' who thinks all things into being."

Fallon could see how the pot might hold the silence of latent creation in its dark interior, accessible to nothing but a small spider. My mother would have wanted to taste this orb of air, Fallon thought.

It was an unusually warm day for December. Teal took Fallon dancing over the mesa through red sand and the sage's slow silver flames. The sunlight was different in Taos: clean, clear, and yellower than the light of the East Coast. Teal began to move in slow configurations of heron extensions, crab crouches, and spider lattice works, as if she were dancing out an alphabet. Her interactions with plants were sentences that spelled out her purpose in the world. She kept trying to pull Fallon into the dance, and at first Fallon resisted.

But the soles of her feet burned with a pleasant warmth that lifted her from the ground, and she found herself matching Teal's gestures. No one could see them where they danced. As she stretched, her fibers filled with oxygen, and she slipped into easeful invisibility, the closest thing to death she had ever experienced. It was a delirious, nameless state she had craved her whole life, a liquid liminality to which she gave herself with relief and and now shared with another person.

Everywhere, orb spider webs stretched between sage branches. Each time they saw one, they danced their version of it. That was how Fallon found herself dancing the strange beauty of Ovid's wind sculpture. Its iridescent strands hummed in the wind, a song of kite strings, string theory, and spider webs, all woven together, a weave that didn't require interpretation or meaning, a weave of life that simply was.

*No object is solid.*

"It's beautiful," she said aloud to no one, but Teal heard her and smiled.

Over dinner the three men told Fallon excitedly that the Dodge Dart was fixed, and Fallon thanked them falteringly. After dinner, she caught Jacob by himself. They sat outside on the doorstep. Od had resumed his perch in the tree, and Teal had vanished. They could hear Kaela and Sammy giggling over a game of mancala in the living room, the sounds of the glass pebbles clattering into the wooden depressions.

"Jacob," she said, "this afternoon I had a revelation while I was out with Teal."

"Oh?"

She began to vibrate inside, the way she did when she was speaking a core truth. "I want to stay here. I want to help you and Kaela with Buffalo Hill."

Jacob turned to look her in the face, and gently took her hand, smiling. "My dear," he said, sighing.

Frightened of rejection, she plunged forward, "I could find a part-time job. I could help with expenses. Will could come out. He'd love it here."

"My dear, you are on a journey. You must complete it. What about your brother?"

"But that doesn't matter anymore." Her words tumbled over each other. "I don't know why I was going to LA anyway. I don't really know Terry. I don't know if I'll find him. He doesn't even call himself Terry anymore. He's Cosmo Kazan. This feels like home, here. I've never known what to do with my life. But here, I don't need to know. I can just live."

"Didn't you say you used to want to be a doctor?" Jacob asked.

"Yeah, but I'm just not smart enough for that. Besides, maybe there's another healing art I could learn, like massage, or herbs or something."

Jacob scraped at the dirt with a stick. "I've been meaning to tell you the story of the Moon Palace," Jacob said. "Mind if I do?" The setting sun painted the hills above the ranch pale gold that stood out against the sky, surreal and impatient. Beyond them, the blue-black Sangre de Cristo Mountains jabbed the sky in jagged pencil points.

Fallon shook her head, trying to quell her impatience.

"There was a young woman who refused all suitors," Jacob said. "None of them were good enough. One day, she fell in love with the head of a man she found in a field, just a head, nothing else. They got on famously. This was the man she wanted to marry. But her father was furious, and when his daughter was away, he stabbed the head in the eye with an ice pick. The head rolled away to the bottom of the ocean, back to his family of heads. When the daughter discovered this, she wanted to kill herself, but instead she was sent to the Moon Palace. This is a place that people go to when they don't want to feel anything anymore, where the light is diffuse, and where the world looks very small and far away.

"She looked down on all the activity in the village, the hunting, gathering, loving and arguing, and thought, 'Why bother?' But one day, she saw three men putting their canoes out to sea. They were standing in the waves laughing. As they talked, they splashed water at each other. The droplets fell all around them, showers of sunlight. Suddenly, the girl wanted to go home.

"There was an old woman in the palace. She told her that all she had to do to go home was close her eyes and climb down a rope, and when she was two feet from the earth, she should let go and jump. She climbed down the rope, just as she had been instructed, but you see, she thought the earth was very far away, and before she knew it, before she opened her eyes, she hit the earth blind, and," he clapped his hands, "turned into a spider."

Fallon just looked at him in silence. "I don't understand," she said. The setting sun turned the mountains to the color of dried blood.

"Because her head wasn't connected to her feet, she didn't know how close she already was to the earth, so she missed it."

The curtain of night fell, and the mountains were now just shelves of darkness against a ridge of dark blue light in which the first stars appeared.

Fallon tried to wipe a tear out of her eye without Jacob seeing.

"This is not a rejection," he said as he patted her knee. "Once you've found your brother and finished this journey, if you decide to come back, you are welcome. Any time. I mean that."

# RECKONING

K nowing a thing and being ready to do it were two different things, so Fallon stayed put at Buffalo hill for a few more weeks. One day, Teal wordlessly conveyed Fallon toward the Dodge Dart. Fallon floated along behind her, unresisting. As she approached the car, shocked body memories poked up their heads like frozen bits of earth, but she pushed them down. She slid into the driver's seat, and Teal into the passenger side, and Teal seemed to restore to the car it's old magic. Eustacia charm. The car started up with a deliciously smooth purr, and they drove out of the Buffalo Hill yard. The road rose to the top of the mesa and grew increasingly rocky and pitted in a manner reminiscent of the road leading up to the *Altiplano*. It dropped precipitously into the deep gorge of the Rio Grande. A 400-foot curtain of wine-red rock folded and unfolded before them. The river, though narrow, roared loudly as they wound their way down into the gorge. At the bottom, they crossed a metal bridge and drove up the other side.

Teal motioned for Fallon to park the car in a dirt area just off the shoulder of a hairpin turn. She scrambled out of the car and jogged down a narrow trail where prickly pear cacti were tucked into the crevices. Fallon hurried to catch up, but Teal was already out of sight. When Fallon found her, Teal had strewn her clothes willy-nilly over the rocks and was immersed in one of the three pools ridged with lava rocks at the side of the river. She gestured for Fallon to do likewise. Although the sun was hot, the air was cold and a slight breeze blew, making Fallon loath to take off her clothes. But she dipped a foot in the water and found it hot. She turned her back to Teal as she unfastened her clothes. Exposed, goose flesh prickling, she stepped carefully into the pool, not looking at Teal, as if avoiding her gaze would hide her nakedness. Hot water jetted from the greenish black mud at the bottom of the shallow pool. Fallon lowered herself into the warm water. Teal scooped up a handful of mud, picked up Fallon's foot, and carefully smeared the mud along her ankle, where it glittered like asteroid dust. As the warmth softened Fallon's muscles and the steam rose, she lay back, looked at the high blue sky, and submitted herself completely to Teal's care.

*If only I could skip all the work and confusion of life and climb the skies,* thought Fallon as the heat gathered and spread throughout her body. *If only my body could be released from its human chains and float like this vapor into beauty, into blue sky.*

*I am a child of the great mother, an ant, crawling between the hairs of her scalp, warmed by her red blood pulsing under her skin. I am nothing.* Her muscles loosened from her bones, her brow ran with drops of sweat, her heart pounded under the labor of the heat.

Teal climbed out of the pool and gestured for Fallon to follow. Fallon noticed how curiously childlike Teal's hips were. She was not saddled with the womanly hips and thighs that Fallon had. Teal's belly protruded like a baby's belly, accentuated by her swayed back. Her fuzzy hair turned dusty silver in the sunlight. Teal led her up over the rocks to a small lake not visible from the road. Though it was winter, the water was at least 70 degrees. It felt pleasantly cool after the heat of the spring, but it was still obviously warmed by the same source. Fallon imagined a fissure at the bottom of the pool that reached all the way down to the earth's molten layer. She climbed in and sat where the pool was still shallow.

Teal giggled, low and breathy, and pulled Fallon off the ledge into the bottomless center where it was hotter, and she lightly dropped her hands around Fallon's neck. Fallon felt uneasy and awkward being so close to Teal, their naked bodies brushing lightly against each other as they treaded water. Teal's arms grew heavier as she pulled her mouth to Fallon's ear.

When Fallon first heard the words, they sounded like another language. She struggled to tread water under the weight of Teal's arms. The vowel sounds were long and spidery, short and silken, hot-breathed and blurry. Fallon finally sorted the sounds out into words, "Stay with me. I want to die with you." It was almost a complaint, a plaintive sigh, sinister in its innocence.

Prongs of fear stabbed her. Teal wrapped her legs around Fallon's waist and transferred her entire weight onto her. Fallon felt the shock of Teal's pubic hair pressed against her hip bone. Her head went under for a second, their bodies melding into each other so that, for a moment, she couldn't tell where hers ended and Teal's began. Fallon spluttered for air as she bobbed up again, her arms pinned to her side by Teal's arms, making ineffectual fin movements. Panic mounted. She tried to maneuver her forearms between their bodies to push Teal away, but Teal's arms were surprisingly strong, wired with madness. Fallon's will to live roared like fire, but the harder she fought to stay above water, the lower she sank. Then something clicked. In one violent, instinctive movement, she sank deep into the water and slipped out of Teal's embrace. In the murky light of the water, she saw Teal's hands grasp for her, but with one powerful scissor kick, she shot shark-like away, her foot accidentally making contact with Teal's body. As she flailed for the rocky ledge and heaved herself out of the water, she was dimly aware of Od, standing over them.

"Teal," he called sharply, his blue eyes burning. Without disrobing he dove into the pool.

"No," Teal screamed. When he emerged next to her, she kicked and hit him, pushing him away.

His voice softened. "I'm not angry. Don't be afraid. Just get out of the water."

Fallon staggered to her feet into the cold air and almost fell to the ground as her blood pressure dropped precipitously.

"No," Teal screamed, flailing her arms, her head whipping back as he grabbed her around the waist.

"Calm down," he gasped, out of breath. "What's gotten into you?"

"I want her. I want to die with her," she screamed, a whirl of fight.

"That's not going to happen," he said as he wrestled her out of the water.

Fallon shook as she tried to pull her clothes over her wet limbs, her wet legs and arms catching on the fabric.

"You better go," he gasped to Fallon when he'd gotten Teal pinned against his chest. "I'll see if I can calm her down."

Breathing hard, Fallon clambered up the rocky path to her car, grazing her knuckles and ankles against the porous lava rock as she passed. When she swung in behind the steering wheel, the heat of the car's interior baked the chill from her skin. She shifted into reverse, gunned the engine, spun the wheel, and raced the car back up out of the canyon toward Buffalo Hill.

---

"She's never pulled a stunt like that before," said Kaela, wringing her hands, sitting in the circular living space. "Do we need to make new arrangements for her?" she asked Jacob. He looked at the floor and rubbed his chin, white stubble rasping under his fingers.

Fallon shrugged and took a deep breath, stretching her arms overhead, pulling her torso up and out of the saddle of her hips. When she lowered her arms, her shoulders hung loosely on either side. "I was terrified, but she woke me up."

"I feel clearer and," Fallon hesitated, "hard. Energized, oddly enough."

Jacob nodded. "Death is a great priority-maker." He shook his head, still looking at the ground.

"And she spoke, you say?" Kaela said, still in shock.

"Yes."

"She hasn't said a word in the two years she has lived here. I wonder what brought this on."

"I don't know. But I think it's time for me to get back on the road," Fallon said.

"I would hate to have you feel like you'd been driven away," Kaela said.

"No, no. I don't. It was time for me to leave days ago. I just didn't realize it until now. It's best for me, and maybe better for Teal, also."

Jacob and Kaela agreed.

Fallon didn't have much to pack, so she was ready to go in a matter of minutes. While Kaela packed a basket of food for her, Fallon called Will. Walter answered.

"Dad," she said.

"Have you found him yet?" Walter asked.

"I'm fine, thank you."

"Oh, yes." Walter sounded a little flustered. "How are you?"

"Is Will there?"

"No, he's at work."

"Tell him I called and that I'm fine. I'm going to make one long push for LA. I'll call when I get there."

"All right, girlie." There was another pause. "Do you need anything?"

"No, I'm fine. Thank you. I—" It was her turn to pause now, her mouth feeling awkward around the words that leapt up of their own accord. "I love you."

"Oh." There was another short pause. "Love you, too."

Od and Teal did not return before Fallon left, and they all felt relieved about that.

Standing beside the car, Kaela wrapped her arms around Fallon and gave her a tight hug. "Come back whenever you want. You're family now."

Jacob patted her on the back and said, "Let us know how it goes when you find your brother."

As she bumped down the driveway, their image jumped and vibrated in the rearview mirror, with Sammy waving cheerfully.

The Dodge Dart sounded better than it had in years, but it felt impersonal and mechanical. With a mixture of relief and sadness, she couldn't feel Eustacia's or Teal's spirit inside it. Maybe now it carried a trace of Jacob and Kaela's spirit.

Her mind buzzed as she turned onto the highway, heading west. The air she breathed into her lungs had never felt so good. She adored this earth, this sky, this dear, faithful, strong body that had taken years of her abuse and always came to her rescue.

Just like Spider Grandmother's perfectly round, black and white pot with its tiny hole at the center, the cool space inside her had been sintered by the coals of Teal's attack, and it had made her stronger. She didn't know if finding Terry was the right thing to do, but some roads had to be traveled before one could determine whether they were right or wrong.

## COSMOLOGY

The brown hills of Los Angeles turned into a mass of tangled freeways and arterials. Mid-morning traffic crawled steadily. Fallon's eyes burned from invisible smog. High on the banks of the freeways, bungalow-style houses overflowed with bougainvillea vines and palm trees. Terry's old address was on San Pedro Street, which Fallon knew from her map was downtown LA, off the San Bernardino Freeway. She took the exit for El Pueblo de Los Angeles State Park and parked her car in the first space she could find. She was hoping that he hadn't moved, or if he had, that someone in the building could tell her where he'd gone.

She took a few wrong turns and ended up in a section of town consisting only of wide boulevards and tall gray buildings, one of which was city hall. Spears of red aloe flowers stuck out around the city hall entrance. Huge billboards on the sides of the buildings advertised Levi's jeans and Cosmology Health System. When she turned the corner onto Olvera Street, she encountered a Mexican street market. Royal blue, orange, and natural-wood stalls lined both sides of the red-tiled street, filled with sweaters, copper pots, toys, candy, strings of red peppers, and Christmas lights. Brightly colored posters in Spanish and English plastered the sides of the smaller brick and brownstone buildings. She felt comfortable there. She stopped before a row of posters advertising "Embra and the Sunfire Circus," remembering the only circus she'd ever been to, in Chile. The slinky silhouette of Embra danced at the center of a flock of yellow birds that burst upward into flight. Fallon touched her sternum, remembering the heat of life that flared inside her when Teal almost drowned her.

She couldn't resist wandering down the street and into a few stores. Religious and abstract murals enlivened stucco walls high and low. One store had wooden floors, high ceilings, and a shrine near the entrance. In fact, most of the stores had a shrine at the entrance. Just inside the front door of a store crammed with ceramic and paper-mâché Christmas ornaments, stood a wooden armoire, doors flung wide open. To one side, a statue of Virgin Mary looked down on a fresh bouquet of flowers. In another store, filled mostly with silver and gold religious medals, a shrine devoted to St. Francis bore an inscription typed on a manual typewriter: "To have everything stripped from you is to enter the state of perfect joy. For then, nothing stands between you and God." Fallon fingered the hole in the right pocket of her jacket. She had had everything stripped from her, and she had found life by sinking into the hole made by Teal's ensnaring legs.

The most interesting piece she found was an armoire that appeared to be a shrine. Tacked to the back of the armoire amidst pink tulle and a strand of white Christmas lights, was a late 1800s photo of Señora Sepulveda with a caption describing her contributions to the Olvera Street community. She had come to Los Angeles as the wife of a Mexican ranchero but had left him and had been largely responsible for the creation of the Olvera Street Foundation, which had preserved the first street of Los Angeles. Los Angeles did not become part of the United States until 1846.

Fallon and her fellow "Americans" were the immigrants, and the Mexicans were the indigenous ones. America was like a cubist painting when it came to reality. This woman's answer had been to unite a community to preserve her people's story. Fallon longed for a community she'd never known. Maybe with Will and Jacob and Kaela, she could start building one.

At the end of the market, she strolled onto a stone plaza dominated by a giant fig tree with multiple trunks and wide, spreading branches. Here, the Sunfire Circus trailers were parked, and a few people milled about, hammering in stakes for a large tent. It made sense that Terry would live here. He, too, must have yearned for Chile.

When she located his address on San Pedro Street, it turned out to be an apartment above a Chicano grocery store, with brightly colored fruits displayed on tables on the sidewalk. Her heart hammering, she pressed the doorbell next to a grillwork over the door. She couldn't tell if it even worked, and there was no name on the mailbox. No one answered. She went into the store, where unusual spices and canned goods with labels printed in Spanish lined the shelves. Again, she felt more like an immigrant in a foreign country. It took her a few minutes to work up the nerve.

"*Perdoname,*" she asked the young woman in a bright pink sweater behind the cash register. "*Busco un hombre que se llama Terrence Kazan. Vivía allí.*" Unable to remember the word for upstairs, she pointed upward. The woman eyed her and rattled off a long question in Spanish to someone in the backroom. The man answered her in Spanish.

"He doesn't live here any more," the woman said.

"Do you know where he went?" Fallon asked.

"No idea," she said and turned away in disinterest.

Fallon wandered down the street, asking a few more people, but no one knew anything. She went into a pharmacy on the corner.

"Have you ever heard of Terry Kazan?" she asked the acned male pharmacist at the back of the store.

"Never heard of Terry Kazan, but everyone knows Cosmo Kazan," he said, pointing to a sign behind her. She turned around and saw a cardboard advertisement showing an almost life-size celebrity holding up a bottle of Cosmologie Shampoo. Fallon's eyes widened as she read in fine print the words, "Brought to you by Kazan Laboratory." She remembered something Walter had said about Terry being in a new line of business—some kind of nutritional products that he said were selling well. Very well, from what she saw. There were vitamins, syrups, skin lotions, and even a line of cosmetics, all guaranteed to keep you young.

"Have you got a phone book?" she asked.

The pharmacist pointed to the phone booth in the corner. Attached to a metal cord was a phone book six inches thick in a binder. She thumbed through until she found the address for Kazan Labs. The pharmacist gave her directions to what turned out to be Venice Beach.

Venice Boulevard was a wide, six-lane boulevard typical of much of Los Angeles, lined with two and three-story gray and pink buildings with arched windows. She found the lab and, entering a reception area, all glass and Danish furniture, made her way to the front desk.

"Excuse me," she asked the manicured receptionist, suddenly feeling greasy and travel worn. "I'm looking for Cosmo Kazan."

"Do you have an appointment?" The receptionist looked her up and down suspiciously, her styled hair miraculously keeping its shape.

"No, I'm from out of town. I'm his sister."

The receptionist's tweezed brows came together in disbelief. "Your name, please?"

"Fallon Kazan."

"Just a minute," she said, not even bothering to smile. She pressed a button and disappeared through the doors behind her desk.

When she returned, she said Mr. Kazan would speak to her on the phone, handing her the receiver.

Fallon's hands shook. Her stomach caught fire.

"Hello?" she said tentatively.

"You the one calling yourself Fallon Kazan?" came a low, curt voice from the phone.

"Yes? Is this . . . Terry?"

There was a short silence. "Put Phoebes back on the line," the voice said.

She handed the phone back to the receptionist, who listened, nodded, glanced up at Fallon, and hung up.

"You can go in," she said, and buzzed the door.

The soles of her feet burned orange, and she seemed to levitate slightly through the doors. A white hallway telescoped away from her.

A tall man with long, almost black, hair stood in the doorway of an office, with light streaming from behind him.

"Falloopia!" his voice boomed. He was much bigger than she remembered, and this nickname was entirely new. "How the hell are ya?" The square-jawed man sauntered down the hall toward her with his arms held wide.

She hardly believed she was standing before her brother, Terry. It had been far too easy to find him, like the girl in the moon palace bumping into the east too soon. This man's voice was so loud and confident, and his gestures so exaggerated, that she couldn't tell if he was acting or he just had an expansive personality.

"It's been a long trip," she said as he gave her a crushing squeeze that lifted her off the ground. She felt frayed. Before she could get a word out, she burst into tears.

"Hey, hey," he said. "What's this?"

"I'm sorry. I'm just tired. I've come a long way to find you."

He drew back and looked at her, a guarded expression in his deep-set eyes. "To what do we owe this visit?"

"Yo, Cosmo, dude," said a small man who popped out from behind him, "introduce me, man." He wore faded jeans and snakeskin cowboy boots with toes long enough to double as Q-tips. His apple-round cheeks and shock of springy white hair made him look elfen.

"This is Fallon, my sister, named after my mother's fallopian tubes. Should have been Fallopia, Falloopia. Just call her Loop, man.

Fallon was disconcerted by the sudden familiarity and surprised that he remembered the origins of her name, which she herself tended to forget.

"And Loop, this is my good man Billy Baroo. We're partners in slime, so to speak."

"Ooh, Cosmo. You never told me you had such a hot seester," said Billy in a Frito-Bandito accent. "How much will you sell her for?" Billy shimmied his shoulders and walked toward Fallon with his arms raised to hug her. Internally pulling back, she woodenly stood her ground and summoned a smile to her face. But when she looked into Billy's eyes, they were glittering with such innocent pleasure she relaxed.

"Oh, you bad man," Billy said when he saw the tears on Fallon's face. "You've made her cry, already." He wrapped his arm around her shoulders and gave her a squeeze.

"It's not that," said Fallon. She turned to Terry. "There isn't any good way to tell you this, but . . ."

"What is it?" Terry dropped all his accents and inflections. His voice became soft, and his brown eyes serious. "Here, come in," he steered her into his office, white and airy, dominated by a glass desk and a white leather couch.

"Sit," Cosmo said. It was more command than request. He remained standing.

"It's Ovid," Fallon said, rubbing the sore spot between her brows, trying to freeze her facial muscles to hold back an emotional avalanche.

"How is the asshole?"

"Terry—"

"Cosmo," he corrected automatically.

"He's dead."

Cosmo froze. His eyes went dull, his face blank. His head pulled back as if he were receiving a blow. He lowered himself onto the leather couch in silence.

Billy whistled softly in the silence. "This calls for a stiff drink." He went over to a glass bar she hadn't noticed until now.

"I tried to reach you by phone, but—" she said.

Cosmo lowered his head and rubbed his temples, then wiped his whole face with the flat of his hands, as if washing.

"How did it happen?" he asked in a monotone.

She held her hand to her mouth as if to stop the words that escaped through her fingers. "He killed himself."

Cosmo shot off the couch. "That *asshole.*" The force of his voice slammed Fallon back onto the couch. He took three paces in one direction, stopped, turned around, and paced back. "Fucking bastard," he exclaimed again. "How?"

"He had been hospitalized because he was swarmed by his bees, and something went wrong. They think it was the adrenaline, or whatever it is, and it triggered—he was delusional, he jumped. From the roof of the hospital."

"What a total douche-bag," Cosmo said. "I can't fucking believe it. Then again, it just fucking figures."

Fallon was so taken aback by his reaction that she didn't know what to say.

"I've got to get out of here." He picked up a leather jacket and swung it over his back with such vehemence that it sent a lamp crashing to the floor. "I'm sorry." He opened the door to his office so hard the doorknob punctured the wall behind it, and he strode down the hall.

Billy stood there looking after him, still holding three shot glasses, his eyes wide, blank, and waiting.

"Don't worry about us!" Billy called to the empty hallway.

---

Billy took her to Cosmo's apartment in a three-story, contemporary house right on the famous Marina Del Rey boardwalk. She was impressed by its elegant balconies, round windows, and scored cement. Every time she worried aloud about Cosmo, Billy told her not to. This was Cosmo's way of handling things. He'd taken his motorcycle and was probably winging it up and down Highway One, letting the ocean breeze "clean the cobwebs" from his brain.

He'd be back, and he'd be fine. She should settle in and not to expect to see Cosmo for a few days.

Fallon wandered Cosmo's apartment looking at his choice in furniture and decor trying to understand this brother-come-stranger. His preference for modern furniture with clean lines was obvious. She was surprised to see that he had matching dishes and silverware, because her own kitchen was filled with mismatched hand-me-downs and curbside rescues. The idea of having matching cutlery had never been a financial option or even a goal. Where her walls were filled with thumb-tacked pictures, he had no pictures of family or even friends, only framed photographs of landscapes, and quite a lot of expensive camera equipment. He also had a lot of humorous marijuana pipes and bongs, like a ceramic hand holding up the middle finger, and bong made out of a plastic Kewpie Doll.

She got in touch with Will and Walter and told them she'd found Cosmo. They were both glad but concerned when they heard how he took the news. Fallon and Will spent most of the evening cradling the phone, talking and not talking as the mood hit them.

"When do you think you'll come home?" Will asked.

"I don't know. It depends on how things go with Cosmo."

The next day, Billy came by and took her out in Cosmo's red convertible Mustang to show her some of the sights in LA. He explained all about their products: organic diet pills, cosmetics, and lotions that were all the rage in LA right now. He assured her they were making money hand over fist. She, in turn, filled him in on some of their family background, leaving out the manner of their mother's death, of course.

When Cosmo returned two days later, he came into the room with forced cheerfulness and reeking of cigarettes and marijuana. Fallon was just polishing off a plate of Billy Baroo's "tastiest huevos rancheros north of the border," if he did say so himself. She had to discipline herself not to lick the plate. She looked up apprehensively as Cosmo walked in the door, but he held out his hands, smiling. "Hey, Loop. Whaddaya say I give you the grand tour of LA? We could go to the tar park—"

"Already been," Billy cut in.

"Or Griffin Observ—"

"Been there, too," Billy smiled.

"—vatory." He went on as if Billy hadn't spoken. "Or I could take you "chopping" in Westwood." His words came fast and loose, but his eyes looked hollow. "How about those canals? This whole place used to be canals. That's why they call it Venice. Most of them are filled in, now."

"Billy, have you taken her to Catalina Island? Come on, waddaya say?"

Fallon searched his eyes for some clue of emotion and found none. Nevertheless, she agreed.

They ended up getting stoned and tooling around West Hollywood. Later, sitting at an outdoor café, Fallon and Cosmo had fallen silent as they watched the people walk by. Billy was off somewhere. There was an above-average number of thin, large-breasted women wearing neon miniskirts and "fuck-me heels," as Cosmo called them. "Plastic," was Cosmo's comment about the breasts. "You can get that look naturally with my products. That's how your little brother is gonna get stinkin' rich."

Fallon was struggling a little with the marijuana high. She didn't feel necessarily happy, just a bit more befuddled and confused, second guessing everything she said, wondering if it was the product of the weed or if it was something she would have said naturally.

During another silence, Cosmo leaned over and whispered in her ear, as though they were continuing an interrupted conversation, "Ovid's not dead, Loop. He just joined the great cosmic soup. Like Mom. You'll see. He'll pop up all over the place. Look. There he is now!" Red veins crazed the whites of his eyes, and he pointed to a man walking out of a shop who had Ovid's familiar leopard walk. "And look over there," he pointed to a dimpled man in a black tank top leaning over a café table and sweet talking another man. "There's another," he said, pointing to a mason with finely drawn features kneeling on the pavement by a shop that was being renovated. Cosmo grinned, fanning out his arms. "He's everywhere!" Floating in a weed haze, she had to admit he had a point. His eyes went vacant, and he shrugged, looked away, and lit a cigarette.

"It feels like it happened so long ago," Fallon said. "But it was only," she paused to count on her fingers, "seven weeks."

In silence, Cosmo continued to watch people walking up and down the sidewalk.

"How do you remember him?" she asked.

"From childhood?" he asked, watching the mason on his hands and knees, placing bricks into the entrance of the store. With each stone he positioned, he scraped some sand from underneath or tamped a corner with the butt of a mortar knife to level it.

She nodded.

"Not much. He was the guy I built rockets with, out of tinfoil, match heads, and paperclips . . . a guy I sometimes skateboarded, windsurfed, and skied with . . . a guy who occasionally beat the crap out of me."

"What about adulthood?"

"After our brief stint in D.C. I never wanted to see him again. Guess I got my wish," Cosmo snorted smoke, mildly nonplussed.

"What happened?"

Cosmo continued to eye the crowd and took another drag of his cigarette. A middle-aged woman in "distressed" jeans and high-heeled sandals exited a clothing boutique holding several paper bags with tissue paper streaming from the top. Her expertly exercised thighs looked more like those of a twenty-year-old. Her blond, perfectly styled hair floated and bounced with her jaunty walk.

"I bet she's one of my customers," Cosmo said.

Fallon waited, debating whether to prompt him again.

"When did you two live together in D.C.?" She'd forgotten. Or maybe she never knew. She either passed her adult life in a fog or memory was playing its usual bizarre trick, filing things under obscure associations, omitting what it didn't understand, and even colonizing other people's memories and late-night movies as though they were its own.

"Let's see. After I got kicked out of school, I lived at home for a while. Ovid moved to D.C. and I joined him for eight torturous months. We did a lot of handyman work, some construction, painting, roof repair. No matter who we worked with, he would fuck the job up by getting anal about totally unimportant details and trying to talk the clients into spending way more money than they wanted in order to do things they never intended, but which he insisted they should do.

Fallon did a mental calculation. She guessed that was her senior year in college or the year after. He was still watching the mason, who was bending low to eye the leveling the string against. "He'd argue with the homeowners about their renovation plans, always pushing them to follow some grandiose design he had in mind that would have tripled the cost, telling them what idiots they were when they refused. Of course, we'd get fired. And he was such a slob to live with. I'd shop, cook, and clean, and when I asked him to clean up, he'd tear me a new one. Then he'd have the nerve to tell me I was his best friend and that he knew me better than I knew myself." He chuckled bitterly. The other Ovid look-alike with the dimple leaned in and kissed his lover across the café table. "That's when I moved out to LA and told him I never wanted to see him again."

"But we're family."

"What does that mean?" It was a rhetorical question, but she gave a shot at answering it.

"Family is supposed to be the people you can always fall back on, who will pick you up when the chips are down." Even as she said it, the cliché rang hollow, especially in connection to their family. "Yeah, right," she ended.

"To me," Cosmo turned his dark eyes on her with some hostility, "family is a fabrication of closeness between randomly generated people, bound not by choice, but by shared genetic material. It's an illusion. All our family ever did was confuse me, knock me down, and throw me for a loop. Best to be rid of it all."

"But what about shared history, shared blood? Doesn't that give us a kind of bond that no one else has?"

"A very fucked up bond. Who needs it?"

"What about Dad?" Fallon asked.

"What about him?"

"Do you feel any connection to him?"

"I'm going to need a few more drinks if we're going to have this conversation," Cosmo said. He signaled to the waiter. "If you were looking to excuse people, which I'm not, you could say Mom and O. were nuts, but Dad was basically sane. He just totally abdicated taking any responsibility for anything. As far as I'm concerned, Dad was the worst of the lot, because he could have done something differently and chose not to."

"Really? My biggest beef is with Mom."

"Well, you can't blame her for an accident."

"What do you mean?" Fallon sat forward in her chair, all senses alert. He was opening the door to the topic that had always sent the family into a soporific labyrinth. The waiter came by and dropped off two shots of tequila for each of them.

"The fire," Cosmo said, downing a shot. "Drink up."

Fallon took a shot. "You think that was an accident?"

"What else?" Cosmo was looking at her now, warily, his eyes lost in a cave of brow bone.

"Wait. How do you remember that day?"

He shrugged, downed the second shot, glanced at her quickly, and looked away. "I don't know. The car was on fire, or something. It was confusing, there was a lot of scrambling and shouting. Somehow, Mom set the car on fire, caught fire herself, and ran."

"Wait," Fallon said again. "You thought the car caught fire?"

"I only remember fragments. That's what I pieced together. I remember Dad wrestling Ovid out of the car."

"That's not what I remember at all." The street and cafe faded. Her senses zeroed in on the memory.

"How so?" He looked at her now full on, stubbing out his cigarette.

"The car was never on fire. I'm still driving it. There's no fire damage."

"Hm. Could have been fixed. Anyway. What do you remember?"

"You honestly don't remember?"

"Well, I thought I did. Come on, hit me."

"Mom spontaneously combusted."

"What?" He laughed explosively. A few people glanced in his direction.

Fallon's face burned. Could she have gotten it so totally wrong? Was *she* the crazy one, after all? "I always thought it was some kind of weird accident, too, but I recently pieced together that she was planning it all along."

"For fuck's sake."

"She was obsessed with parting the atoms and walking through walls. She must have figured out how to do it—or thought she did—and something went wrong. Maybe she didn't realize parting atoms meant fire, and fire meant death—"

"Fallon. I'm surprised at you." Cosmo's face creased with an exaggerated grin. "I thought you were somewhat sane. A pansy. But a sane pansy."

Fallon said nothing, her mind cycling through all the details. "She left notes, you know. They're in the car. I'll show you."

"I don't want to look at any notes. Look, it's over. I don't know what happened, and I don't care. But I'll tell you one thing, for sure. She didn't spontaneously combust." He laughed again and looked over at the mason who was now standing back and surveying his work. The man looked briefly his way, sensing he was being watched the way people mysteriously do.

"Don't you remember we ran to the place where she went up in flames?" she said. "There was nothing left." She leaned forward, her voice drilling into him. "If she had just caught on fire, there would have been a corpse. Don't you think we'd remember that?"

"We could have blocked it out. I thought we left her there."

"Left her there?"

"Well, that's what the Tarantula Man was doing when we left."

"The Tarantula Man?" Now it was her turn to be incredulous. She sat back in her chair.

"Yeah. He was there. At the end. When we were towed away. I looked out the back window and he was burying her in the sand. He had a broom."

"What would the Tarantula Man be doing there?" She raised her palms skyward.

"I don't know. That's just what I remember."

"Then you remember we *were* in the car that wasn't burned."

"Oh yeah," Cosmo said softly, looking puzzled. "Anyway. What does it matter? She has gone the way of all flesh. Given up the ghost," he said in a mock British accent, "Kicked the bucket. Croaked. Perished. Conked. Let's have another drink."

But for Fallon, this changed everything.

## SERPENT IN THE CITY OF ANGELS

S he wasn't that surprised that his memory was so different from hers. Memory was notoriously unreliable. What surprised her was that they had never, until now, been able to compare notes on what happened. What had been unbridgeable had been as easy as drinking shots, and just like a shot, the effect crept up on her later. Over the next few days, she was disoriented and had to look at everything twice to make sure the bed was still a bed, the door still the door. It didn't help that Billy Baroo-with-jigger-too constantly plied them with tequila and cannabis as the three of them sailed around the city in Cosmo's red '67 Ford Mustang convertible. Wherever they went, men and women of all shapes and sizes constantly stopped to shake Cosmo's hand and slap him on the back, either because they knew him through business connections, or because they just liked his expansive, sardonic style. Periodically, Fallon surreptitiously peered at Cosmo's face in the rear-view mirror for signs of hidden grief over Ovid's death. His face seemed to be made of malleable rubber that could wrinkle and twist in the most flexible ways to convey a broader range of human emotion than Fallon ever thought possible. But if grief was one of the emotions, she didn't recognize it, and after a while she forgot to look, enjoying the feeling of being part of a three-person posse again. When a good song came on the radio, the three of them rocked the beat. She'd found the missing piece of the human jigsaw puzzle.

It was Billy's idea to go to the Sunfire Circus. He had noticed how Fallon eyed the posters glued all over the city.

"She has a devoted international following," Billy said, referring to Embra. He was riding in the back seat, and the top was down. He stretched across the seat and rested his pointy-toe boots on the open window ledge. "The circus comes every year around Christmas and performs in the Pueblo. They're from Mexico or somewhere like that. She does this whole serpent-bird-dance thing with birds and feathers. Some people say she's Quetzalcoatl reincarnated as a woman."

"Quetzal-who?" Cosmo asked, twisting his head in an exaggerated way to look at the back seat of the car before snapping his eyes back on the road.

"The plumed serpent," shouted Billy over the road noise. "Union of bird and snake, sky and earth. Toltec god of civilization, life, laughter, and art. People love old Embra. She's considered the spiritual mother of millions. We should go."

"Wherever there's a cult, we shall follow," Cosmo said wryly.

"You're a cult unto yourself, dude," Billy said, smiling broadly and winking at Fallon, who sat in the front passenger seat. He nudged the back of Cosmo's head with the tip of his boot. "He's the father of millions. People love this big handsome lunk."

"I don't know why," said Cosmo. "They don't even know me."

"It's those big brown eyes," Billy said. He sat up, leaned forward, and mock-whispered into Fallon's ear, "When people look into them, they see no fear."

---

That night, as they followed the crowd into the yellow and blue tent and climbed the bleachers, Fallon asked Cosmo if he remembered the circus they went to in Chile.

"Not really," Cosmo said, his voice blank. "I told you. I don't remember much about any of that."

They took central seats halfway up and on the aisle.

"It's better to forget, don'tcha think?" Cosmo added with forced cheer.

"Yes—no—I don't know. Maybe."

"Wow. That answer covers all the bases."

"I'm a little concerned about you, actually."

"Me?" Cosmo tilted his head, arching his brows exaggeratedly, his eyes bulging slightly.

"Yeah. You seem to deal with things by cutting them off."

Billy sprang out of his seat. "I'm going to get us some of that *delicious* caramel popcorn." They both looked at him blankly.

"And?" Cosmo asked. "You think it's better to hold on to memories until they grow moldy and fester?"

"I don't know about festering, but—"

"Look. You deal with life your way. I'll deal with it my way. Everyone in our family thought we were all the same person. This just in," he held his hand to his ear and spoke in a mock newscaster voice, putting his face up close to hers, *"we're not."* His resonant voice easily rose to the volume of a shout.

She colored, torn between anger, shame, and confusion. She clasped her hands tightly over her denim-clad knees. That moment of floating across the mesa with Teal returned of its own accord, and her shoulders relaxed.

"You're right," she said, "but you don't have to yell."

Cosmo looked at the crowd and took a deep breath. "Sorry. I don't know why I got so touchy."

"Forget about it," she said, imitating his mock Italian accent.

She felt good, actually. This was one of the first times she'd made a mistake, taken a hit for it, and acknowledged it without falling into a pit of shame and melting a hole right through the center of the earth—or launching a counterattack. Yes, she could admit it. She was guilty of trying to fix Cosmo instead of minding her own business. That didn't make her a worthless person.

"I'm back, beautiful," said Billy, bouncing up the stairs with a giant tub of popcorn just as the lights dimmed. "Miss me?"

The circus was similar to others at first, with clowns and trapeze artists in glittering sapphire suits who flew through the air like light inside a jewel. But Fallon's eyes wandered, hooked their gaze upon the sloping canvas seams, and followed their curves up into the dark where the cloth gathered around the center pole like a spider's web. Beneath the smell of crushed popcorn and cotton candy, she could smell the musty canvas of the tent and a hint of armpit odor.

A flock of screeching canaries burst into flight and startled her nearly out of her seat. The crowd gasped in delight and pointed as a cloud of yellow shimmered around the tent, thinned and swooped to go through a hoop, then widened, and spiraled in ever-changing formation. It was just like that day they arrived in Santiago. But now, the birds flew through a hoop held by a thin, gray-haired man with wrinkled brown skin and glittering black eyes. Fallon fixated on this man. He wore an old riding outfit of a cream-colored, button-down shirt, brown velvet pants that billowed before they tucked into black boots, and a burnt-orange cummerbund wrapped around his waist. The worn but commanding dignity of this figure sent tarantula legs up her spine. *Nothing is impossible.*

Unconsciously, she laid her hand on Cosmo's forearm. She was about to ask him if the ringmaster reminded him of the Tarantula Man, but the lights went out. The crowd quieted in anticipation of the big act. Drums began to beat. A voice boomed out of the blackness with a thick Spanish accent:

"Ladies and gentlemen, I give you Embra, the Burning Woman." The crowd erupted into a wild frenzy, but when the spotlight lit a curtained opening at the back of the ring, they ceased so abruptly the resulting silence hit like a club. A woman clad in a suit of green-tinged, iridescent scales emerged with her hands raised. The crowd erupted again. She bowed. A circle of torches burst into flame around the perimeter of the ring, and a red carpet unrolled at Embra's feet, signaling the crowd to pay close attention. The crowd quieted. Embra danced sinuously down the red runner. Once in a while, her hands burst into flames and, with the flamenco twist of a wrist, went out. Four pillars stood near the center of the ring. Like an elegant snake, she slid and wove in and out of the pillars. Each time she circled a pillar, it burst into flames at the top, and each time she left a pillar, it went out, so it seemed like she was in a dialogue with the fire. Next, a bed of flames erupted between the pillars, and she danced onto it. The flames went out wherever she stepped and rose up again in her footsteps while the entire bed of flames rose between the pillars, until it formed a flaming tabletop on which she continued to dance. Eustacia's words flickered through Fallon's mind. *I unravel to ingest the sun. I fear no darkness. My magic is my alchemy.*

Embra danced faster and faster, spinning and stepping, the flames coming and going at a faster and faster pace. The entire crowd clutched their seats and leaned forward as the drumbeat built to a mind-crushing thunder. Then in one great inhalation, Embra burst into flames. The crowd gasped, and Fallon screamed and gripped Cosmo's arm, her hands, now talons. But the crowd roared so loudly no one heard her. Cosmo winced and glanced down at his arm. The look of a sleepwalker suffused his face as he returned to the burning woman who whirled and gesticulated with increasing irregularity, so it appeared that something had gone horribly wrong and she was twisting and turning in agony.

Fallon leapt to her feet as images formed and reformed in her head, a kaleidoscope of colors, yellow birds, blue rags, tarantulas, hands playing an olive soccer field. Then Embra turned around, and the flames were gone. She turned again, and she was aflame in green. Each time she turned she was a flame of a different color, now woman, now blue fire, now woman, now burning woman, now most articulate tongue of fire among the least articulate flames of earth. *What is magic? What is holy? Numinous life.* Embra danced faster and faster, drawing herself up into a white cyclone. Then in great puff of smoke, the flames went out, and she disappeared. When the smoke cleared, there she stood, with her arms raised, her green scales replaced by iridescent feathers, and a host of yellow canaries sitting all along her arms. The crowd leapt up, screaming with pleasure, clapping their hands, and stomping their feet. The yellow birds burst into flight behind her as if the fire had turned to feathers, and they all flew away. The bleachers shook and swayed so much, Fallon was afraid they would collapse. Embra held her position, smiling serenely, bowed low and spread her feathered hands wide. She bowed again, holding her hands to her heart, and threw kisses to her adoring fans, thanking, and blessing them.

Far away, in Fallon's mind, a hurricane of images began to rise, a woman ran, shoulders raised, elbows slicing the air, head thrown back, newly giddy, loose with laughter, free. Shards of glass, fragments of the kaleidoscope fell into order, and an image coalesced of the Tarantula Man sweeping up a pile of ashes. The fragments of the image rippled and refit themselves more closely. Fallon narrowed her eyes as she strained to see a memory appropriated from Cosmo. Had the Tarantula Man been sweeping, or had he been pulling up a board that hid a pit in which her mother crouched? *Just so, magicians lie to set the mind free, to reveal the invisible magic at the root of existence.*

When the ringmaster in velvet pants and orange sash emerged to clasp hands with Embra and bow with her amidst thunderous applause, Fallon knew. That was the Tarantula Man. And Embra could only be one person. Her mother.

"I know her," Fallon screamed, a wind in her mind drowning out all other thought. She pushed past Billy and Cosmo, shrugging off their hands as they reached for her, only dimly aware of their surprised faces as they fell backward. She leapt down to the next bleacher seat, pushing people aside. "That's my mother!" she screamed. Other people surged forward in her wake, moving behind her and with her. "Madre!" they called. "Madre!"

"No, that's my mother!" Fallon screamed, pointing at Embra above the crowd, clawing at the people around her to get past them. She became the hurricane, leaping from bleacher to bleacher as the crowd surged and the roar rose. Her legs tangled with the legs of others as she crawled, twisted, folded, and turned. She placed her hands on other people's shoulders to heave herself past them, maybe even stepping on a few people's laps to get over them.

"Madre," a dark-haired woman next to her screamed with arms outstretched and tears streaming down her dark cheeks.

"Goddamn it," Fallon screamed again, wedging her body closer to the stage and squeezing past, "that's my fucking mother."

Embra looked up startled, comprehending that this was not the usual audience response, that something was out of balance. She was older at closer range, with thick eyebrow pencil melting on her wrinkled face. The Tarantula Man pushed her behind him protectively, and other circus personnel came out, locked arms around her, and shuffled awkwardly toward the back exit. Security guards, holding batons horizontally between their fists, pushed back at the crowd. Fallon hooked her leg over someone's shoulder, grasped a baton, and heaved herself into the ring just as two other guards grabbed her by the arms.

"No, you don't understand," Fallon screamed again, kicking her legs, and yanking her arms. "That *really is* my mother." Then something heavy hit her on the back of her head, and everything went black.

Male voices were shouting on and on in her head, in fevered circles. When she opened her eyes, she found herself lying on a hard cot in a holding cell. It wasn't like the metal cages she'd seen on TV shows. It was just a room with a locked metal door. But even through the thick safety glass, she could hear Cosmo's voice arguing. Her tonsils felt swollen and sore, and as she rubbed her throat, she pictured two grayish, blue-veined oyster lumps.

"Look, she should be in the hospital. Not jail," Cosmo was saying.

A quieter, more restrained voice explained that she'd already been looked at by a doctor.

She lay on the cot looking at the ceiling, thinking about the circus. If she had gotten to the center of the ring at that moment, she was certain she would have killed her mother. She could imagine her hands closing around that soft crepe-paper neck, stopping the flow of air and blood. It turned out that old woman in Dodge City, Bobby, had been right: a murderer had lurked inside her all along.

She curled on her side and looked at the palms of her hands. They were empty and pink. They said nothing. They were not made of feathers. They did not fly or burst into flames. She felt nothing except, surprisingly, a tiny stream of relief. If that was her mother, she could finally point to someone who was made of flesh and blood and say, "That is what happened to me. That is what drove Ovid crazy. That's why I could never be happy, never believe in myself. My mother didn't just neglect us, she didn't just walk out on us. She twisted our brains so far out of shape that we could never put reality back together again." She would be able to say, "She wasn't just a narcissistic liar. She was a monster." She *is* a monster.

The inside of her head prickled with the snowy sound of a television station gone off the air. She got up, walked over to the door unsteadily, and knocked on the glass.

The guard, who was seated at a desk in front of the door, turned around and looked at her.

"Loop, how the hell are ya?" Cosmo shouted, with that cheerfulness that no one else seemed to realize was hollow. The glass grayed his voice as a sedative dulls the mind. "What the hell got into your loopy head? You nearly took an officer's eye out. I'm trying to get you outta here, but I'm having a hard time convincing the nice man here that you're not a lunatic. Tell him you're not a lunatic, will ya?"

"I'm not a lunatic," Fallon said in a matter-of-fact tone.

"There, ya see?" Cosmo said, smiling at the guard and gesturing to her. "Does she look like a criminal to you? Come on, Jim. Be a prince and let 'er out, why doncha?"

"Look, Cosmo, you know I would if I could," the man explained, his back to Fallon now. He seemed to know Cosmo. An awful lot of people in this city knew Cosmo, she thought, not for the first time. Her mouth was dry, and she felt groggy. She wandered back to the cot and sat down.

A spot of light shimmered on the ceiling. She looked around for its source. It quivered like a reflection of water. There was no window to the outside. Maybe it came from the door lite. She waved her hand in front of the spot. It didn't flicker. She sat up and waved her hand in front of the door lite. Still no flicker. Its source was inexplicable.

If Embra was her mother, she wouldn't have to try to explain the inexplicable anymore. She wouldn't be the daughter of absence. Her life didn't have to compete with perfect mystery, and she didn't have to live up to the extraordinariness of Eustacia's disappearance. On the other hand, if her mother was alive, everything she knew about herself was based on an illusion. It made all the difference whether she was the child of a miracle, or the child of fabrication.

That ordinary truth was so much worse than the extraordinary. If Embra was Eustacia, that meant her own mother had thrown a bomb into their lives and left her to sort it out. The gall of it was harder to imagine than the combustion.

She didn't know how she was going to make sense of it, how she was going to be able to pick up and move on, but she knew one thing: Doing it alone was not the answer. The only way reality made sense was if you put it together with other people.

She knocked on the glass. The guard swiveled to look at her.

"Do I get a phone call?"

# ZERO ENCHANTMENT

At Cosmo's apartment, Billy brought Fallon a bag of ice wrapped in a towel. Will, who'd caught a redeye as soon as Fallon called, smiled at Billy, took it from him, and held it up to the lump at the back of her head. Billy stepped back, eyes darkening and tilting down at the edges.

"So, Loop," Cosmo was saying, leaning close to her and fixing her with a stare. "Seriously. You're going to sit there, look me right in the eye, and insist that Embra is our mother?"

"I know it," Fallon said. But she wasn't as sure as she made out. She looked uneasily at Will. He sat close to her, leaning forward with his arms resting on his knees, at home no matter where he was. The California sun had already bleached his long light-brown hair to a reddish blond, as if reclaiming a long-lost son.

"I believe you," Will said.

She was surprised and gratified.

"Jesus, Loop." Cosmo shook his head and looked at the floor. "I thought you were the sane one in the family."

"Quit being so hard on her," said Billy. "She's obviously taken a nasty blow."

"I'm not crazy," Fallon said. "That was Mom. Don't you see? It was all a trick."

"What the hell are you talking about?"

"Why don't you give her a chance to explain," Will said.

"It makes a lot more sense if you look at the notes she left in the Dodge Dart."

"Again with the notes," Cosmo said. "What fucking notes?"

"I'll get them," Will said. "Where are your keys?"

"Will somebody please tell me what y'all are talking about?" Billy said, reverting to a Texas twang that was apparently his natural accent.

Fallon told Billy her version of the final day on the *Altiplano*, getting stranded, the strange lights in the distance the night before, her mother scooching farther and farther away from the car, randomly sprinting off into the desert and launching herself into flames.

"Wow. Hit me with a sledgehammer," Billy said. "Cosmo, dude. You never told me this."

Cosmo shrugged. "What was I going to say—my mother spontaneously combusted?"

"I'd have believed you, man. I saw a show about it on the Discovery Channel."

"That's not what I remember, anyway," Cosmo cut in. "I remember her setting the car on fire and catching fire herself."

"We've been over this," Fallon said. "There's no sign of any fire damage in that car, inside or out."

"I can confirm that," Will said. "I checked it over pretty thoroughly before Fallon left. All original panels, parts, and paint."

"And there was nothing left of her," Fallon said.

She remembered how the calligraphy of her mother's soul seemed to have etched itself into the *Altiplano*, how the wind blew.

"Shit. I put all that behind me. Why do you have to keep bringing it all up again, Loop?"

"Because I've got to know. Don't you want to know?"

"Nope. What's bothering me, to tell you the truth, is all this drama, this digging into things, rehashing the past. It got you thrown in jail, for crying out loud. It's over, Loop. Get over it. Let it go. Move on." He heaved each phrase out like a bag of sand over a cliff.

"I can't move on if I can't figure out what's real. Look," she said, doggedly pursuing her train of thought. "I think they dug a pit in the sand and covered it with something—a board covered with burlap—whatever. Mom went running off to a pre-designinated spot. I mean, maybe that's what she was doing when she was scooting away from the car on the campstool. She was waiting for the signal from the Tarantula Man to run and in that direction."

"But Loop, she couldn't have planned for the car to get stuck where it did." Cosmo's memory now seemed intact.

"Why not?" Fallon said, talking fast now. "The Tarantula Man could have gotten there ahead of time and dug the tracks down a little deeper. It wouldn't have been that hard to arrange. Remember she said she was going to take us to a place where she could demonstrate *the greatest mystery man has ever achieved?* She said, *It will change you forever.* Maybe she carried some kind of explosive with her and just threw it down when she was ready to vanish. In the smoke, there would have been enough time for her to jump down into a hole. The Tarantula Man could have covered it over and jumped down into some other dugout of his own."

"But you said we stood over the spot where she disappeared," Cosmo said.

"We stood over the spot where the *explosion* occurred. And we were so dazed, we didn't really see anything."

"But I saw her on fire, running."

"Didn't we see Embra engulfed in flames on stage? And you're the one who told me you saw the Tarantula Man as we were towed away. That's when it all came together for me—when the ringmaster came out. Didn't he look the least bit familiar to you?"

The whites of Cosmo's eyes showed all the way around his brown irises making him look crazed. His mouth was pulled back in a grimace.

"And now that I think of it, didn't we see a car or truck driving off in the distance? We tried to flag it down, and they ignored us. What if that was him?"

"I know our mother was crazy, but why would she do such a thing? Why would *anyone* do such a thing?" He scowled.

Will came back into the room, slightly out of breath and handed her the notes.

"Look at this note," Fallon said, unrolling the delicate yellow scroll she'd stashed in the glove compartment. '*Einstein said, Logic will take you from A to B, but imagination will take you everywhere.*'"

"So?"

"To me that says she was setting up a trick to get us to imagine her apotheosis. It fits who she was so perfectly. She saw herself as a piece of God. What better way to leave us?"

"You lost me."

"Look, here's another one, even more telling:
*No one has ever seen the particles.*
*Yet scientists make predictions based on the idea*
*and prove them over and over again.*
*This idea, this fiction, is the building block of life.*
*Just so, magicians lie to set the mind free,*
*to reveal the invisible magic at the root of existence.*"

Cosmo pulled his head back into his neck like a turtle pulling back into his shell and rubbed his bulging brows with a large thumb and forefinger.

"And here's another, '*It is easier to see illusion than it is to see reality. For me there is no difference.*'"

"I'm not saying I believe you, but if she did this . . . " he was silent for a while, absorbing the immensity of such a deception. "If Embra is really Mom, and she did this, I just don't want to know." He smiled, shook his head, and pushed the idea away with his hand.

"How's the ice pack, Princess? Want me to refresh it?" Billy said, cutting the tension.

I got it," Will said amiably, but pointedly.

Billy turned so Will couldn't see his face and silently imitated him and threw him an imaginary punch.

"I've got to talk to her," Fallon said.

"They'll never let you see her," Cosmo said. "You know how many people want to talk to her?"

"After all, she's the spiritual mother of millions," Billy chimed in.

"And don't forget," Cosmo said, wagging his finger at her, "you've got a record now."

"We'll find a way," said Will, covering her hand with his own.

---

Cosmo was right. When Will and Fallon tried to so much as walk up to one of the trailers and ask for Embra, a beefsteak of a man accompanied by two German shepherds stopped them.

"The lady takes no visitors," he said in a rich Mexican accent. He folded his arms over his chest and planted his feet wide. His eyes drifted momentarily in the direction of a certain trailer before he corrected himself, but it was too late; she knew which one was Embra's.

Fallon and Will pulled back and sat in the square under the ficus tree, its trunk like the strained neck tendons of a 60-foot giant.

"Should I send her one of her notes to prove who I am?"

"I don't know," Will said. "It will put her on guard. Might be better if she doesn't know you're coming."

"Perhaps we could pose as reporters."

"Little late for that. I say we sneak into her trailer during the show tonight. Didn't you say her act was last? From what you told me, I'm guessing everyone will be on high alert. They will be distracted. You can speak to her when she comes back to change. I'll watch the door and run interference."

"What will I say?"

"I don't know. Just don't kill her."

That night after Fallon had rehearsed what she wanted to say with Will, and while the show was going on, they snuck out to the trailers. The muscleman with the dogs was on patrol, but he was the only one, so it wasn't hard for Fallon to sneak up to the trailer door. It was locked. She and Will circled the trailer until they found an open window. The music, the roar of the crowd, and the buzz of the generators provided great cover. It was easy to pop the screen out, and with Will giving her a boost, Fallon dove quickly through the window.

She took a deep breath and looked around at Embra's things. Fluffy costumes stuck out of a half-closed closet, and the vanity was covered with pots of makeup and cream. Paper flowers, creased photographs, and newspaper clippings adorned the mirror. Fallon touched Embra's brush, feeling for her mother's energy. She looked for objects that might betray Embra's true identity. She opened the vanity drawer, looking for anything with her handwriting. Nothing. There were nail files, a ball of twine, a few screwdrivers, a light bulb, and a pinecone. Nothing said Eustacia specifically, except maybe the pine cone. What if she was wrong? What if she was about to scare an innocent woman to death? She'd get arrested again, for sure.

As she backed away from the vanity, she almost tripped over the marble bust draped in a scarf on the floor. She pulled the scarf off to reveal a bust of Einstein. Her heart, which had migrated to her stomach, drummed dizzyingly along with the muffled sounds of the circus drums. The intensification of the applause and foot-stomping indicated that Embra's return to the trailer was imminent. Her mouth went dry, and a burr materialized in her throat. She coughed involuntarily and froze. Footsteps. She hid herself in the costume closet.

"You were more brilliant than the stars, as always, *querida*" a man's voice said.

"*Caro*, what would I do without you?"

Was that her mother's voice? Fallon scanned her memory. The memory was mute. Endearments were uncharacteristic of Eustacia, though, as well as the slight accent. Fallon couldn't remember

Eustacia expressing affection of any kind to Walter. The door opened, the trailer shook slightly as Embra mounted the steps. The man's footsteps crunched away.

Embra sighed, unzipped her costume, and let it drop to the floor. She whirled a fringed kimono around her slender, aged body. She pulled off her black wig and put it on Einstein's head. Fallon stayed hidden, watching.

Embra was smaller than Fallon remembered her mother to be, and older. But that made sense. Her hair was completely white. As the woman sat facing the mirror and opened a jar of cold cream, Fallon thought she could trace her mother's features, even through the heavy makeup. Until this moment, she hadn't realized just how large Eustacia had been to her. She had covered the sky, yet she was so small. A longing as large as the sky sprang up inside her. The ground undulated to make room for this new reality, but disbelief numbed her. Her plan had been to call her by name to see how she reacted.

"Eustacia Kazan," Fallon said, stepping out from the costumes.

Embra started, her hand flying to her chest as she looked up at Fallon's face in the mirror. Fallon thought she saw a flicker of recognition, immediately masked.

"My God." She half-rose from her chair. "Marco— Antonio—" but her call was half-hearted, almost a show.

"Shh." Fallon said. "You know me, don't you?"

"I have no idea what you are talking about. Get out of my trailer. How dare you intrude. I'll—"

"Have me arrested? No. Even you wouldn't go so far."

"You have mistaken me for someone else. What do you want?"

"I want you to confess."

"Confess what?"

"That your name is really Eustacia Kazan. That you abandoned your family and staged your death."

"I am Embra Menendez, spiritual mother of millions." As if to prove that she wasn't perturbed, she sat back down and whipped a tissue out of the box, thought better of it, and smeared a glob of cold cream on her face with her hands.

Fallen felt lightheaded. Her hands shook as she unraveled the scrolls.

She read aloud, *"Einstein said, Logic will take you from A to B, but imagination will take you everywhere.* Sound familiar?"

Though Embra kept her eyes lowered, they darted to Einstein's bust and back. Her hands stopped circling for just a minute and continued caressing her cheek and neck adoringly. She picked up a discarded tissue and dreamily rubbed the cream off her face. "I'm sorry for whatever happened to you, but I can't help you."

Fallon's head felt like a balloon, floating away from her shoulders. Embra was so cold. Her mother had been self-absorbed, not cold. Even considering Eustacia's self-absorption, Fallon couldn't believe that a person confronted with a truth so naked would not so much as quiver. Perhaps she was wrong, after all. Perhaps she was delusional. She tried to feel the ground but couldn't. Silenced, she watched Embra wrap a new tissue around her finger and carefully wipe away the thick black eyeliner. When she uncovered the mole on the lower lash line of her right eye, time expanded to fill the enormity of the moment. Fallon's feet found the ground, and bending her knees slightly, she regained her balance. She breathed and jumped forward.

"It *is* you." She raised her hands to grasp Embra by the shoulders but thought better of it at the last minute, teetering over her and regaining her balance again. "I knew it. I knew it when I saw the act, but I needed proof. I would know that mole anywhere."

Embra held both her hands to her cheeks, looking up at Fallon's reflection in the mirror with a complex mixture of expressions: dread, joy, embarrassment, relief, pride.

"All right. I'll give you this. Parts of me were once part of Eustacia, but she exploded. Antonio taught her how to part the atoms, and it was just as I—she thought! So much space between the electrons. She just flew apart . . . and . . . Antonio reassembled her into me. No one has ever parted the atom and lived to tell the tale!

But now that my parts are reassembled, I belong to everyone, not just to you."

"He reassembled you right down to the mole under your right eye?"

"He's very good at his job," she said without irony. "It took him a long time."

Fallon almost laughed. Her own emotions ran the gamut from hysterical amusement, to melting love, to nuclear rage, all wadded together in a wordless concoction.

"Mother," was all that came out.

"She would never have just walked out on you," said Embra. " She loved you too much."

"Love?"

Embra/Eustacia twisted around in her chair, and looked up at Fallon, for the first time, face to face. She reached up to touch Fallon's cheek but hesitated. "Of course, she loved you. How could she not? So much, so much! Why else would she have brought you all those shiny bits of the world, day after day?" She turned back to the mirror and looked off through the window behind her, reflected in the glass. "But sometimes a different kind of love comes. When it comes, you obey."

For a second Fallon could almost hear the strains of "I Have a Love" from *West Side Story* and wanted to laugh, but too many different emotions battled with each other as Eustacia continued.

"That woman, Eustacia, didn't understand love until she met Antonio. She knew the indescribable beauty of life's mystery, but without love, she couldn't experience it, couldn't become it. She had to die and be reborn. 'Love is not love which alters when it alteration finds, or bends with the remover to remove: O, no; it is an ever-fixed mark, that looks on tempests and is never shaken; It is the star to every wandering bark.'"

"You're quoting Shakespeare to me?" Fallon found herself panting.

"You wouldn't understand true love unless you had found it yourself. I—she had to leave . . . to fulfill her destiny with Antonio."

"To become a circus act?"

Embra drew herself up tall in her seat and said, "To become art! The perfect blend of art and science in a form that reaches the masses. I bring wonder to everyone." She gesticulated with her arms into the mirror, her eyes flashing at Fallon with anger and excitement. "People love the world more intensely because of what I do. You have seen how I feed their hunger."

Fallon laughed.

Embra's voice cooled. "But you have to be a genius to truly understand the importance of what I do. No one understands it like me."

"Genius," Fallon said. She wanted to hurl the truth of Ovid's death at her. She wanted to hurt her as much as she had been hurt, but some fragment of herself knew this vengeful feeling was cruel and wrong. She breathed deeply to still herself. She looked at her feet and felt how solidly they touched the floor.

Still, she wanted—needed—to wring some acknowledgement of the truth from her mother. The "Battle Hymn of the Republic" began to march through her mind . . . *He hath loosed the fateful lightning of His terrible swift sword; His Truth* became a shining sword in her hand, raised over Eustacia's head.

"Do you have any idea what you did to us?"

"I told you, I am not that woman."

Fallon longed to bring the blade of truth down, to slice through all the years of bullshit, to cut clean and cauterize at the same time.

"You twisted our brains, our hearts."

"I had so much to give the world," Embra replied, hands swirling around her now, as graceful and expansive as peonies. "If I didn't find a way to give it, I would have smothered you. I loved you too much. That's why I had to leave."

"That is such bullshit," Fallon said. Words flew from her mouth now like revolving blades. "You *did* smother us, but not because you loved us. Because you loved yourself loving us, and because your so-called 'self' extended about two miles out from your body. You never even *saw* us," her hands chopped the air.

"You don't understand," Eustacia rose to her feet and faced Fallon.

"And it's not just your inflated super-egotistical apotheosis that was so galling—it's the way you raised us. It's even in our names. God *damn* it, Mother."

Fallon looked up and caught her own reflection in the mirror, and it caught her back. The skin was drawn tight and white as a drum, the eyes were jagged obsidian blades that conducted electricity to every spot they fell upon, the nostrils flared, the body pumped ten thousand watts of energy. She had never seen this face before. This face was beautiful, powerful, fully present. She loved this face as she had never loved her face before.

"Why didn't you just leave? Why did you have to do this whole act?"

"Would you have preferred the banality of infidelity? How would you have felt if I told you that running away with the circus was more important than my own flesh and blood? The way I did it was so much better. Eustacia was a phoenix; she had to die to embrace the universe, and she died giving you the gift of mystery. Look how well you turned out. You are so competent. After all, you found me. How did you do it?" With a sharp intake of breath, Eustacia's eyes lit up. "It was Ovid, wasn't it—"

"Mom," Fallon said, breathless. The word felt foreign in her mouth.

"—My sweet, brilliant boy—"

"*Mom*." She tried the word again. The truth was blazing in her hand now, too hot to hold. All at once, the difference between reality and truth became clear: Reality could never be pinned down, but truthfulness could. It was hard enough to figure out what was real, even when people weren't trying to deceive you. In the face of all life's twists and turns, people had an obligation to tell the truth as they knew it.

"—He figured it out, didn't he?" Eustacia continued on her tangent, "Oh, I knew he would. He's just like me, he—"

"*Mom! Ovid is dead.*"

Embra/Eustacia/her mother collapsed inward as if stabbed in the stomach. She stopped breathing, clasped her breast and abdomen, and curled around the wound in silence. "You're lying. You're just saying that to hurt me," she choked out.

"He died trying to follow you. Right off the fucking roof!"

"How dare you!" Embra rose from her chair, holding her breast and gut as if she truly bled. "Antonio!" she called, "Antonio!" It was a piercing wail, more cat than bird, the universal cry of the lost Fallon remembered so well from the campsite in New Mexico. The door to the trailer flew open. Antonio the Tarantula Man strode in, a small but intensely burning force.

"*¡Fuera! Fuera de aquí!* " His glittering black eyes in his time-etched face stripped Fallon of her self-righteous anger and propelled her from the trailer. She stumbled down the steps into Will's arms, and he guided her out of the circus camp to the parking lot.

## A DIFFERENT MAGIC

"What?" Cosmo jumped off the couch when Fallon and Will told him the truth the next morning. The sunlight bounced off his eyes, making them crackle like fire. "I'm going to tear Esmeralda a new asshole!" He commenced to pace, his vibrant voice filling the room.

"Embra," Billy corrected.

"Please don't," Fallon begged. "For one thing, she has guards, and you'll get arrested. But also—"

"One asshole is enough," Billy Baroo chimed in. "Imagine the kind of shit she'd make with two."

Cosmo stopped for a second and half-laughed before anger overtook his face, and he fell back to pacing in front of the balcony windows. "What an unbelievably worthless piece of shit she is. The fucking coward. The manipulative, narcissistic, mind-fucking bitch." His voice was so round and resonant that it left little room for them. He ran both hands through his long hair, pulling it back from his sweating brow as he paced, his eyes wide and staring at some middle distance below him. "Fucking Imelda—"

"Embra," Billy corrected again.

"Whatever the fuck her name is. Eustacia Kazan. *That's* her goddamned name. She's alive? She's been fucking alive this whole time?" He whipped around. "Not for long."

"She claims she really did explode and was reformed as a new person," Fallon said, but she didn't know if she was trying to calm or feed his rage.

"What utter horseshit. And that—that—*spider* man—"

"Tarantula Man—Antonio, actually—" Billy corrected.

"That cocksucker stole our ever-lovin' cunt of a mother! I'm going to pulverize him."

"How about a drink?" Billy said, holding a full glass of tequila up to him.

Will raised his hand to intervene, but Cosmo downed it too fast.

"Whoa," Cosmo said, swaying slightly. "Empty stomach."

"That's the stuff," Billy nodded approvingly.

"She makes me wanna puke. She makes me—" His eyes opened wide, and his brows wrinkled in puzzlement. "I think I'm actually gonna puke." He dashed to the bathroom. The three of them sat looking at one another, listening in silence as the sounds of retching echoed off the toilet bowl.

"Oops," said Billy.

After that, Cosmo said he had to lie down. He hadn't gotten enough sleep, he felt like shit, and he suddenly couldn't keep his eyes open. He was going back to bed and would deal with that witch-cunt-whore later. Fallon winced, hearing Eustacia referred to that way. Will quietly pulled Fallon out of the apartment.

"We need to take a break from all this. Just cool off and forget about it for a few hours."

"Easier said than done," Fallon said.

"Let me rephrase. Let's connect to something bigger."

"Sounds good to me."

It was only a forty-minute drive to Long Beach and a one-hour high-speed ferry ride to Catalina Island, which felt like a world away. They docked in Avalon, a city that could have been in the Mediterranean, with its white, red-tiled cottages studding the hillside, punctuated by columnar poplar and cypress.

"I grew up in Long Beach, but my family never went snorkeling," Will explained as they got out of the car. "Their idea of a good time was a Sunday afternoon drive down a hill. Discovered a whole world under the water on my own after I left home. Ever been? Some of the best snorkeling in the world, right here." He pointed to the marina.

"I don't know." Fallon looked at him dubiously. She didn't feel like she had the energy for anything new, and she didn't want to get wet. A blanket and bed sounded like the best cure at the moment.

"Come on. Trust me."

"Why do I trust you?"

Will watched her and waited.

"Because you listen to me. Because when we talk, we are really having an exchange. In my family, talking was more like someone giving a speech and me trying to figure out how to give a better one."

"Come," he said. He bought tickets for a snorkeling expedition.

As they sat on the boat with the saltwater breeze ruffling their hair, Fallon had trouble absorbing the beauty of the turquoise water and brilliant sunlight. "I'm disappointed, in a way, that it was all a trick," she said.

Will nodded sadly.

"I mean, of course I'm glad she's alive. But as disorienting and dangerous as it was to believe she spontaneously combusted, she was right that it made the world seem more miraculous."

"Look," Will said, pointing over the rail of the boat.

A pod of dolphins frolicked in the water beside them. The water was absolutely clear, and the dolphins rippled through it. Those closer to the surface were slate gray, and those deeper down luminescent gray-green. The deepest ones were quicksilver spirits. The sunlight bounced across the water and dappled them in mesmerizing patterns too fast for the eye to retain.

The rules had changed, and reality had thrown her a new bone to chew. She was the child of two unbelievable stories, the real one more unbelievable than the lie. Did she really fly Ovid and Eustacia as kites? Was it coincidence or a vast spider web of design that brought two blue women into her life and that orchestrated her steps so that she would literally bump into her mother?

Later, underwater, as their ears filled with air bubbles and the watery hum of ocean vastness, as schools of black, white, and yellow sunfish surrounded them, as they swayed among the myriad forms of blue sponges, lavender corals, and spiny sea cucumbers, nature's infinitely varied weave of order and chaos impressed itself upon her and sifted a new knowledge into her body: that she would never have and didn't need to have all the answers. Between nature, self, community and a beloved other, the obscurity of an order edged with chaos, like the fractal patterns of a coastline, was enough. It was more than enough; it was a blessing.

On the ferry ride back that evening, Will pulled a bottle of champagne wrapped in a bag of ice out of his duffle bag.

"What is this for?" she asked, her eyes shining.

"Your independence." He unraveled two glasses from an old shirt.

"When did you get it?"

"I have my ways," he winked.

"So, you are capable of deception," she said.

He laughed and poured.

"Here's to not being a prisoner of your mother's mystery anymore," he said, holding up a glass.

"Here's to letting Ovid rest in peace," she said as she clinked hers to his. For just a second, grief surged inside her and swam away like a dolphin deep under water.

As champagne fizzed down her throat, she knew she could spend the rest of her life with Will. She had always thought love was desperate and all-consuming. The root of the word *passion*, after all, was "to suffer." She didn't suffer with Will, she thrived.

As they approached Los Angeles from the water, strands of light spangled the darkness. She remembered a night camping with her parents long ago beside a lake called Todos los Santos, all the saints. A lava flow had hit the water a hundred thousand years ago and formed hexagonal columns of black basalt that rose and fell irregularly like random steps approaching infinity.

It had been hard to get to sleep because beetles were flying everywhere, their heavy bodies constantly crashing into their faces, ricocheting off their arms, and getting tangled in their hair.

They awoke in the middle of the night when Eustacia yelped, jumped out of her sleeping bag, and leapt toward the cliff, twisting her body, and flapping her arms. *Oooo, ooo, ooo!* she called, slapping her head and lunging on ostrich legs from one hexagonal step to the next. The moon had risen and glittered in the black waters of the lake.

Hopeful that it was some sort of wild incantation, the children jumped out of their bags and fell in behind her, imitating her twisting, spastic movements with the greatest accuracy, to support her cause, whatever it was—just four silhouettes against the shimmering background of the lake, dancing under the stars.

It was only after Walter managed to catch up to them and made a flying tackle worthy of the most aggressive football player that the children found out that Eustacia had a bug in her ear. The frantic scratching of legs and wings on the sensitive membrane of her eardrum had been maddening.

It reminded her of the words to a Jewish round she had learned in college: "If the people live their life as if they were a song for singing out the light, they'd provide the music for the stars to go dancing circles in the night."

That night when she was ready, Will touched her, and her body opened to him with such simplicity and honesty, that it was another revelation. In the past making love had been a struggle. Her mind flew around like a trapped bird, darting, perching, and ricocheting off illusions of space that turned out to be neck-breaking windows. She had never known why this happened and had been too ashamed to ask anyone about it. However, with Will, her mind stayed connected to her body. In fact, her mind *became* her body, and lovemaking became an open dialogue where her hand on his chest was a question and his hand on her thigh an answer. Never before had sex been call and response in such a sacred space. Making love to him was like taking a sponge bath with hot sunlight.

Afterwards, she felt like someone from the Acoma creation story, who had long been trapped in a dark first world, and who had only just now climbed a tree through a hole in the sky to find a new expansive world, full of light, a world she knew she could live in for the rest of her life.

## A NEW STORY

A small crowd surrounded Cosmo outside Eustacia's trailer. He was shouting and shoving someone. As Fallon got closer, she saw it was Antonio. Their mother was cringing and holding her hands to her ears, and Marco, the muscleman, was grappling with Cosmo.

Cosmo grabbed the front of Marco's shirt and pulled his face in close to his own. "You're going to sit your ass down, or I'm going to tell the whole world that Evangeline, the mother of millions, is a fraud."

"Embra," Eustacia corrected. Marco backed off and looked to Embra and Antonio for directions.

"How's that gonna play with your fans, huh?" Cosmo said. "Immolation Embra the adulteress. The liar. A woman who abandoned her own children."

"¡*Cálmate, cálmate!*" Antonio said, stepping between Marco and Cosmo. "We take this inside."

Fallon and Will stepped to Cosmo's side, and Fallon placed her hand on his forearm.

"Come on," Will said.

Eustacia, Antonio, Fallon, Cosmo, and Will ducked into the

trailer, their collective weight jostling it. Antonio stepped in front of Billy as he mounted the trailer step.

"I'm with the big guy," Billy said, pointing over Antonio's shoulder.

Antonio stepped back, dark eyes glittering, the lines around his mouth deeply etched. "*Siéntense*," he quietly commanded.

"I don't have to listen to you, spider man," Cosmo said, his big voice lifting the trailer off its blocks. "You fucking stole my mother. This whole thing was *your* idea, wasn't it?"

Eustacia gasped indignantly. "I am no follower. You know I've always been my own woman."

Cosmo whipped around and thrust his face into hers. "I don't know you at all. And whose fucking fault is that? As far as I'm concerned, you're a piece of shit that doesn't deserve to be stuck to the underside of my boot."

She cringed and clasped her head again, and Antonio stepped between them. Cosmo grabbed Antonio by the shirt.

"Cosmo, please," Fallon said, pulling on his arm.

"Listen, big guy," Will said, coming up behind Cosmo. "I get it. You're totally within your rights. Just take a breath."

Cosmo took a breath, and the trailer fell silent, except for the sound of their collective panting.

Eustacia spoke up. "All I ever wanted to do was create beauty."

"Does this face look beautiful to you?" Cosmo shouted, pointing to his face, eyes bulging, veins on his forehead, frothy spittle in the corner of his mouth. "Your so-called beauty drove Ovid right out of his mind. You encouraged his total bullshit. Nursed him on it. You as good as killed him."

Eustacia's face contorted and tears fell. "I'm sorry." Her voice came out as a dry rasp.

"You better be sorry," Cosmo interrupted her.

"Cosmo . . ." Fallon placed her hand on his arm again.

"My beautiful boy is gone. I broke his heart."

"Oh, my fucking God, don't make me puke, again."

Will drew Cosmo out of the trailer, and Billy followed.

Fallon rose to leave but turned back and looked at Eustacia

weeping in Antonio's arms. She wanted to be better than Eustacia. She wanted to be able to forgive her. Her mother babbled quietly through her tears, muffled by Antonio's arms, "Maybe my boy figured it out, maybe he parted the atoms and he is everywhere."

"*Sí, sí. Por supuesto,*" Antonio murmured.

Fallon left the trailer. Life was too short and too valuable to waste on any more lost causes.

Back at the apartment, Cosmo was still digesting it all.

"I'm going to call the press and ruin her fucking career."

"Please don't," Fallon said.

"Why do you keep defending her?"

"I'm not. I'm not trying to excuse her, either. I'm not even telling you to stop being angry about it. I'm just saying," she rested her face in her palms for a second and raised her face to Cosmo, "It's hard to know where mental illness ends, and responsibility begins."

"She's a monster. She should be punished."

"She's her own punishment," Will said.

Fallon, thinking of how many times she'd blamed Ovid for his outbursts, said "Maybe this is truly the best she can do. Maybe Embra is the sum of all her Mom's parts, the way she makes the best sense."

Cosmo shook his head in silence, looking at the ground. A thought struck him. "Did you call Dad?"

Her complete failure to even think of Walter in all this time opened inside her like a black hole.

"I'll call him," Cosmo said.

Warmth for Cosmo flared, revealing as it did, that she had been a little afraid of him until now.

Cosmo went off to his own room, and through the open door she heard him dial.

"Dad?" he said, in a chastened voice. "It's me. Terry." He closed the door.

He emerged fifteen minutes later, totally deflated. "You're not going to believe this."

They all looked at him expectantly.

"Dad said he suspected it all along."

"What?" Fallon said. "But why didn't he say anything?"

"He said he knew it was what she wanted us to believe, and he didn't say anything out of respect for her."

"But that makes him almost as guilty as she is," Fallon said. "He colluded with her."

Cosmo just shook his head and rubbed his stubbled jaw, the loud whisking sound emphasizing their collective silence.

---

After a few days of lounging and sleeping, Fallon and Will packed to go.

Will reminded Fallon to call Jacob Sweet before they left.

When she got Jacob on the phone, she said, "You know, you were right."

"About what?"

"That I needed to finish my journey."

"Did you find your brother?" Jacob's voice quickened.

"Yes. But that's not all I found. I found my mother."

"No kidding." Jacob sounded astonished.

"Yeah, and she's alive."

"Amazing."

Fallon gave him a blow-by-blow account of how she'd made the discovery, and telling the story both heightened it and put a containing wall around it. "If I'd ended my journey there, at Buffalo Hill," she concluded, "I never would have found her."

"It just goes to show you," Jacob said.

---

When Terry hugged Fallon goodbye, his squeeze-lifted her off the ground.

"It was good to see you, sister. Stay in touch."

"Okay, Cosmo," she croaked.

"Terry," he corrected and set her down.

"That's going to take some getting used to," said Billy, looking quizzically at Terry.

"Are you going to be okay?" Fallon asked Terry.

"I feel like I could sleep for a hundred years."

"That's how he handles trouble," Billy chimed in. "A regular sleeping beauty.

Now, Princess," he turned to Fallon, took her hand, and made an elaborate show of kissing it, "if this big lug mistreats you, I'd be more than happy to come to your rescue."

Fallon smiled and shook her head.

As they got into the car, Will said, "Where to?"

"Home, I guess."

"Where's home?"

"Well, there's this place in New Mexico I'm dying to show you. I wonder if there are any medical schools nearby."

"Sure you want to hang out with a dumb old guy like myself?" Will asked.

"You'd better stop insulting the man I love," she said.

Will leaned over and kissed her.

As she leaned close to him and looked into his dark blue eyes, she remembered the sea sponges waving underwater, spider grandmother's black and white pot, and the tarantulas moving across the plain like the hands of an unseen body, the earth itself talking in one of its many languages. The invisible barrier between herself and life gently fell away, and the expansiveness of the mountains, dolphins, and Eustacia's pantomime opened up a space inside her big enough to contain them.

# DISCUSSION QUESTIONS

1. What passages stuck with you the most?

2. How would you characterize Fallon's relationship with each family member? Which family members are most strongly connected, and how does this change?

3. How does travel to other cultures shape Fallon, her family, and her perception and reality?

4. How is nature a healing force in the novel?

5. What does Bobby symbolize in the novel? Is she right about Fallon? Are they similar? Why and why not? What is her impact on Fallon?

6. Why does the story of what happened with George come up right after she meets Bobby? How does her understanding of that event change?

7. What is Teal's impact on Fallon? Is she the same as the blue woman Ovid saw?

8. How does Fallon change as a result of her stay with Kaela and Jacob?

9. Why does Jacob tell Fallon the story of "The Moon Palace" at that juncture?

10. In what ways are all the main female characters in the novel either the blue woman or the burning woman? How many different things might the "blue woman" symbolize?

11. What role do magic and/or coincidence play in the novel? How does that role change?

12. How does she Fallon ground herself in a reality she can depend on toward the end of the novel?

13. In what ways does Fallon both conform to and rebel against feminine roles? How does this play out with her relationship with Will and with herself?

# ACKNOWLEDGEMENT

Many thanks to my writing friends who have supported and encouraged me, to my SUAWP group (Shut Up and Write—Please), Anntonette Alberti, Karen Bjornland, Jacki eGoodwin, Elaine Handley, Darla Miklash, and sometimes Bob Miner, and to the WMD's (Women of Mass Dispersion), Nancy White, Marilyn McCabe, Kathleen McCoy, and Mary S. Shartle. Thanks to Katie Bowen, who never stopped believing in this novel and calling it forth, to my husband Charley Brown for his wise love and support, to Kate Moses for helping make sense of the "palimpsest," and to my childhood writing partner who started me on this journey, Catherine Ambrose. Thanks also to my family of origin for adventures in distant lands, arguments and inspiration and—their forbearance— as I borrow family stories and likenesses, and change them *wildly*. Thanks also to my acquisitions editor Nika Rose, and to the Head Penguin, Stephanie Larkin, whose generosity and good cheer never fail to amaze me. Thanks, finally, to all who wrote blurbs, tweets and reviews. There are more to thank, too many to name. I only had three things on my bucket list, a beloved partner, a healthy child, and this.

# ABOUT THE AUTHOR

Lâle Davidson's stories have appeared in *The North American Review*, *Big Lucks*, and *The Collagist*, among others. Her short story collection *Strange Appetites* won the Adirondack Center for Writing's People's Choice Award. Her story "The Opal Maker" was selected by Roxane Gay as one of the Wigleaf top 50 (Very) Short Fictions of 2015. She is a Distinguished Professor of English who has taught writing for nearly 30 years at SUNY Adirondack. She earned the Chancellor's Award for Scholarship and Creative Activities in 2018. More information is available at laledavidson.com.

Made in the USA
Middletown, DE
29 November 2021

53731142R00165